“A debut novel focuse … lo’s sports novel reads like … ove of the story’s setting, … ens to before races to Sara’s punk aesthetic…the author clearly did his research on track and field and is able to successfully convert this visual, fast-paced sport into vivid writing that will leave readers on the edges of their seats. A gripping, highly nostalgic dive into a decade and a high school sport.”

—*Kirkus Reviews*

“*A Reason to Run* is a captivating coming-of-age story that transports readers back to the 1980s with its vivid blend of music, nostalgia, and youthful exuberance. Sam Bagliarello’s journey from tragedy to triumph through the world of competitive running is a thrilling and inspiring tale that captures a specific moment in time with incredible accuracy and heart. A must-read for anyone who loves a good underdog story!”

—Erik Lindsay, screenwriter of *American Pie: The Naked Mile*, *American Pie: Beta House*, and *Last Call*

“Mike Magluilo’s novel navigates the challenges of family, friendship, and aspirations while underscoring the spirit of resiliency and repair. Exceptionally well-written with characters that are complex, flawed, and very human, *A Reason to Run* flows effortlessly and clearly to a finish line that is as exhilarating as the races run by its main character. There’s much to love about this book, and much that will remain with readers long after the final page is turned.”

—Greg Fields, award-winning author of *Through the Waters and the Wild*

“Whatever hurdles you’ve taken on in life, you’ll see a piece of yourself in Sam ‘Bags’ Bagliarello as he pursues finish lines both literal and figurative in *A Reason to Run*, the impressive first novel from author Mike Magluilo. Magluilo’s snarky take on late-1980s Chicago recreates a world of checked-out parents, post-punk mix-tapes, and blow-dried teenage awkwardness. Ultimately, this story will resonate with anyone who has had to find a way back from adversity without a training plan."

–Chris Jenkins, communications professional and former sports writer at *USA Today* and the *Associated Press*

"*A Reason to Run* is a deeply thoughtful and inspiring story of a teenager's journey set off by a tragic event one fateful summer night–and the long uphill battle to find his own internal peace. Magluilo writes with ease—a page-turner through and through—and each step of the adventure reminds us all of the lessons we come to learn through the personal struggles, internal setbacks, and disappointment in our own lives.

But this story is much more than a tale of personal triumph and how Bags searches endlessly for his inner balance...the story explains, in detail, the entire journey and how true friendship, ample doses of humility, and extreme generosity can all be part of our very own healing process whatever we are seeking to reconcile.

Magluilo's *A Reason to Run*, peppered with good-natured humor and relatable teenage hijinks, provides us with non-stop opportunities to reflect on what truly matters in our lives—family, teachers, friends—and the hope that we can all find our own secret weapon inside us."

—Brian Shell, Chick Evans Caddie Scholarship alumnus and golf industry executive

"As a coach, competitive cyclist, former high school and college athlete and, as a father, I loved *A Reason to Run*. Magluilo takes you on a trip back to the late eighties with spot on details and the heart pounding race that is high school sports and coming of age. We can all relate in some way to Bags's goals, trauma, training, and toughness. My high school senior daughter lives in a vastly different world today, but many issues and circumstances facing teenagers remain. We can all learn a thing or two from Bags, while the thrilling races will keep you on the edge of your seat and inspire you to your own personal best!"

—Greg Waggoner, USA Cycling licensed coach, former professional XC MTB racer and competitive road cyclist, former DI collegiate diver

"Magluilo's debut novel is hard to put down. This compelling story includes a spot-on portrayal of what it's like to recover from traumatic injury. As a pediatrician and sports medicine and concussion specialist, I interact with patients in these situations every day. *A Reason to Run* takes readers on a journey through the thoughts, emotions, and fears of a teenager navigating the aftermath of a life-threatening injury. The book accurately portrays a common discussion I have with my adolescent patients about engaging in the hard work required to recover across all areas of your life: physical, emotional, academic, and personal. This is a story that will resonate with young readers and the adults in their lives and has the power to help survivors of tragedy find purpose and change their lives in a positive way."

—Kevin Walter, MD, FAAP, medical director of the Sports Medicine Program at Children's Wisconsin and associate professor at the Medical College of Wisconsin

"A combination coming-of-age story and self-help allegory, *A Reason to Run* is a compelling reminder that it is never too late to uncomplicate our lives and discover that what we need most has always been right in front of us. Just as *Who Moved My Cheese?* did for managing life's changes, *A Reason to Run* reveals profound truths for regaining control of our lives in the tumult of others' expectations and demands."

—H. Edward Wynn, bestselling author and founder of We The People Project

"Reading about Bags's journey was inspirational and reminded me of all the skills I try to instill in my students—perseverance, inner strength, indomitable spirit, self-confidence, and self-worth—and reminded me I needed to tap into those skills too.

Bags as a high school senior thought he had his whole future mapped out, and then in a single moment everything changed. How many of us can relate to that? I certainly can. I found myself cheering for Bags throughout the whole book, hoping and praying he would find his new passion and direction.

We all have 'Spirit Hills' that appear in our lives, and we have decisions to make. We can change our route to avoid the hill. We can sit at the bottom of the hill and give up. Or we can charge up the hill as many times as it takes to reach the top—the view is always amazing at the top. May you all gather strength from reading *A Reason to Run* and charge up your own Spirit Hill."

—Master Kellie Thomas, 6th-degree ITF Taekwondo black belt and owner of TaeKwonDo K.I.C.K.S.

"*A Reason to Run* is a must-read for any parent, sibling, or friend of a young person with Down syndrome. As a mother of a child with Down syndrome and one who serves the community in nonprofit leadership, I couldn't put down this story of overcoming obstacles and the search for identity...This is the best work of coming-of-age fiction featuring a character with Down syndrome since *Champions* and *The Peanut Butter Falcon*."

—Evelyn J. Walter, board president of Rocky Mountain Down Syndrome Association

A Reason to RUN

A Reason to RUN

Mike Magluilo

Rootstock Publishing

Montpelier, VT

Release Date: October 3, 2023

Printed in the USA.

Rootstock Publishing, an imprint of Ziggy Media LLC
www.rootstockpublishing.com
info@rootstockpublishing.com

Softcover ISBN: 978-1-57869-145-6
Hardcover ISBN: 978-1-57869-146-3
eBook ISBN: 978-1-57869-147-0

Library of Congress Number: 2023909996

Cover art by Abby Clark Creative.

Interior and book design by Eddie Vincent, ENC Graphics Services.

Author photo by Noëlle Bourgault.

For permissions or to schedule an author interview, contact the author at mike@madgorillawrites.com.

"The real purpose of running isn't to win a race, it's to test the limits of the human heart."

—Bill Bowerman

"Maybe it *meant something*. Maybe not, in the long run . . . but no explanation, no mix of words or music or memories can touch that sense of knowing that you were there and alive in that corner of time and the world. Whatever it meant."

—Hunter S. Thompson, *Fear and Loathing in Las Vegas*

For Eddie and James. Keep pedaling…

1989 Illinois High School Track and Field Regional Finals

3200-meter race (eight laps), minutes before the start

Nine months ago I was dead. That's no excuse if I fail today. I need to place in the top four to make it to state next weekend. Before rehab, I never ran continuously for more than ten minutes. Today's race will be over in nine.

I toss my warm-up gear behind Coach Rip and slip through the carnival of athletes crowding the grass infield on my way to the starting area. The buzz from the stands makes it all so real and confirms I have nowhere left to hide.

Family and friends look on as I join my competition in a final shake-out of pre-race jitters. Lots of people helped me get here. Many are everyday heroes, some are everyday assholes. The taste of iron in my mouth triggers a fear of what awaits—like in the minutes following my accident. Questions of survival have become questions of identity. I began running to recover. I kept running when I discovered I was good at it. I'm running today to slay the self-destructive flaws that led me to the sport in the first place.

The starter takes his position and calls us to the line.

"On your mark!"

I lean forward, draw a deep breath and smile in the torturous pause between the starter's command and the firing of his gun.

BANG!

1

AUGUST 1988 [NINE MONTHS EARLIER]

The stench of disinfectant scrapes the lining of my nose, jolting me awake to the rattle of wobbly wheels and the squeak of rubber on vinyl. I want to scream, but the strobe of ceiling lights passing overhead lulls me into submission. I mistake the people pushing my rolling bed for pallbearers until I notice their urgency and matching blue uniforms.

"C-cold," I bleat.

"Hello there!" A woman shrouds me in a coarse cotton blanket, no thicker than a beach towel. "We lost you for a minute." Her gesture warms me more than the fabric.

I attempt to sneak back into unconsciousness, but the chills and pain and all the squeaking and rattling and those goddamn strobe lights make closing my eyes impossible. The guy at the front of the gurney kicks open two swinging doors, and we roll into a hushed room, dark except for a large disk-shaped lamp directly above me. Beeping sounds fire from beyond the curtain of light encircling my bed. A rotation of doctors and nurses jam their heads into my face and ask questions.

A man introduces himself as my anesthesiologist. He's going to *add a drip* to my IV to relax me. A second dose will *put me under* so the surgeon can operate. *Beep . . . beep.*

One nurse punches a needle into my left arm like it's a juice box and asks how old I am. Seventeen. *Beep.* Another Capri Suns my right and asks my name. Sam. Samuel Bagliarello. *Beep.* How do you spell that? She must be kidding. The first one asks where I go to school. Enough with the questions . . . and all the noise!

Fragments of memory return, and I tell the doctor I drank a few beers tonight. "In case you need to know. Before the drugs."

"Oh good," he says. "Then you will really enjoy the happy juice I'm about to serve you."

I release a muffled laugh with my last bit of energy. The juice kicks in and from behind my closed eyelids I float through a slow-motion replay of how I got here.

2

Cars line both sides of the street, forming a landing strip to Charles O'Toole's house. Jed and I hop off our bikes and try to blend in with the kids walking from their vehicles. We fool no one.

"Does that come with a bell?"

We should have parked our bikes on another street.

"I guess it's better than getting dropped off by your parents."

Social lines are drawn before we reach the party.

"Can you believe they're seniors?"

We ditch our Schwinns on the side of the garage and join the teenager-shaped hormones flowing into the O'Toole family home. The cool kids have cornered the kitchen, swapping gossip, giggles, and ganja. Charles emerges from the smoke.

"Hey dorks, thanks for coming! Keg's out back." If the yearbook awarded a Biggest Asshole superlative, Charles would be on the short list given he never fails to make you feel you don't belong.

The backyard smells like a late-summer swamp of trampled grass and sweat, masked by cigarette smoke, Drakkar Noir, and Skin So Soft, the moisturizer with the unanticipated benefit of repelling mosquitoes. Jed and I split up at the keg in the center of the patio. Distant thunder drowns out the bassline of a Violent Femmes song while I pour myself a beer and scan the crowd, careful to avoid getting pulled into an undesirable conversation. My concerns prove unwarranted, since no one pays any attention to me.

Fortune cuts me a break by sending Zoe Devine my way. Zoe

lights up the backyard with style, sophistication, and being hot as hell. Whenever I get close enough to speak to her, my knees wobble and my antiperspirant fails. Knowing I'll be a senior in three days emboldens me to beam as brightly as the red Solo cup of Milwaukee's Best in my hand and offer her a refill. She sweeps past without a glance and walks right up to David Boardman, captain of the diving team. His chiseled features resemble a certain eponymous marble statue in Florence. He and Zoe exchange giddy smiles, suggesting they expected to see each other.

A handful of football players interrupt my contemplation of fortune's fickleness by blitzing the patio in search of beer. They surround the keg, and a voice booms, "Hey, Hooch, is it time for a keg stand?"

Dan Hutchinson simultaneously defines and defies the high school jock stereotype. Enrolled in honors classes since freshman year, boundless enthusiasm is his tragic flaw. Picture Animal from *The Muppets* being told to put down his drumsticks for a book with no pictures. The attention span of a squirrel means Hooch won't be making any valedictorian speeches, but it helps him spice up a party.

Hooch scans the crowd for a recruit. "Boardman! Get over here."

Boardman waves off the invitation while shaking his head politely, as if saying, "Not tonight. Can't you see I'm standing next to this beautiful young woman?"

Hooch is having none of it. He barrels across the patio, slings Boardman over his shoulder and carries him back to the keg.

His teammates chant, "Handstand! Handstand! Handstand!"

Boardman raises his hand again, this time in surrender. He spreads his arms in front of him to clear a path, stands tall, and takes a deep breath. In a single graceful surge, he bounds toward the keg and inverts himself above it, supported only by his extended arms. A kid plugs the tap into his mouth as gently as a baby's bottle. Boardman swallows while maintaining his self-supported handstand, and the crowd cheers.

I look on like a starstruck groupie.

He finishes with flair by launching his body above the keg into a backflip before landing softly on his feet and drawing an approving roar from the crowd.

Hooch slaps Boardman on the back and calls out like the ringmaster at a circus. "Who's next?"

While Boardman juggles the approval of the crowd and Zoe's puppy dog eyes, I shout, "Right here!"

Jed grabs my arm. "Dude, you're gonna make a fool of yourself."

I brush him away. "Why don't you stop being a buzzkill, Jed?"

"Why don't you stop trying so hard, Bags?"

Jed MacGregor and I met in kindergarten when he was still known as "Jimmy." One afternoon I overheard his mom scolding him with his given names, James Edward, and the next day started calling him Jed. Other kids piled on, and that became his official nickname. Along with Sara, we're the only kids from Saint Edward the Confessor's Class of 1985 to exit the Catholic school track for high school and have remained best friends since.

"Bag-OOO-lee-OH!" Hooch calls out, exaggerating one of the common mispronunciations of my last name.

Hooch drops into an athletic stance, ready to lift me by my legs. I wave him off like Boardman did and take a running jump at the barrel. My feet fall well short of vertical, arcing sideways in an imitation of a drunk rodeo clown. I land clumsily on one foot, then stagger backward until a flower bed bordering the patio breaks my fall. My attempt to join the ensuing laughter backfires when it becomes clear nobody is laughing *with* me.

"Just call me Bags!" Hooch shouts as he runs over to help me to my feet. He pulls me up with one hand, then takes off like a caveman in search of dinner. Hooch's jibe has haunted me since freshman year. Frustrated with the inability of my new teachers and classmates to pronounce my last name, I started suggesting everyone "just call me Bags." A few alpha fourteen-year-olds looking to establish their rank within the freshman class pounced, mocking me for promoting my own nickname. The quip resurfaces on nights like this, whenever I do something deserving of ridicule.

I head indoors to escape the embarrassment. More jeers greet me in the kitchen and chase me to the front of the house, where I find Sara standing calmly at the door as if deciding whether to enter the jungle.

Sara is impossible to miss in a crowd. She's the only girl I know with lime-green hair, having ditched her natural shade of black when she became a drummer in a punk-rock band freshman year. Curls would make her look radioactive, but Sara's hair falls straight to her shoulders in two smooth brushstrokes that accent her freckled complexion.

"What'd I miss?" she asks.

"I'm getting out of here."

Sara is also the only girl I know with a tattoo. A percussion note with its stem passing through the loops of a treble clef is inked on the inside of her right arm. It expands and contracts with her bicep each time she beats a drum. It's fully flexed when she leads me out the front door by the wrist. I share an uncomfortable recap of the last twenty minutes, while the sky delivers on its earlier threat and hammers the roof of the front porch with rain.

"I don't know what's worse, making a fool of myself or being a jerk to Jed."

"Jed will get over it, but you flailing around the keg sounds a little desperate."

"I know. The night sucked from the moment we arrived." I fill her in on my failed attempt to attract Zoe's attention and getting taunted for riding our bikes.

"This isn't the first time your desire to be cool has backfired, Bags."

"How was your show tonight?" I don't need a reminder of my chronic social flaws.

"Our singer's a loser. Loves to be onstage but makes no time to practice. He stumbled through his lyrics and couldn't keep up with the rest of us. I'm done playing with high school boys."

"Well, I'm done with Linden Grove. I can't wait to get out of here next year."

"What'll leaving Linden Grove change?" Sara's smiling gray eyes turn into a scowl.

Damn, I walked right into it. "Oh, don't start," I say. "The last thing I need is one of your lessons on how to accept mediocrity by giving up."

When Sara gets mad, her freckles disappear as she flushes with emotion. Standing under the artificial light of the front porch, her face transforms into the same shade of tart cherry as her Sex Pistols T-shirt.

"Isn't that what you're doing by blaming others for your problems?" Sara says. "For someone who wants to escape, you seem to only want what the people around you have."

"I'm just tired of being a low-budget nobody, watching the happy people make life look easy."

"The happy people . . . hah! Their happiness is as real as Zoe's hair color."

"Says the girl with the green hair!" I gloat in calling Sara out until she fires back with principles.

"I'm going for art, not fame." Since the great sorting process that was freshman year, Sara's green hair, passion for loud music, and a body I'd describe as comfortably curved have placed her on the fringes of the high school social scene. The difference between us is, Sara enjoys being left alone.

"Whatever. Life seems simple to me. Money and status make the world go 'round, and life sucks when you're on the sidelines watching it spin by."

"Bags, if you want freedom from Linden Grove, stop chasing what other people value and go after something that gets you excited." Sara exhales, and the irritation fades from her cheeks. She turns toward the house and before giving up on me, she looks back and adds, "What you need is to figure out the difference between happiness and meaningfulness."

In my best dramatization of a self-absorbed teenage boy, I stomp past Sara with a growl, yank my bike from its lonely post at the side of the garage, and pedal away in what's now a full-blown downpour. The absence of Jed's bike means he's laughing in his dry bed knowing he beat the rain.

Three blocks from home I reach the top of Spirit Hill. My Chuck Taylors are two water-logged sponges, and my legs are caked in the street grit spinning off the wheels. Shaped like a steep ramp, Spirit Hill connects the northern and southern halves of Linden Grove. People who live north of the hill refer to it as the upper half, even though we all go to the same church.

I ride close to the center lane to avoid the runoff flooding the side of the road and gain speed over the top of the hill—unfortunately, not enough to outrun the car fast approaching from behind. By the time I realize the driver isn't slowing, the car's front fender smashes my back wheel and sends me soaring into the wall of trees lining the edge of the road. For a brief instant, my world freezes in a colorless silence.

Sound returns in a snap of light and the crack of bone as my head and hands break my collision with an unyielding elm tree. My body compresses into itself before the tree tosses me to the ground like a bag of rocks. I open my eyes to a thick canopy of trees brushing the clouds above. Raindrops leak into my eyes in a scarlet blur, and I wipe a handful of blood from the top of my head.

"Shit! Oh shit!" I yell at my hand before rubbing the blood into the dirt, as if that will make the problem go away. A burn rises from my gut, and I pull a sticky red ooze out of a hole in my shirt, wondering if rubbing an open wound with muddy fingers will cause a problem.

My breaths become labored wheezes, and I pull another handful of blood out of the hole in my shirt, no longer worried about hygiene. My shoulders shiver, and thirst overtakes me, despite the rain soaking my body. I tell myself chills are normal when you get caught in the rain, but the thirst is unreal. My breathing quiets down as blood, water, and air leak out my body.

The ground underneath comforts me. Spirit Hill has towered over my life. As a kid I spent hours trying to ride to the top without stopping before turning around to fly back down at faster and faster speeds. When it became clear I had little talent for mainstream sports like football, baseball, and basketball, Spirit Hill turned exclusion into escape. As I got older I ventured deeper into the world beyond Spirit Hill by bike, and cycling became therapy when my nuclear family detonated four years ago.

Spirit Hill has been my personal sanctuary since childhood, and here it is consoling me as I lie powerless in a mangled, bloody mess staring up at its trees. I don't want my life to end here in a hug of mud and leaves—left on the sidelines for good. Sara's words are fresh in my mind, and there are too many people I want to prove wrong. Before giving any thought to how I am going to do that, my world goes dark.

3

Consciousness returns in waves, as if everything's happening underwater. I wake and puke over the side of the bed and again on a jerky gurney ride through a maze of hallways that look and smell like old cheese. Mom looks into my eyes with tears in hers and a weary face of helplessness. Images and sounds sharpen as I rise through lighter and lighter layers of distortion until I break into the cool air of a hospital room.

"Thirrr-sty," I say.

"Can't give you any water right now, love," a nurse says. "But I'll bring you some ice chips."

She returns with a piss-cup full of crushed ice. An attempt to sit upright fails miserably due to the IV caught in my left arm like a barbed fishing hook and the sling constricting my right. The aborted effort electrifies my abdomen with a bolt of pain.

The nurse rushes over shaking her head before pressing a button on a controller wrapped around the bed's guardrail. The top half of the bed folds upward and suspends me midway between lying flat and sitting. I shake a few ice chips out of the cup. Doing this at a forty-five-degree angle sends most of them onto my chest. The few chips that make it into my mouth are refreshing despite tasting like gutter water. The nurse tears open a package containing an oversize yellow cotton swab and rubs it across my lips. Lemonheads laced with rubbing alcohol.

My surgeon, Dr. Padrone, marches into the room. I remember little of our interaction last night, other than in his scrubs, cap, and mask he looked like a cartoon doctor through my blurred vision. This morning he resembles a hitman in a red and black tracksuit, and his gold chain completes the caricature. I'd laugh if my belly wasn't on fire.

Mom rushes into the room and darts around with high energy and low utility. "Jesus, Mary, and Joseph! I thought you were dead."

"He was—for nearly a minute." Dr. Padrone explains my heart flatlined after I stopped breathing in the ambulance. Massive blood loss is no joke. One of the paramedics brought me back to life with CPR fifty-one seconds later.

I always thought of death as the most significant event in life. Having no memory of my own feels anticlimactic. Mom has a different take on the situation. She sobs away in the chair next to me, showing no interest in celebrating the fact I'm alive.

Upon hearing I stopped breathing, my mind rushes to assess possible brain damage. I say the alphabet in my head. When I get to *z*, I do it in reverse. Then I play around with numbers. The first that comes to mind is my address: 612. Twelve divides into six. Six plus twelve is eighteen, which divides into three, and my address has three digits. I get tired, probably due to the drugs and Dr. Padrone's mention of a concussion. While Mom mourns my death, I force my squishy brain to absorb the highlights of Dr. Padrone's recap of our time in the operating room last night.

I follow Dr. Padrone's movements, which are few, as the man operates with the precision of a Swiss watch. Broad shoulders and thick legs bulge from under his loose-fitting get-up. The sinewy muscles of his jaw ripple beneath his skin as he speaks. It's like the trauma Dr. Padrone lives through everyday has chiseled away all his soft layers and left behind a hard marble core. I realize he doesn't give a shit what anyone thinks about his outfit. This guy collects dying bodies scraped off pavements and puts them back together. He's a badass ER surgeon who saved my sorry ass a few hours ago and has earned the right to dress however he wants.

Mom stops sniffling as Dr. Padrone explains I fractured my collarbone. More importantly, fifty shiny staples hold together a vertical incision stretching from my sternum to my navel, courtesy of the branch that punctured my belly. He sewed the layers of tissue underneath my skin with stainless steel wires that will remain inside me. A tube pumps nutrition directly into my stomach through a small hole cut into my belly, while two small plastic bags cover open incisions on each of my love handles in order to collect *drainage*—the poison and other discharge from my gut. Another tube called a catheter disappears under my hospital gown to collect my urine. This last item catches my attention.

"How did you—" I start to ask.

"Very carefully. Be glad you were unconscious."

"How are you going to—"

"Quickly. Don't worry about that for now."

"When can I go home?"

"As soon as possible. Lying around here won't do you any good. We need you up and walking as soon as you get out of the ICU and into Pediatrics."

"Any idea what happened to my bike?"

"Your bike? No clue," he says. "Alright, your family doc will take over from here. Who's your pediatrician?"

"Dr. Moroni," Mom says.

"Never heard of him."

"He's a nice young man. Building his practice."

"Whatever. Let's hope he knows what he's doing. If there are any problems, I'll be downstairs."

"Thank you so much, doctor," Mom says.

He nods, cool and smooth like he just killed all the bandits and is about to leave Mom and me to rebuild the cabin.

"I'll have the nurse bring you something to deal with the pain and help you sleep," he says.

Dr. Padrone turns to the door, and I ask, "What are you going to give me?" A couple aspirin will be no match for the sensation of a rusty blade churning my insides.

"Morphine," he says without looking up from his clipboard.

"Huh." Before I can give it much thought, a nurse enters the room and empties a syringe into my IV. My head pops like a cork and a warm effervescence floods my body. The happy juice transports me to the comfort of a home I've never known, far removed from the last argument I had with Mom before my accident.

4

The clatter of silverware and porcelain greets me when I walk into the house.

"What are you doing washing the holiday dishes?" I say.

"They get so dusty. They'll be a nightmare to clean at Thanksgiving."

"It's August, Mom. And nearly midnight."

"I didn't ask for help, did I?"

Today's mail is stacked neatly on the counter. The distinctive black and red logo on the envelope from the American College Test distracts me from Mom's neurosis. I took the ACT a second time six weeks ago after scoring a twenty-six on my first try. Upon learning my AP classmates put up scores in the low to mid thirties, I feared the nuns at Saint Edward's were correct—I *am* a slow learner, and they were wise to sentence me to Sister Kenneth Agnes's remedial reading classes in grade school.

Sara thinks this is all bullshit and the entrance exams have little to do with measuring raw intelligence or predicting college success. "The only thing they assess is your skill at taking the tests," she says. While I'm no fan of bullshit, my target schools require a score above twenty-six. My parents weren't able to cover the cost of a private prep course, but I discovered the Jewish Community Center offers free classes and doesn't discriminate against Catholics.

Holding the envelope in my fingers, I'm about to find out if studying for the test made a difference. I work the envelope open, squint hard in the ceremony of it all, and unfold the paper inside. Math: thirty-two, Reading Comp: thirty, Overall: thirty-one.

Wow. I feel . . . smart. And vindicated. The nuns can stuff it!

An image of Sara appears on my shoulder, hammering her fist at me for thinking better about myself because of a test score. I still need to write my essays but finally checked the box on this bullshit test so someone will read what I have to say.

"Any luck with that bullshit test?" Mom shuts off the vacuum after going over the already spotless kitchen floor one last time before bed. She realizes it's a silly question when she catches my grin. "Okay, let me see."

She rips the paper out of the envelope, then looks at me with a flush of pride. "Congratulations, Sam. You deserve this." She hesitates a beat before adding, "Now, how about you settle down this fall? Enjoy yourself but do so with less booze and horsing around than this past year."

Her dig catches me off guard. She's been paying more attention than I give her credit for. I grab an opened bag of potato chips from the cupboard and sit down at the kitchen table, a small rectangle of fake wood designed for four child-sized people. In order to fit in our butler's closet of a kitchen, one of the table's long edges is pushed against the wall. It's barely comfortable for two adults, but that's not a problem since Mom and I are the only ones who use it.

Mom sees I'm trapped and doesn't waste the opportunity. "So, have you given any more thought to a major?"

It's the question I've grown tired of discussing. "I mean, I'm still torn between finance and journalism."

"Well, you know my opinion," she huffs while reattaching the cord to the vacuum. "And stop rocking that table, you're going to damage the wallpaper." The table has two uneven legs. The bolt securing one leg to the table's top is stripped loose, and the second has always been a quarter inch shorter than the others.

"Okay, Mom." Ever since Frank flunked out of college and Dad moved out four years ago, "Okay" is a button I press to get Mom off my back. It rarely works as intended, but it helps me ignore her when she tries to pull me into an argument.

"Oh, Samuel. I don't want to crush your dreams, but you're gonna need a paycheck when you get out of school."

"Okay, Mom."

"Do you know how much a journalist makes?"

Okay-okay-okay.

"And I asked you to stop it, Sam. You keep banging that leg into the floor, and you're gonna dig a hole in the linoleum. You know, rent in a city like Chicago or New York ain't cheap."

Rock-bang-rock-bang.

"Listen, Sam. Your father and I grew up poor, but we didn't know it because the world was a different place twenty years ago."

"Yeah, but it's not like you had a lot of options. I want to make money, but I don't want a job that makes me miserable. I still need to figure things out." *Bang-rock-bang-rock.*

"Don't be afraid you're gonna end up miserable like your father. He's always let others push him around, and that's made him an easy man to ignore. You've got something he never had—ambition."

Bumping the table against the wall is like a tic that can only be soothed by forcing the table to stay in place.

Mom fires up a cigarette.

"I thought you were quitting." I say.

"I *am* quitting. That means I am *in the process of* getting to the point where I *have* quit. This one is to help me relax before bed."

Bump-rock-bang.

"For Chrissakes, Sam. Look what you're doing to the wall!" Mom pulls a rubber door jamb from the wicker basket she keeps on top of the fridge. The basket holds everything that doesn't have an assigned place in Mom's kitchen, which makes it a small basket. She drops to her knees and wedges the jamb under the short leg of the table.

"The wall's already dented, Mom, and there's been a hole in the linoleum for years. The problem is the two broken legs."

Mom collapses into the chair opposite me and takes a deep breath.

Silence cools the tension.

"Sorry, Mom. I wasn't looking for a fight today."

She raises one of her bushy eyebrows and watches me squirm.

"That reminds me, do you want to talk about Teddy's call this afternoon?" I say.

"According to your caddie master, Teddy, that slob Charles O'Toole started it. You don't need to get beat up a second time by me. Besides, everyone knows Charles O'Toole is a douchebag."

5

"Sam?" I hear the whisper from the side of the bed but can't turn my head without irritating the sutures down the center of my body. The room glows in blue light from the equipment preventing me from dying a second time.

"Daaad . . ."

I have no idea how long I've been awake. It's nighttime—the least worst part of the day in the ICU, when sleeping patients moan less, and weeping visitors are at home. The beeping equipment no longer bothers me, having receded into my subconscious like a ticking clock. This leaves only the occasional cardiac arrest alarm and startled screams of confusion to interrupt my morphine-induced slumbers.

"Samuel. Are you okay? I mean, are you in any pain?"

"It only hurts when I breathe," I say, no sarcasm intended. The fact is, pain shoots through the gash in my belly with each inhale.

"Is there anything I can do?"

"I'm so thirsty."

Dad returns with more ice chips and lemon swabs, and I want to complain to the manager. Most of the chips end up on my neck and chest as usual. Dad brushes them onto the floor, then delicately wipes my lips with the lemony antiseptic swab. The loneliness of my hospital room gives us the space to enjoy each other's company like when I was a kid and unaware my dad lived in a world beyond pony rides on his back and walks for ice cream. He may be what Mom describes as an easy man to ignore in that bigger world, but in this melancholy little room, at the present moment, he's everything I could ask for.

I wake most mornings in a sweat. The sun burning through my unshaded window distracts me from the thirst, hunger, and pain. I'm done with the ice chips and lemon swabs. The ice never stopped tasting like an underarm and, based on the volume of urine flowing through my catheter, the saline solution in my IV provides all the hydration my body needs.

Since I won't be able to eat solid food until I get out of the ICU, breakfast consists of twelve-ounce cans of something called NewTrition. The first can they gave me featured a picture of a frosty vanilla milkshake in an old-time soda-fountain glass on its label. Starting the day off with dessert sounded like a good idea. Unfortunately the contents taste nothing like a vanilla milkshake—more like a sugary, chalky goo. The labels note the product's "full day supply" of all the vitamins and minerals my body requires. The shakes have it all, including fine print that reads, "contains artificial colors, flavors, sweeteners, and preservatives" and a long list of ingredients. I can only pronounce the first and last ones—high fructose corn syrup and FD&C Yellow #5.

The only thing working as advertised is the morphine. It's a wet dream that never ends. I struggle to understand how such an intense high can be legal, even in a hospital. The nurses pump it into my IV with the same indifference as they change my bandages. I keep meaning to ask about it, but whenever I see the small clear vial with its distinctive blue cap, all I do is drool like a dog conditioned to the smell of his food.

Studying the picture on each day's can of NewTrition has become my morning entertainment. Today, it's two smiling grandparents dressed in tennis whites. The picture reminds me of the country club, and the milkshake of a life I lived before my accident.

6

The steel pedal cuts into my shin. That's not the worst of it. Nor is the sunbaked blacktop searing my skin after Charles O'Toole stiff-arms me in the shoulder, hurtling me sideways over my bike. Charles started it, but I'm just an employee of the club, and the O'Toole family pays dues. The funny thing is, I caddie for Mr. O'Toole regularly, and based on what I overhear on the golf course, he thinks Charles is a shit, too.

Charles is a prime cut of Midwestern beef. He stands well over six feet tall, weighs two hundred fifty pounds and, from my immediate point of view, fills the space between two rows of parked cars blocking my path.

Several factors may have caused Charles to go out of his way to heckle me: the suffocating humidity of a Chicago summer, another aimless afternoon sunning his boobs at the pool, or an urge to treat me like the hired help since my dad works for his. Whatever the trigger, Charles reacted by leaning over the fence of the pool deck as I rode toward the club exit, shouting, "Hey, looper, make sure to wash my balls before you leave!"

"Sure, asshole. Let me know when you've pulled them out of your . . . your quiche!" I have no idea what that means, and I didn't intend to say it loud enough to be heard, but it gave Charles what he was looking for. The next thing I knew, he cut through the clubhouse, and a crowd gathered on the terrace.

"Caddies need to walk their bikes in the lot," he announced, as if reciting from a manual. "Get off the bike, and I'll let you pass."

So here I am, after deferring to a guy nearly twice my size, pinned between my bike and the sizzling blacktop, while the crowd on the terrace erupts in laughter.

As I peel my skin off the asphalt, the caddie towel draped over my shoulder falls into my hands. Those frayed orange rags from PE class are perfect for twisting into thin, four-foot-long whips.

Charles bellows. "What are you going to do, snap my ass with that?"

He charges, and I let the towel rip—aiming for the creamy filling of his belly. Charles catches my ragged excuse for a bullwhip before it makes contact, pulls me toward him like a spinning top, and locks me into a chokehold. While preparing to jam the towel down my throat, Charles twists his dagger past the point of mere humiliation. "Why are you and your old man such losers?" *That* is the worst of it.

The pool manager breaks up our schoolyard charade before Charles force-feeds me a summer's worth of dirty golf clubs. He dismisses Charles with a "Back to the pool, O'Toole!" before sizing me up. "Over here, Indiana Jackass." He drags me by the collar to the caddie shack and leaves me in the hands of Teddy Lincoln, my caddie master.

Based on the name they gave him, Mr. and Mrs. Lincoln expected great things from their son. After six years financing Teddy's study of golf and leisure at some country club college in Florida, his parents gave up on their dream, and managing the caddie program at Linden Grove Country Club became a suitable plan B for Teddy. The job provides plenty of opportunities to get out on the course, and the workday ends when happy hour begins.

While Teddy spins the rotary dial of a phone I can't believe still works, I dread Mom's white-hot temper on the other end of the line.

"Bags, remind me how you pronounce your last name."

"BAG-lee-uh-RELL-oh." Teddy, like most people in Linden Grove, struggles with names that have more than two vowels and do not start with an *O* or a *Mc*.

"Hi, Mrs. Bagliarello—" he hits three of five syllables correctly—"it's Ted Lincoln, the caddie master at Linden Grove." Teddy pauses and looks over at me before grunting. "Yes, your son is fine." It's a laughing grunt in response to a mother's intuition her child did something wrong. "Sam got into a disagreement with the son of one of the members, and I'm calling to inform you—"

"Charles O'Toole, ma'am."

"Yes, he was defending himself."

"Sure." Teddy hands me the phone.

I know less is better and open with a cheery "Hi, Mom!"

"I'm in the middle of something, Sam." Mom speaks in her work voice, which has a volume and tone that suppresses the sarcasm and curse words characteristic of her everyday vernacular. "Let's talk about this later." Mom works as a secretary at a fancy ad agency in the Loop, the commercial center of downtown Chicago. Lucky for me, we called during her turn working the reception desk. Personal calls, dealing with family drama, and cussing are no-goes in front of the firm's clients.

I hang up the phone, and Teddy looks as relieved as I feel about how the call went. "Hey, whaddaya know," he says. "It's beer-thirty. Stay out of trouble, Bags, and I'll see you in the morning."

Teddy bolts for the door before pausing to look back at me. "On second thought, any interest in joining me at Riley's?"

Doc Riley's is the one place you can grab a drink in downtown Linden Grove. Unlike the sports bars dotting the commercial roads on the edge of town, Riley's is sociable, safe, and sterile, appropriate for a town with the motto "Where Families Return Home."

Before we leave his office, Teddy reaches into a cooler and pulls out three cans of Natural Light, still connected to the plastic rings of what was once a six-pack. Three beers for a ten-minute drive to a bar seem excessive, but the summer of 1988 has been one long carnival of underage drinking for me. I follow Teddy and his three beers in their plastic rings to his car—a metallic-blue Porsche 911. The soft leather passenger seat smells as sweet as a shoeshine, and I do my best to suppress thoughts of the damp basement-carpet odor of my family's secondhand Buick Skylark.

Teddy secures the beers in the center console between us, opens the sunroof, and asks what kind of music I want to listen to.

"Anything. Something indie or alternative."

"Take a look." He gestures to the glove box.

A handful of cassette tapes fall to the floor, ejected by the usual mix of junk forgotten in a compartment used for everything but gloves. The music all predates the eighties but is an impressive selection of classic rock. I grab *Who's Next* and rewind to the first track, "Baba O'Riley."

"Right on!" Teddy resembles a dad in a station wagon when he lets loose on the air drums following the song's trippy electronic organ intro. "This song was *meant* to be played with the windows open!"

"Especially while cruising a teenage wasteland like Linden Grove," I say. Once his hands return to the wheel, I ask Teddy where he got the car.

"Hand-me-down from my old man. It's the first turbocharged Porsche to be imported from Germany since the 930 in seventy-nine. This baby gets to fifty miles per hour in first gear, which is all you need in Linden Grove."

Teddy lost me at "turbocharged." The Skylark is the first car my family owned with automatic transmission and sorely lacks the aesthetic and performance characteristics of Teddy's 911.

Teddy opens the center console and looks over. "Road soda?"

"Sure. Can I buy you one?"

"Absolutely."

I fetch a can for each of us.

That first sip of cold, hoppy carbonation plays in my mouth like a soundtrack to this steamy August evening before flooding my throat with the cool mountain stream images of the beer commercials from my childhood. Exiting the club in Teddy's car gives me an unfamiliar feeling of self-importance, and I cross into a world as comfortable as the car's bucket seats. It's a taste of the life I hunger for, and I want to stuff my belly full of it.

The hostess at Riley's recognizes Teddy and leads us to what appears to be his regular table out back. While the bar's location on Main Street makes the front entrance busy and loud, the beer garden is quiet—except when the freight train passes every hour. It has the intended feel of a backyard deck, complete with picnic tables sporting Budweiser umbrellas, overhead lights mounted on the deck posts, and a speaker system playing "Your Love" by the Outfield. An unseen chorus of crickets and cicadas fills the space between songs with their rhythmic melodies, punctuated by the constant scratching of the bug zapper. While the trees shade the retreating sun, the air remains muggy. A breeze would be welcome, but that would carry the smell of rotten garbage from the corn processing plant in the next town over.

A waitress arrives like a gnat on sweat as soon as we take our seats. "Hi Teddy, how ya' doin'?" she asks between chews of bubble gum. She looks me up and down, offers a "Hello, hun," then turns back to Teddy. "I never knew you had a son, Ted." She chuckles at her own joke through gritted teeth that somehow keep the gum in her mouth.

A cheap haircut and lanky build peg me for a teenager still growing faster vertically than horizontally. My navy-blue Linden Grove Country Club shirt with its *Honor Caddie* logo doesn't help. While the appearance of propriety is important in Linden Grove, the Irish Catholics that run the town revere beer like a village of friars, and the Polish family that owns Doc Riley's treats nanny-state restrictions on commercial activity like yield signs. So, despite her sarcasm, our waitress follows up with, "What can I get you gentlemen to drink?"

"Pitcher of Michelob, Susie," Teddy says.

We work through our first pitcher over burgers and fries while watching the Cubs win their first night game in the history of

Wrigley Field. It's the sort of night a high school kid dreams about, but likely a disappointing consolation prize for a twenty-something caddie master.

"Sorry to cause all that trouble today, Teddy."

"Forget about it, Bags, but you need to keep your nose clean if you don't want to risk losing that caddie scholarship."

"You know I didn't start it, right?" Fear of pissing away my ticket out of Linden Grove spooks me into contrition. "Sometimes I get sick of carrying everyone else's bag, you know?"

"Do you realize what carrying those bags got you? You're the kind of kid most members wish they had for a son. That's why Mr. O'Toole sponsored your application for the scholarship. Shit, that's why he gave your dad a job when he learned about your family's situation."

My family's situation. That's a polite way to put it.

"Well, after seventeen years in Linden Grove, I'm ready for something new."

"Oh yeah? What are you planning to do with that scholarship?"

The tables in the beer garden are full, amplifying the conversation and laughter. The simple chords of a couple Tom Petty songs keep things cool despite the temperature. We finish our food, and Teddy orders a second pitcher.

"I'm getting ready to apply to college this fall. I have it narrowed down to four or five schools, but I need to figure out what I'm going to major in."

"What's on your shortlist?"

"This week, finance."

"You mean like trading?"

"No, investment banking."

"Like a stockbroker?"

"No; investment bankers advise companies on raising money and making acquisitions."

"Ah, Wall Street stuff. Is that as exciting as it sounds?"

"Not when you start out. You enter the industry as a financial analyst and learn the business by doing all the grunt work. It's two grueling years of hundred-hour workweeks doing whatever the senior bankers tell you, then asking for more with a smile."

"Sounds like a miserable two years, if you ask me. Actually, it sounds a lot like being a caddie—with less sleep."

"It's not about the day-to-day. It's the prize at the end." I've been waiting to use that line I read in an article about a guy who grew up like me before making millions on Wall Street.

"Let me ask you a question," Teddy says. "Do you know why there are eighteen holes on a golf course?"

"Because they invented the game in the place that gave us yards instead of meters?"

"No—although that might explain why it's not twenty holes. The point I'm trying to make is, golf wouldn't be much fun if you hacked your way through the course for four hours only to enjoy one green at the end. It's about how you spend your time on the course, Bags."

"I hear you, but if I bust my ass for a couple years, I'll be free to do whatever I want after that."

"Good luck chasing your freedom." Teddy's sarcasm surprises me, although working at a golf course seems to be all he needs.

We finish the second pitcher and drive back to the club. Before getting out of the car, I thank Teddy for dinner. "My friend Sara says I need to stop acting like a steakhead by chasing superficial goals. She keeps pushing me to think about what excites me. I'm still trying to figure that out."

"Sara sounds like a smart girl," Teddy says. "You should listen to her, but I wouldn't freak out about it. All seventeen-year-old guys are steakheads."

Teddy answers my earlier question about the third can of beer by cracking it open before pulling away. "One more for the road!" he yells out the sunroof.

Why he needs a warm beer for the drive home after the two

pitchers we downed at Riley's is unclear. Then again, I don't own a car.

I hop on my bike and pedal less steadily with a pitcher of beer in me. My fight with Charles O'Toole seems like days ago, and passing the club exit a second time today reminds me of my *family's situation.*

Four years ago, my older brother Frank set off a chain of misfortune when he flunked his freshman year of college and lost his football scholarship. After Frank went college crazy, Dad's life fell apart, too. He took Frank's failure hard, got fired from his middle management job in the Chicago grocery industry and moved out. Mom went to work full time and started raising me on her own. After a year of struggling to pay the bills, my parents defaulted on their mortgage, and Mom and I became renters to the investment firm that bought the house in foreclosure. While Mr. O'Toole did a generous thing by offering my dad a job, I became the kid whose father runs the local car wash.

I regain my balance a few minutes after leaving the club and approach the top of Spirit Hill. A ride down Spirit Hill always jams my senses. The flood of objects rushing by overloads my visual field. I notice the pressure of air and how the slightest adjustment of my body affects my speed. The ground shoots erratic vibrations through the bike and into my joints, and the wind howls at a pitch that increases with my speed.

The air blasting my face as I fly down Spirit Hill tonight is still warm and fails to cool my sun-crisped skin. Thankful for the lack of traffic that usually races up and down the hill, I use the full lane to float between the random pattern of manhole covers designed to throttle a cyclist descending at over thirty miles per hour. Drowning in stimulation, I have no capacity for thought—and my mind grows quiet.

The background noise in my head has tormented me since childhood. An inability to ignore my thoughts kept me awake at sleepovers long after the lights went out, and my wandering mind earned me a slow-learner badge and that seat in Sister Kenneth Agnes's remedial reading class in grade school.

At some point, in an effort to manage my restless mind, I created an alter ego and called him Bad Gorilla, a phonetic play on my last name. I feed Bad Gorilla all my negative thoughts: worry, fear, insecurity, anger, envy—you name it. While this helps quiet the chaos in my head, now and then Bad Gorilla busts out of his cage, foaming with all the negative energy I've sent his way, and forces me to grapple with him on the wrestling mat of my mind. Clearing my head while tearing down the narrow two lanes of Spirit Hill is one way to calm Bad Gorilla when he throws his weight around.

The noise in my head tonight is an endless loop of negative thoughts about Charles O'Toole, my family, and where I fit in the world. As usual, Bad Gorilla is no match for the hill, and the ride to the bottom leaves me with a temporary feeling of freedom and detachment, like a little kid enjoying the simple thrill of a bike ride.

7

Frank surprises me with a visit in the ICU one morning. I wasn't sure when I'd see him again after the Fourth of July when, in a sign Dad was getting his life back together, he took us to watch the fireworks downtown. By the time the three of us worked through the clumsiness of not having seen each other in a while, Frank reached the bottom of his flask and passed out in the grass.

I fill Frank in on the events leading up to and following my accident with more guilt and shame than I shared with my parents, as if confession to the reigning family screw-up might absolve me of my sins.

"I wouldn't mention Dad's visit to Ant'nette."

Frank ceased referring to our mother as "Mom" in middle school. He got a kick out of mimicking the way friends and family from the old neighborhood pronounced the hard vowels and truncated middle syllable of her name. Mom thought it was cute at first, but the gag grew old when Dad and I joined in.

"You think she'll find something to resent about Dad visiting me in the hospital?" I ask.

"I can already hear her saying, 'Everyone loves ol' Joe. Bless his heart, but guess who had to pull up the slack while he was playing Mr. Nice Guy all the time?'"

I don't need to hear more complaining about our parents, and since I never ask Frank questions about his life I don't already know the answers to, I simply thank him for visiting.

"Well, get used to seeing more of me. I quit my job and am moving back home for a while."

"Really?" Moving back home is a major concession for the guy who refused to admit failure after flunking out of college four years ago.

"Working for Mr. Callahan's moving company and living in a crappy apartment aren't what you'd call a life goal. I need to take a breather and figure out what I want to do with my life."

"Mom's okay with this?"

"Ant'nette said as long as I help out, I can stay at the house for a little while."

"I'm sure she has a few ideas for how to put you to work, right?"

"As it turns out, I volunteered to oversee your PT program."

"My *PT program*?"

"Physical therapy. Rehab. You're gonna need to rebuild your strength and put a lot of weight back on. Mom can't take care of you while she's working, so that's where I come in."

"Well, you might be taking on a bigger challenge than you think. Check this out." I pull up my hospital gown and show him my emaciated legs.

"Damn! What've they been feeding you?"

I hand him an empty can of the vanilla-flavored plaster.

"New . . . Trition? What the hell is this?" He scans the label. "This isn't food. There's not one naturally occurring ingredient in this *all natural* shake."

"They footnoted that."

"What a scam," Frank says.

"You mean this nutrition shake isn't nutritious?"

"I can't believe the hospital serves this to its patients. It's as bad as the McDonald's in the lobby."

"Or eating like every day's a tailgate party at Soldier Field, right?" I say. The last thread holding our family together unraveled with Dad's heart attack shortly after my parents lost the house.

"Mom still refuses to blame the beef and brats," Frank says.

"Mom prefers to blame people," I say. "She needs someone to be mad at." Frank is well aware Mom blames Dad for the inconveniences in her life—and Frank for the problems.

"Anyway," Frank says. "Dad's problems inspired me to take a look at my own health. I started eating healthy and working out again. I also realized my drinking was out of control and cut out the booze."

"You mean blowing up your life in college wasn't a loud enough wake-up call?"

"Low blow, Sam, low blow."

"Sorry, Frank, it's the drugs talking. How's sobriety going?"

"I've been dry for a month now."

"Are you in rehab or something?"

"Nah. I'm not one for sitting around with a bunch of drunks talking about my feelings. When I put my mind to something, I get it done."

"I guess this means we'll be roommates again?"

"Yeah, sorry to crimp your style. You know Ant'nette isn't big on guests messing up the living room."

"Don't worry, your posters are still on the wall, and no one's touched your old bed."

"Thanks."

"Just let me pick the music."

8

The knock on the door is barely audible. A man who forgot to shave below his lower lip pokes his head in.

"Samuel? May I enter?" It's my pediatrician, Dr. Moroni. I'm wide awake and don't understand why he's whispering.

He asks how I'm feeling. "Good," I say.

He smiles and claps enthusiastically as if I just wee'd in the potty for the first time.

I reconsider, too sore and bored to let anyone think I'm enjoying myself. "Actually, Dr. Moroni, my head hurts, and my memories are like broken glass I keep stepping on. My belly's on fire yet I'm starving, and the only thing I look forward to are the morphine hits twice a day."

He stares at me like a startled doe before responding. "Thank you for sharing, Samuel. And by the way, you can call me Dr. Blakely."

"Why Blakely?"

"Because that's my first name."

"Blakely?"

"Yes."

I try to say, "Dr. Blakely," but it only makes me resent his parents. "I'm gonna stick with Dr. Moroni," I tell him.

"May I?" He approaches with extended arms like he's expecting a baby to pop out of my hospital gown.

"Go for it."

He checks out my scars and makes a few sounds of approval. "Dr. Padrone does fine work," he says.

I have no idea what he's pleased about, given my torso resembles an omelet.

"I'm sorry to hear you're uncomfortable. I'll take another look at your medication regimen and see if we can do something about the pain."

I appreciate Dr. Moroni's concern for my feelings and comfort, but Dr. Padrone filled the room with a technicolor energy that reassured me I'd get out of here alive. Based on first impressions, I'm glad Padrone is the guy they called from the ambulance Saturday night.

"Dr. Padrone called," the ICU nurse says. She's scouring my face and neck with a damp washcloth. These daily hospital baths clear the opiate fog most mornings and make me dream of standing under a hot shower once again. "You're all clear to move to Pediatrics today."

I'm so thrilled by the news I forget to ask how, exactly, my catheter will be removed before transferring to Peds. Two unassuming nurses answer my question with a bucket and what looks like a basketball pump. One nurse deflates the small balloon that secures the catheter inside my bladder before the other extracts the tube with an unceremonious yank. I've spent enough time in the boys' locker room to know I have no reason to brag about the visible portion of my reproductive gland, but the length of the tube they pull out of my pecker looks like it was sized for a horse. The intrigue is, unfortunately, not enough to distract me from the barbaric scraping of the tissue lining the most sensitive organ of my body as the catheter—and deflated balloon—travel the narrow path from my bladder, through my urethra, and out my Johnson.

Sara and Jed show up later in the day. They stand in the doorway to my room holding supersize fountain drinks from the McDonald's in the lobby, gazing at me with expressions I've grown used to.

"Do I look that bad?"

"Uh . . . you look like you got hit by a car," Jed says.

"The scary thing is, I look better than I feel." I give them the show-and-tell of my sutures and describe my daily routine of sleep, liquid meals, and morphine.

"We brought something to help you pass the time." Jed hands me a Walkman and mix tape with *Recovery Songs* scrawled in Sara's handwriting on the label.

"This is so cool. Thanks, guys! A little music is what I need. I'm losing my mind lying around all day. Tell me about the first week of senior year. What's the hot gossip?"

"Bags, *you're* the hot gossip." Sara's overdressed for the Pediatrics wing in a secondhand corduroy blazer from Goodwill covering a Velvet Underground T-shirt.

"Yeah, you've become a *legend*—at least this week," Jed adds.

I let out a horsey laugh, like Horschack from *Welcome Back, Kotter*, which scares my friends. Use of my abdominal muscles stretches the incision down my belly, so I have to force laughs through my chest to minimize the pain.

"On a serious note, today's mass was dedicated to you," Sara says.

"And the football team dedicated Friday night's game to you," Jed says. "Unfortunately, they got clobbered, but Hooch said some nice things about you in his pep rally speech."

"Except he called him *Steve*," Sara says to Jed.

"Yeah, but he also called him a *badass*," Jed replies.

"That was after he described him as 'a kind of quiet, nerdy guy worth rooting for,'" Sara says.

I don't want to tell my two closest friends to shut up, so I try refocusing the conversation on me. "I didn't realize I was such a big deal."

Jed turns back toward me. "Not many of us know someone who escaped death, Bagman."

A Pediatrics nurse wearing a Cinderella crown taps the door with a wand coated in glitter. "Sorry to interrupt," she says. "But Sam needs his rest, so I'll have to kindly ask you to leave."

Cinderella twirls away, and Sara says, "I think she likes you, Bags."

"You should have met the one who pulled the three-foot tube out of my wiener this morning."

I pop the mix tape into the Walkman after Sara and Jed leave. Since I was a little kid lost in the thoughts in my head, there's always been a song playing in the back of my mind. I wish I could say music helps me *make sense* of life, but despite the forty-two issues of *Spin* magazine stacked in my closet and a dresser-full of cassette tapes pirated from the library, the best I can say is music helps me *get through* life.

My world froze when that car hit me. After Jed and Sara's visit, I realize my life and the world are two different things. The world isn't waiting for me to get out of the hospital. This complicates things, like keeping up with school so I can graduate and keep my scholarship, applying to college, and joining my classmates as they live out senior year. I let Bad Gorilla work on these worries and instead savor the attention my accident has attracted. *Badass legend* might be the sort of "recovery" I need to break my curse as a quiet nobody.

"Teen Age Riot" by Sonic Youth starts up. The song is beautiful and terrifying and sarcastic and hard to understand. It reminds me of the last few years. The lyrics speak about rebellion, hyperactivity, and other extremes of teenage life. I think the point is to see the nuance between the extremes if I want to make sense of it all. The song makes me think I could solve a lot of my self-inflicted problems if I stopped letting the extremes get to me, like the last time I hung out with Jed.

9

"You're not the only one who wonders if their parents were ever teenagers, Bagman."

Jed and I ride no-hands alongside each other on our way to Charles O'Toole's house for one last party of the summer before school starts on Monday. The smell of ozone and rumble of thunder mean rain is on the way.

"I don't want to talk to a teenager," I say. "I need some adult wisdom."

"At least your decision about college is a conversation, not a command," Jed says. Mr. and Mrs. MacGregor are as cold and repressed as my mom is hot and emotional. Whereas Mom can't let an opportunity to argue pass her by, the MacGregors say little but insist on controlling everything. As far as Jed's plans for college, he'll be allowed to freely choose his major—as long as it's in the field of engineering—and he can attend any school he wants—as long as it's a Big Ten university, preferably in the state of Illinois.

"I think my mom's burnt out," I say. "She still feels my dad and Frank gave up without a fight when things got tough, and all she got was a steeper hill to climb."

Jed cruises along on his lime-green Schwinn Suburban, and I ride the bike I bought in eighth grade with money from my first summer caddying—a royal-blue Schwinn Deluxe Varsity ten-speed.

"Speaking of hills, see you up top," Jed whistles. Since we were kids, Jed has pronounced his *s*'s and *z*'s with a wheezy twang, somewhere between a drawl and a lisp, as if he was born in southern

Illinois instead of southern Linden Grove.

We turn the corner, and Spirit Hill rises like a drawbridge. In contrast to the descent, time slows when climbing. My legs pulse with liquid pain in a battle to complete each pedal stroke and keep the bike upright. Before my body gives in to the alarms from my lungs and heart, the road flattens at the summit, and I believe I can do anything for a minute.

Jed pushes his heavy cruiser bike to the top, and we ride alongside each other once again.

"Everyone's going to be at O'Toole's tonight," Jed says. Jed lives for parties. Ironically, the social lubrication of alcohol so many of us rely upon to "be ourselves" doesn't interest him. Jed's simply wired to have fun, which is plenty, given he kicks up enough trouble with nothing more than the sophomoric creativity of an aspiring engineer. "You know, last bash of the summer and all."

Jed's propensity for high jinks originated in grade school, and his Christmas Eve prank in eighth grade remains a Saint Edward the Confessor legend. The two of us served as altar boys for the Christmas Eve family mass that year. Jed somehow gained access to the two floor-to-ceiling banners embroidered with the letters *S E C* used for holiday celebrations. When the banners dropped from the ceiling at the front of the church during the priest's final procession, the *C* had been replaced with an *X* thanks to two strips of excess felt cleverly sewn into each banner. Our church's celebration of *S E X* was immortalized when one of the pictures processed at the local drugstore ended up in the *Chicago Tribune* the following week.

"I'm thinking about going to homecoming this year," Jed says.

"What? Aren't you the guy who sabotaged last year's parade?"

"Dude, that's *alleged* saboteur. The school never found any evidence, and they issued a public apology for accusing me."

"You still won't admit to your oldest friend you swapped the music on the king and queen's float?"

"Are you referring to the hidden tape player that replaced the music the pom-pom team selected with songs like 'Sexual Healing' and 'The Stroke?'"

"Among others . . . I recall 'Darling Nikki' was the finale," I said.

"Oh, the one about the sex fiend who happened to have the same first name as our homecoming queen?"

"Yeah, *that* mix tape."

"Listen, I resent homecoming as much as the next kid who's grown tired of syrupy teen cheer, but I don't know any more about last year's ruckus than you."

"Whatever, Jed. You still haven't answered my question."

"You know better than anyone, Bagman, I don't drink, I don't play sports, I don't even know the school fight song. I figure I could try fitting in for a change and create some normal high school memories before we graduate."

"It's funny you say that, because I've been thinking of going to homecoming too."

"You actually plan to ask someone out?"

"What's that supposed to mean?"

Jed's look tells me girls are another sport in which I lack natural talent.

"Okay, fine," I say. "This may sound crazy, but I've got a thing for Zoe."

"Zoe Devine? What makes you think you've got a chance?"

"Well, I had PE with her last semester, and I know from caddying for her mom that she and Fitz broke up earlier this summer."

"Dude, you have no chance in hell with Zoe Devine."

"Tell me why I don't deserve the most amazing girl in school."

"It's not whether you deserve her, Bagman. You have nothing in common with her, and that pisses you off. Bagging Zoe would be your ticket into the club of kids with more money, fancier clothes, and more popularity than you."

Jed has a point. The line of suitors will be long, and knowing her mother isn't much of an angle.

"You're right," I say. "This is more of the same crap I've dealt with my whole life. Always on the outside looking in."

"There's no need for self-loathing. Just try focusing on someone in the same orbit as you."

"I've got a few weeks. Let's see how tonight goes before I lower my standards."

"If I had to put money on it, I bet she hooks up with one of her pretty-boy friends," Jed says.

Ugh. The pretty boys and girls. Teenagers with no acne and great clothes who excel at nothing academic, athletic, or extra-curricular. A living Benetton catalog with a charisma I admire given I'm such a social klutz.

"My money would be on Chad," he says.

Chad Jones was my first encounter with a pretty boy. We took the same Intro to Typing class the summer before freshman year. I'd never seen a fourteen-year-old boy with blow-dried hair, a spray tan, and a waxed chest visible through the open buttons of a clean, unwrinkled shirt. Four years later, I now know the kid was born that way.

"Have you asked Sara for her thoughts on Zoe?" Jed asks.

"Sara already offers more advice than I can handle. I stopped asking her about girls."

"Well, you haven't left yourself many options." With a mischievous grin he adds, "Maybe we should think about sabotaging homecoming again?"

I take a friendly swat at Jed, and the conversation ends there because we hit a traffic jam of teenagers a block from Charles O'Toole's house.

10

A woman named Nurse Cooper sets a large tray in front of me containing a pack of Saltine crackers and a bowl of Jell-O.

"Welcome to fine dining Pediatrics style, Sam." Nurse Cooper's humor is one sign I'm no longer in the ICU. Perhaps too many patients never make it out of Intensive Care to improvise. Even when not cracking jokes, Nurse Cooper speaks with a colorful lilt to her voice, and despite the early signs of crow's feet, she's kind of sexy. Smooth skin, crystal-blue eyes, and the way she ties back her silvery-blond hair give her an ageless beauty that complements her soothing voice. She's an angel dressed in Snoopy scrubs.

"How come I'm not starving? I haven't eaten since my accident."

"Your stomach shrank. Like any muscle, you need to use it or lose it. You'll slowly rebuild your appetite as you begin eating real food again."

After dinner, Nurse Cooper takes me on my first walk since entering the hospital. She warns me to not expect much. Like eating, I'll be rebuilding my physical strength from scratch. She helps me slide my legs over the side of the bed and scoot onto the floor using one working shoulder. I stand too quickly, and the gash down my torso shoots a jolt of pain through my body. I hunch over to relieve the tension and lean on the IV stand with my good arm. All I can manage are heavy, deliberate baby steps, like walking against the current in a river, and I wheeze from the exertion.

"Let's take a breather here," Nurse Cooper says when we reach the door of the room next to mine. "How do you feel?"

"I . . . I'm exhausted." I take shallow breaths through my chest. Any more pressure on my belly risks splitting my crusty scar open.

"Not a bad start, Sam. Let's head back so we don't miss dessert!" Again with the jokes, but defeat keeps me from laughing.

Bound once again to my bed, another nurse brings my nightly ticket to Morphineland. As the liquid swaddle warms my veins, an invisible weight presses down like a lead blanket. The soft mattress cradles my body, exhausted yet too agitated to sleep, and I can't tell if I am experiencing surrender, addiction, or destiny.

The next morning brings a small box of Cheerios and an intruder. He's a pudgy kid, a little over five feet tall, with a salad bowl of light brown hair that falls to his eyes. I don't know what to make of him when he bounces through the door like a lit firecracker. He leaps onto the second bed in a single bound with the enthusiasm of his Superman onesie pajamas—an odd outfit for a kid who looks to be a teenager. After a few bounces on the mattress, he drops to his butt and springs onto the floor. He pauses when he notices me in the other bed, then grabs his crotch.

"Hi, my name is Marty." He speaks in a slow monotone.

"Hi, Marty. I'm Sam."

Marty releases his penis and walks over to me. He takes a close look at my disheveled hair and cloudy eyes, and I notice the upward-slanting eyelids of a kid with Down syndrome.

"Are you dying?" he asks.

"Uhh . . . not any more. What are you in for?"

"I have a bad heart. I come here a lot."

Marty returns to the other bed and proceeds to rip the sheets off it. Once he gets them on the floor, he pulls the cases off his pillows and returns his hand to his crotch. A woman pops her head into the room and exhales when she sees him.

"Marty? I wasn't sure where you wandered off to." She turns to me. "I'm so sorry if Marty interrupted you."

"I don't mind visitors."

"How do you feel about roommates?"

While Marty gets tangled in his sheets and imitates the Abominable Snowman, the woman empties a bag of clothes into a drawer. She turns back to me. "My name is Evelyn. Mrs. Koppen. I'm Marty's mom."

Marty resurfaces and fluffs the loose sheets on his bed into what looks like a giant Hostess Snoball. He kicks off his shoes, climbs aboard, and makes himself comfortable.

"We're going to have a great time," he says. "Thanks for being my roommate."

Marty's constant motion presents no window to complain. He asks one last question after turning off the light above his bed. "Have you ever seen *Star Wars*, Sam?"

The Summer Olympics in Seoul distracts me from thinking about my next dose of morphine, competing only with Marty for my attention.

"Are you watching a bike race?" he asks.

"Yeah, the men's road race. It's the Olympics."

"I love bike racing!" he says with the enthusiasm displayed while tearing apart his bed the day he arrived.

Marty tells me how he became a cycling fan while watching a stage of the Tour de France back in July. The majestic scenery, sunshine, colorful jerseys, and primal drama of watching two hundred riders destroy themselves in pursuit of glory seduced him, like the millions of other fans who get it. By the final stage in Paris, Marty convinced his mom to remove the training wheels from his bicycle. After hours of falling and getting back up, he learned how to balance and ride by himself.

"Do you play sports, Sam?"

"That's a sore subject." Without wanting to get into my ineptitude with ball sports, I tell Marty about my short-lived experience racing bikes. Freshman year, Coach Wolfe organized LGHS's first-ever cycling team as a form of off-season conditioning for his football players who weren't playing a spring sport. He was convinced improved cardiovascular fitness and muscle endurance would give his players an edge on the football field.

I showed up to the first workout on my Schwinn, and Coach Wolfe took an immediate liking to me. Besides being Frank Bags's younger brother, I was there to ride, whereas the football players showed mixed degrees of enthusiasm for his unconventional approach to off-season training. Over the course of the season, I grew to appreciate competitive athletics for the first time in my life. I trained hard, got faster, and excelled at something outside the classroom.

I wasn't the only one who got stronger and fitter, and the football team made it to the quarterfinals of the state playoffs that fall. Unfortunately for me, Coach Wolfe's off-season conditioning program caught the attention of multiple collegiate athletic directors, and he accepted a position with one of the Big Ten football programs that winter. His replacement viewed off-season training outside the weight room with suspicion and scrapped the cycling team. Along with it went my career in organized sports.

Marty hops onto my bed and worms his way around my IVs and the sling supporting my collarbone until he's resting his head on my good shoulder. We watch the American, Bob Mionske, compete in the Olympic road race. Mionske is a local Chicago boy from Evanston, Illinois. He finishes fourth, less than a wheel's length behind a West German rider. Although he missed out on a medal by inches, Mionske's finish is the best ever Olympic performance by an American cyclist.

It's also the beginning of a special friendship.

Marty and I spend the afternoon watching replays of various track events. You couldn't have scripted a better matchup for the men's 100-meter race. Carl Lewis, defending Olympic champion, lines up against Ben Johnson, current world champ. In a close finish, the Canadian Johnson breaks our hearts by taking gold over the American Lewis.

Johnson later loses his gold because of a failed drug test. I'm happy to see Carl Lewis get the medal he deserves, but the circumstances leave me feeling empty and deceived. Johnson cheated Lewis and everyone watching out of the emotion that can only be experienced at the finish line, not days later through some procedural victory.

"Mom calls that 'fair play,'" Marty says.

"I call it bullshit."

"It's like Twister," Marty says.

"Twister?"

"Twister. We played it at my birthday party. I love to see how far I can twist before I fall."

"That's why this is so disappointing. Cheating makes it all about winning, instead of the race itself."

"At my party, my friend Kevin started pushing people so they'd fall over. Everyone stopped laughing and more friends started cheating. Then everyone got mad because Kevin won."

"You mean everyone except Kevin?"

"No, he got mad, too, because nobody wanted to play with him anymore."

11

Each morning brings one less sucky day until I get out of the hospital. My mind is suffering the same deterioration as my body. I've given up on schoolwork. My attention span is shot, and reading gives me a headache. I spend most days doing nothing more than getting interrupted by bandage changes, sponge baths, walks around the Peds floor, and mushy food that all tastes like potatoes.

Dr. Moroni visits for his daily checkup. Marty started responding to his timid knocks on the door with one-liners from the daytime television he's been gorging on. "Just a moment, we're washing our hair!" he hollers today. We both laugh like a live studio audience.

Dr. Moroni tiptoes to the side of my bed and asks, "How are you today, Samuel?"

"It's Sam." We go through this every day.

"Right . . . Sam. Everything okay?"

I describe my inability to concentrate while reading.

"That should pass in the next few days."

"Is there a test or something?"

He looks down at his clipboard and says, "Anything else?"

"Uh, well . . ." I'm tired of Moroni's routine. All the touchy-feely interest in my emotions yet no concrete answers to my questions. *How do you feel? Are you enjoying the food? Are you comfortable? What's new in your life?* What does he think I'm up to? I'm in the hospital wasting away while senior year passes me by. So I ask him about the guilt I'm feeling over my enjoyment of the morphine.

"We don't want you to be in any pain, Samuel."

"I flew into a tree! Shouldn't I expect *some* pain?"

"We've been tapering your dosage since you got out of the ICU. This is a regulated substance, and everything is carefully monitored. You can trust the drug companies and your medical team know what we're doing."

I want to protest. I want to tell him my physical suffering is nothing more than the itching of my incisions as they heal. At this point, my body has adapted to the pain. But I don't tell him that. He makes it too easy to play along, and I already miss the liquid blow jobs I'll say goodbye to when I go home. So I give in and take another trip away from my atrophied body and brain and the life I wanted to escape right up until that car crashed into me.

Nurse Cooper reads *The Little Prince* to Marty. She invited me to join, but I refuse to be read a children's book. So while I lie alone in bed, Marty giggles and gasps as Nurse Cooper's enchanting voice retells the story about living a rich and unselfish life. She pauses when an orderly walks in with a bouquet of flowers for me.

"Those aren't from me," Nurse Cooper jokes. The surprise delivery makes a typical day in the hospital as exciting as my birthday. She notices I can't keep my eyes off the unmarked envelope attached to the vase. "I'm not continuing until you read that card."

I open the envelope and read the note out loud:

> *Dear Sam,*
>
> *How are you? I pray daily for your speedy recovery. I can't begin to tell you how many sleepless nights I've had since our accident and wonder why the Lord chose me to drive over that hill at the exact moment you were on the other side.*

While this tragedy may have been avoided if you had not been drinking that evening, there is a reason for everything, and the Lord's Prayer reminds us to forgive those who trespass against us.

After many hours of prayer, I've decided to forgive you and would like to cover the cost to repair your bike in the hope you will be able to ride it once again.

God bless you,
Marjorie Craven

"Well, if *that* doesn't restore your faith in America," Nurse Cooper says. She picks up where she left off with Marty and leaves me to ponder Marjorie's note. I read it a few more times, wondering what kind of nut believes my near-death experience was the Lord's doing.

Discharge day. Nurse Cooper removes the tape securing the IV to the crook of my elbow, then slides the bloody needle out of my rigid vein for the last time. The tube leashing me to a bag of saline solution since the paramedics wheeled me into the ER drips along the floor as she carries it away.

Mom arrives later that morning, and I change out of my hospital gown. Marty laughs when I step out of the bathroom, and I get the joke when I look in the mirror. I can now cinch my belt to its tightest hole, and my loose jeans make me look like MC Hammer.

"You might want to think about getting a haircut, too." Mom's humor often involves a sarcastic barb about something she's trying not to complain about. It's been so long since my last visit to a barber, I can now tuck my hair behind my ears.

Dr. Padrone enters. He's dressed in clean surgical scrubs, taking a break from repairing the damaged and dying.

"Big day, buddy," he says.

I detect a grin underneath the intensity of his game face.

"Let's get you ready for the beach."

I cringe when I realize he's ready to remove the staples from my belly.

Padrone slides one of his shovel-sized hands behind my shoulders to help me sit up and swing my legs over the side of the bed, then pulls a futuristic-looking pair of scissors out of his pocket, squeezing them a few times in his meaty hands.

"What do you call that thing?" I ask, as if the staples might magically disappear while I stall Padrone with questions.

"A staple remover." He senses my anxiety and hands me the tool. It looks like an oversize nail clipper with a pincer at the tip, presumably for grabbing and bending the long edge of each metal staple.

He lowers my gown off the front of my shoulders, exposing the minefield that is my torso. "This should tickle more than hurt," he says, before snipping the topmost staple on my incision.

The ends of the staple pop free with a warm pinch, like pulling a hair out of my skin. The staple lands in the stainless-steel bowl next to him with a gentle *ting*.

He works his way down my torso, popping staples patiently and efficiently.

Snip-ting-snip-ting-snip-ting.

The man is an enigma. A mysterious beast who brings bodies back from the dead with his bare hands, yet is capable of working the canvas of my torso with the delicate brushstrokes of an artist.

After the final staple drops into the bowl, Padrone steps back to survey his work. Fifty pink dots border each side of the vertical incision running from my sternum to my navel. The scar looks like crispy bacon, and the holes left by the staples itch like crazy.

"Try not to scratch," he says. "Hydrocortisone cream will help the itching."

He presses a finger to the scars left by the drainage holes on each of my love handles and the gastronomy tube above my stomach.

"These have sealed up nicely."

He rests his fists on his hips and gives me a smile for the first time since we met. "You ready to get back out there?"

Before I answer, Nurse Cooper swings the door open. "Dr. Padrone, you're needed downstairs."

He turns back to me. "I'll see you in three weeks for your checkup. In the meantime, keep moving and try to put on some weight."

Mom thanks him as he makes his way to the door, and the artist with the delicate hands transforms back into the hardened gladiator, ready to return to the mess of life and death downstairs.

Nurse Cooper runs me through the usual battery of tests and weighs me one last time. One hundred twenty-five pounds—same as when I was a freshman, four years, five inches, and twenty-five pounds ago.

She asks if I have any questions.

"Yeah, uh . . . what do I do now? Go home and have lunch?"

"That's exactly what you do," she says. "Go home and eat something. Take a walk. Do some schoolwork. Visit with friends. You need to return to daily life, and that starts today. Then you do the same thing tomorrow and the day after that."

"It all seems so sudden." I've been looking forward to this day for weeks, but I didn't expect things would feel so messy once it arrived.

"Sam, there's no cure for tragedy. You've survived an experience you'll find has changed you. It might not be obvious how, but when you notice it, don't fight it. Embrace the change and find a way to allow it to make you a better human being."

"Thanks for that, Nurse Cooper." If there's one thing I am ready to embrace, it's change for the better. "You've really been . . . an angel."

I walk over to Marty's bed and give him a hug. "Thanks for being my roommate, Marty. I hope you get out of here soon."

"Thanks, Sam. See you at school!"

As I walk past Nurse Cooper on my way out the door, she puts her hand on my shoulder and looks at me one last time with those diamond eyes. “You’re going to be okay, Sam.”

“Will I ever see you again?”

“That would be wonderful. Do me a favor though.”

“Yeah?”

“Let’s meet somewhere else next time!”

1989 Illinois High School Track and Field Regional Finals

3200-meter race, first five laps

I pop off the line with a violent exhale and marvel at how easily Cooper Assell and Rich Duffy—the two race favorites—jump to a three-meter lead. While there's little doubt they'll finish in the top four and make it to state, neither will be content merely meeting expectations.

The field settles into a pace I can barely sustain after the first turn, and Duffy and Coop maintain their lead over the rest of us. Little changes over the course of the first 1600 meters as I try to hang on and not screw anything up.

Coop and Duffy lift their pace as we start lap five, and a group of seven chasers, including me, matches the increased effort. We're past the point of posturing, and the runners near me pant like a team of sled dogs.

Fear within the chase group provokes the junior from Ernie Banks High to attack on the back straight of lap five. I'm stuck behind the bunch when he makes his move. My teammate José is well positioned at the front and joins him. They catch up to Coop and Duffy, creating a lead group of four.

The stands tower over the second turn of lap five, and a multicolored cloud of energy and noise propels us down the near straightaway. Three laps to go, and I remain boxed in by the chase group, like the hospital bed that restrained me nine months ago. If I don't find a way to break free, my season will be over in less than three minutes.

12

I celebrate my homecoming with a nap. The doorbell jolts me awake from a nightmare about watching TV in a hospital bed.

"That must be Frank," Mom says to herself from the kitchen. She opens the front door and shouts, "Go around back!"

I'm unaware of Mom ever allowing a family member to enter the front door. This enables her to keep the public areas of the house uncomfortably spotless. If years of frostbite, scraped knees, and urgent pleas for the toilet never tempted Mom to open that door, the return of two sons after extended absences stands little chance of softening her up.

I take a shower to shed the hospital stink from my body. Despite the removal of the staples, tubes, and drainage bags, my abdomen remains tender and caked with dried blood. My skin bears the leathery yellow stain of the Betadine antiseptic the nurses applied to my sutures each time they changed my bandages. Those bandages stripped my wounds raw, and the pressurized water from the showerhead stings the exposed tissue like rubbing alcohol.

I return to my room and find Frank has already settled in. His leading quality as a roommate is a lack of possessions. Other than clothes, all he brought home is a stereo and his high school football helmet. The gold plastic shell still sizzles with the heat of the battlefield like some ancient warrior's armor displayed in a museum. In an adult's bedroom, however, Frank's high school trophy is a sad reminder of an incomplete victory.

Frank convinces me to join him for a short walk while Mom

prepares dinner. We head to the base of Spirit Hill three blocks to the west. After walking around the Peds floor, I no longer hunch over like an ape-man.

"The first thing we do tomorrow is get you some new shoes," Frank says.

"I like my Chucks." The same navy-blue Chuck Taylor high tops I walked hundreds of miles in while caddying this summer seem adequate for PT walks.

"Is that right?" One of Frank's annoying habits is to disagree by feigning curiosity. "You see what I'm wearing?" He points to his drab pair of gray Adidas. "These are running shoes, which also makes them good for walking. Better support than those Chucks. We'll go try on a few pairs tomorrow and see what you think." Like many conversations with Frank, the easiest way to get him to stop telling you you're wrong is to shut up.

I'm huffing by the time we get to the end of our block and explain to Frank this is the farthest I've walked since August.

"Sure thing. Let's go home and stretch."

The smell of simmering tomatoes, garlic, and oregano greets us at the back door. Mom calls her pasta sauce a "gravy" because unlike an everyday marinara, it contains a cupboard-full of ingredients and cooks for hours. One of its secret ingredients is the mystique surrounding its origin in Naples generations ago and journey to the US in the head and heart of my grandmother in the early 1900s. Frank and I roll our eyes each time Mom retells the stories, but they never fail to enhance the meal.

The three of us sit at our shitty little kitchen table. No one comments on the empty chair Dad used to occupy.

"This sure beats the food at the hospital," I say.

"Amen! Some home-cooked meals will help fill out that waistline." Like all the women in our family, Mom believes a few extra pounds are a sign of good fortune and health.

I exercise my atrophied stomach muscles with two helpings of pasta and a slice of Italian bread to clean my plate. The walk with Frank and onset of a food coma leave me barely enough energy to crawl into bed after dinner. Getting in and out of bed remains a slow, delicate exercise. Really, any movement requiring a stomach muscle sends pain up and down my midsection. I've learned how to roll in and out of bed without flexing my abs, but the pressure of my body's weight still burns the muscles underneath my scar.

The familiarity of my childhood bed soothes my aching body as I stare at the ceiling. Before sleep pulls my eyes closed, a slow tickle in my head, itch in my throat, and tension in my limbs demand something left back at the hospital—my nightly dose of morphine. The craving grows in my bones, stopping short of helplessness when exhaustion sends me into a deep sleep.

An energetic voice from Frank's speakers startles me awake in the middle of the night. It's the announcer for WBBM Newsradio 780 AM. *Welcome home, roomie.* For inexplicable reasons, Frank never adopted the use of an alarm clock. Since seventh grade, he's relied on the station's "Nonstop news, traffic, weather, sports, and business"—interrupted by frequent announcements of the local time—to get up in the morning. "It's twelve forty-eight. Here's traffic and weather together on the eights . . ."

While I wish I could blame Frank for waking me, the problem is the cramp in my belly, the juices sloshing around my stomach, and the burn in my throat. Withdrawal from the happy juice is a logical suspect, but gorging on Mom's home cooking after two weeks of soda crackers, chicken broth, and fruit bowls has more likely shocked my system. My adventures in underaged drinking have taught me to know when I'm moments away from puking, and I make it to the hallway bathroom an instant before dinner splashes into the toilet. Three retches later, and it's over. I stagger back to bed and fall fast asleep once again, untroubled by the report of a traffic accident on the Kennedy Expressway in the background.

13

"It's seven forty," announces the Sunday morning radio host. "Sports is up next."

"Morning, bro," Frank says. "How'd you sleep?"

"Eh . . . why do you keep the radio on when you're already awake?"

"Because I want to eat at eight and need to know when to get out of bed."

We meet Mom in the kitchen, enjoying her morning ritual of coffee and the *Chicago Tribune*.

"Bacon and eggs or pancakes, boys?"

"No fried food for me, Ant'nette," Frank says.

Mom gives him her *whatever* face.

Happy to take advantage of the hospitality while it lasts, I accept her offer.

Mom gives me the week off from mass but insists I join her next Sunday.

"You know how I feel about church, Mom." As soon as the words leave my mouth, I regret giving her an easy target.

"You mean to tell me after all you've been through, you still resent God?"

"I have nothing against God, Mohammed, Yoda or whoever brings people spiritual inspiration. It's all the loudmouths I can't handle."

"Loudmouths? No one even talks at mass," Mom says.

"It's not what they say. It's the showing off that bugs me. All the happy parents acting like they're in some phony smile contest. Then they judge you if your family doesn't walk in looking like a

Christmas card."

"I never feel judged," Mom says. Frank laughs.

"Our family is why I feel judged!" I say. "Don't you remember how people treated us when Dad lost his job or when Frank flunked out of college or all the funny looks we get in the Skylark?"

"The Beet! I always felt embarrassed in that car," Frank says.

Our shit-maroon secondhand two-door Buick Skylark earned its nickname one cold Sunday in January ten years ago when its battery died in the church parking lot. The guy who helped Dad jump-start it gave him a hard time for owning a car that resembled a rotten vegetable. "Like a beet or something," he said.

Mom places her fists on the table while swallowing a mouthful of eggs. "I think you're blaming Saint Edward's for broader problems in society."

"Maybe. But those childhood memories all have Sunday mass in common."

"Believe what you want, but joining me next week is the least you can do, given how many people have been praying for you."

"I appreciate people praying for me, but don't be surprised if I walk out after Communion."

"You know, I planned on thanking God today for saving your life," Mom says. "Now I think I'll have to ask Him to save your soul."

Shortly after the Beet putters out of the driveway, Frank and I head to the running store in his El Camino. The car's brown and tan paint scheme earned it the nickname the "Guinness" when Frank was in high school. Its split personality—passenger car up front, pickup in back—suited High School Frank: all business on the football field, Mr. Good Time off it. The Guinness had a reputation as a party car given the bed in the back got lots of use transporting kegs and boozy teenagers. Now it looks like a dated muscle car driven by someone who can't afford to replace it.

The Runner's Sole is located in downtown Linden Grove, around the corner from Doc Riley's. I've passed it hundreds of times because it's next door to the Tourmalet, our local bike shop, but I've never had a reason to walk in until today. Frank heads to the book and magazine section, and a twenty-something clerk named Summer greets me in running gear that fits her body like a superhero suit. She asks me a bunch of questions. Her light brown eyes are as soft as flannel and muffle everything I say into "Uhhhh."

My eyes twitch so nervously in her presence I fear she'll think I'm stoned. I shift my gaze to her lips and blush because they look like big juicy pillows I want to cuddle up into. If I take my eyes off her face, they lock onto the gravitational pull of her breasts, which I know is wrong. I eventually give up trying to break the cycle of *eyeslipsbreasts eyeslipsbreasts eyeslipsbreasts* and stare at the floor while stammering through an explanation of my accident and need for a pair of walking shoes.

Summer measures my foot and analyzes my gait as I walk along a rubber track inside the store. She pooh-poohs my Chuck Taylors as if I wore Hawaiian shorts to a wedding. She could sell me Moon Boots and I'd leave happy, but instead she recommends the New Balance 1300s as a comfortable, stable shoe to support my walking.

After I pay for the shoes with part of my caddie savings, Frank and I cross the street to Sandy Creek Park for an easy walk on the dirt path circling it. The nauseous feeling returns during our second lap, and two eggs and chunks of bacon end up in the grass.

"What's up with that?" Frank asks.

"No idea. The same thing happened with dinner last night." I fill him in on my nocturnal dance with the toilet.

Frank leans over to inspect my barf. "This ain't normal." He suggests I take it easy on Mom's cooking until my body adjusts to eating again.

I push through an achy walk back to Frank's car, when a juggernaut of energy packed in lean muscle breezes by us. "Hi, Sam. Enjoy those shoes!" Summer waves.

"What was that?" Frank asks.

"My new favorite season. You should have bought a pair of shoes today."

"Now that you mention it . . ." Frank says, looking down at his Adidas.

Mom greets us back home with lunch from the Happy Wiener, local vendor of all the favorite foods of my childhood.

"Beef or hot dog, Sam?" Mom asks. Frank rinses lettuce in the sink behind her and tilts his head to remind me to take it easy on lunch. The aroma from the grease-stained paper bags on the kitchen table brings sentimental tears to my eyes.

"I, uh, I'll just have some fries."

"Fries aren't a meal!"

"I—I'm still full from breakfast."

"Take a hot dog." Mom places the sweet-smelling package of comfort in front of me, and I drool as pickle relish falls over the side of the bun.

"Lay off a bit, Ant'nette," Frank says. "You don't need to force it on him."

"Who's forcing? I'm letting you make your rabbit food over there, aren't I?"

"Come on, guys," I say. The argument about to unfold stirs my gut, already bubbling from my last two meals.

"I don't need to *make* my rabbit food," Frank says. "This is how it grows out of the dirt."

"Okay, wise guy. What's with you and the fancy foods, anyway?"

In the hopeless hope of salvaging a beautiful day outside the hospital, I start singing "Won't You Be My Neighbor?" from *Mister Rogers' Neighborhood*. I don't know where it comes from—although PBS television provided the bulk of my early social-emotional development.

"Since giving up booze, healthy eating has become a more

wholesome outlet for my addictive personality," Frank says.

"Well, you can't survive on salad alone."

"You're right. I eat a lot more than salads. I just don't eat any more fast food."

I continue with "Can You Tell Me How to Get to Sesame Street" from the television show that helped me believe every day could be a sunny day. Frank and Mom give me a quick glance, then continue swinging.

"The Happy Weiner is *not* fast food."

"I should have said *unhealthy* food."

"Don't lecture me on healthy food. Did all that healthy food help Dad?"

"Oh, come on! Dad never stopped eating crappy food."

"I'm the one who buys the groceries. Low fat this, sugar free that, margarine instead of butter, Healthy Choice frozen dinners."

Arguing over Dad makes me nauseous again, so I start singing the chorus to "You Light Up My Life," the Debby Boone song that made me want to barf during car rides with my parents in the seventies.

"Mom, Dad had high blood pressure, diabetes, he was fifty pounds overweight, and his only exercise was reclining the La-Z-Boy. You think he was born that way?"

"Don't start this," Mom says.

"You started it."

"You haven't even been home twenty-four hours."

"What are you trying to say?" Frank says.

"I'm trying *not* to say it."

"Go ahead, Mom, give us your professional opinion as to what caused Dad's heart attack."

I give up. Defeated, I sing "Rainy Days and Mondays," the Carpenters song that reminds me of eating breakfast at this same sad table with Mom on dark winter mornings, wishing I could crawl back into bed instead of facing the snow and ice on my walk to school.

"You broke his heart," Mom says. "He was your biggest fan, and you shattered all the dreams he had for you."

"Yeah, yeah—I blew it, screwed my life up. But Dad's problems ran deeper than disappointment in his son."

"You're welcome to your opinion."

"*My* opinion? I'm only restating the opinion of what every shrink and medical doctor told us."

"None of that matters, guys!" I finally shout. "It doesn't change the fact Dad's not here, and he works at a car wash!"

"Hmmph." Frank takes the opportunity to stand down. "I'll be out back—with my *salad*. Feel free to join me, Sam, I made one for you, too."

Frank lets the screen door slam behind him. Before I respond, Mom puts me out of my misery. "Oh, go ahead and join him!"

Mom stays at the table after I skulk away. Not one to allow something paid for go to waste, she rehashes her conversation with Frank in between bites of a second hot dog and bag of fries.

14

I change the bandages on my belly twice a day. Rubbing the antiseptic swab along my wounds sends a shiver through the young nerves in the new skin. I accept the scars and wires are a part of me now.

Dr. Moroni encouraged me to take Advil for the pain after I left the hospital. Without the euphoria of the morphine, popping pills three times a day isn't worth the hassle. My morphine cravings are the only injuries that still hurt, and withdrawal is a whole different kind of pain. It burns under the skin, hard to pinpoint, but everywhere I look.

Sara stops by with a backpack full of study snacks and textbooks. "How's the homework coming?" She's wearing a Roxy Music T-shirt and a fresh shade of green hair.

"Terrible," I say. "I can't read without getting dizzy."

Sara offers me a powdered doughnut, which I pass on, given my stomach issues. Thirty minutes in, I toss my AP Calculus textbook against the wall.

"This is crazy!" I say. "I can't make sense of the first chapter. How am I going to catch up?"

"Uh—let's take a break."

"I don't have time for a break!"

She shakes her head and returns to her book. A minute passes, and Sara shows no interest in my problems.

"I thought you came to help?"

"I'm waiting for the tragedy to pass."

"You may be here a while. Do you want to know what tragedy looks like?"

She ignores my question, but that doesn't stop me from explaining it looks like a brown gash stretching from my sternum to my navel and hurts like the humiliation of having to relearn how to stand up and walk without holding someone's arm. It's the helplessness of being unable to pay attention and understand what I'm reading, like when the nuns at Saint Edward's convinced me I was stupid until I finally worked my way back into the eighth-grade language arts classroom. Tragedy is the inability to feed my hunger because my body holds a grudge. "It feels like a part of me got stolen."

Sara takes a deep breath, causing me to do the same. It relaxes one of us. I want to break the silence, but I'm not ready to apologize.

"Tell me about homecoming," I say.

"My new band played the dance."

"*New* band?"

"It's the same band minus our narcissistic singer. He wouldn't stop telling everyone he threw us out of *his* band, so we changed our name, found a new singer, and added a girl bassist."

"How'd it go?"

"We rocked. The new chick can play a mean funky bass guitar. It went so well, Miss Homecoming Committee Karen Beager kept nagging us to play more dance songs."

"Sorry I missed it."

"Well, you've been busy studying, right?" Sara grins.

"Right . . ."

"Are you ready to get back to work?"

"Listen, I've got too much hitting me at once. I get tired walking down the street, laugh like a hyena, and puke after every meal. To top it off, my brain is mush."

"Bags, you literally died two months ago. Why are you being so tough on yourself?"

"Because I've worked too hard at becoming a good student to fail now."

"Can you drop any classes?"

"Not if I want to graduate in June. I've always taken a study hall to keep up with the workload, so I have no credits to spare."

"Who says you need to graduate in June?"

"If I don't graduate on time with at least a B average each semester of my senior year, I lose my scholarship—and my plans to get out of Linden Grove."

"Are your teachers showing you any love?"

"Pffft. When my mom went to pick up my books, Mr. Bracovich told her I shouldn't expect any special treatment. And you know he's a stickler for class participation."

"Stickler's one word for whatever's jammed up that guy's ass. Asking questions in AP US History has become a full contact sport."

"Huh, huh, huh," a low chugging laugh puffs out my throat as I avoid straining the surgical wires left in my belly. "I can't wait to get back to school, but it takes me all morning to change my bandages, do my walking and stretching therapy, and wipe my ass without causing the scars on my belly to burn."

"More than I needed to know, Bags." Sara says while covering her ears.

"Sorry."

"It sounds like the easy road through senior year vanished with your bike. You're going to have to get comfortable leaning on others for help even if you don't like the idea."

"Thanks for all you're trying to do. I mean it. And I'll take you up on your offer to help. I'm just not ready yet."

After three days of failing to hold down any traditional Bagliarello foods, Frank prepares a few meals for me. He ditches the take-out and microwave dinners, snack foods, and a butcher's counter worth of processed meats like sausage, hot dogs, brats, and salami. He also scales back the milk and cheese. He claims this will give my hypersensitive system a rest and reduce inflammation to help my muscles recover more quickly from the rehab. It's hard to give up all my favorite foods, but after a few days, Frank's program seems to be working. I haven't had any digestive issues, and my taste buds are starting to enjoy the new flavors.

After Frank cooks me a breakfast of oatmeal loaded with nuts, seeds, and berries and topped with maple syrup, I make it to the foot of Spirit Hill. I'm getting stronger and no longer drag my knuckles like an ape-man when I walk. I look up to the summit, marvel at how the road disappears into the sky, and figure if I can get to the top of that, I can do anything.

Jed calls and wants to welcome me home in person.

"Do me a favor, Jed."

"Laugh at your jokes?"

"Pick up a six-pack on your way over."

"I'll be there at seven."

Asking Jed for help with schoolwork is pointless. He may have a brilliant mind for mischief, but he's not much of a student. He's one of those kids who can pull a 90 on a test without studying and knows that's enough to get him into the schools his parents will allow him to attend. With the efficiency of the engineer he wants to be, he deems any further effort wasteful.

Jed and Sara are fine friends to have if you spend the first several weeks of senior year recovering from a tragic accident. Sara is the friend to turn to in a crisis. Jed can help you forget about your problems over a game of Scrabble, an episode of *Gilligan's Island*, or beers on a school night.

Jed rolls up in his parents' minivan. "Where ya' wanna go?" he asks.

I look him up and down and shake my head.

"Shut up," he says.

"I didn't say a thing."

He's wearing one of his "school outfits." Jed's control-freak mother makes sure he never leaves home without a clean, pressed shirt sufficiently plain to avoid controversy. No concert T-shirts, branded sports apparel, or graphic prints for Jed. When his mom finds a style she likes, she buys it in multiple colors, which Jed rotates through strategically, hoping no one notices he wears the same thing every day.

"Let's check out the benches," I say. The patch of grass at the top of Spirit Hill has a few long wooden seats from which you can catch the sunset. I fill Jed in on things since we last saw each other but leave out the morphine stuff. Until I figure out how to shake my nighttime cravings, I don't want anyone thinking I have a problem with drugs.

"So, why the interest in boozing alone tonight?" Jed asks.

"I'm not alone. I'm with you."

He squints like I kicked dirt in his eyes. Some people give you the benefit of the doubt to avoid confrontation. Jed's not one of them. Seeing as he's my oldest friend and can smell my B.S., I fess up about the morphine cravings.

"That's messed up," he says, whistling his *s*'s.

"Can you get hooked on something if no one tells you it's addictive?"

"Of course! You're talking about chemical changes to your brain. This isn't a matter of ignoring an itch."

"I'm not shaking and sweating like in the movies. It's more like being hungry for something I can't eat, but the feeling's in my head, not my belly. I guess it's also in my throat. And my bones. But not my belly. Well, sometimes my belly."

"Sounds like withdrawal," Jed says.

"That's why I wanted a beer. Maybe an old-fashioned buzz will trick my body and let me sleep tonight."

"Well, you'll be happy to know I picked out an old-fashioned beer for you."

I should have known not to let a teetotaler choose the beer when

Jed hands me a can of Old Style. Here I am celebrating my first night out since my accident on a park bench, watching the sunset with a guy while drinking cat piss.

"You know, I wonder who's to blame for your drug problem," Jed says as we watch headlights zip around lower Linden Grove.

"It's not a problem. I'm sure it will go away on its own."

"I'd be careful. You know, addiction runs in families."

"*You* be careful."

Jed ducks for cover, knowing better than to draw comparisons between Frank and me.

"It's not an addiction," I say.

"Call it what you want, but I'm not sure Old Style is the smartest way to kick a narcotics craving."

Jed's got a point. Frank swapped his addiction to alcohol for diet and exercise. Maybe I need to find a healthier antidote than beer.

"Oh, yeah, I forgot to tell you I found your bike," Jed says. "The cop at the scene of your crash put it in the trunk of his car. It's been in his garage the past five weeks."

"How's it look?"

"About as bad as you the first time Sara and I visited the hospital."

I respond like a drunk Santa slurring "Ho, Ho, Ho." Jed mimics me, but we agree it doesn't sound authentic without the scars to back it up.

"Seriously, though," he says. "I brought it to the Tourmalet. They said it would cost more to repair than replace with a new bike."

"That sucks. I loved that bike."

"Maybe you can see if the lady who hit you will pay for a new one."

"Ugh, Saint Marjorie. I better start praying at bedtime."

"Or you can find a new way to get around town."

Jed drives me home after a second beer. I enjoy my buzz while chilling out to some Hüsker Dü. The Old Style wears off but not in a familiar way. My head's foggy, my stomach's queasy, and my muscles ache—

like the first time I chewed tobacco. This has nothing to do with the dinner I ate. My body is rejecting the alcohol while working hard to rebuild itself. Fearing another barf session, I lie down in the empty bathtub, stretch an arm across my face and fight the spinning room by rocking back and forth while my system flushes the poison. The malaise passes within a couple hours, and I crawl back into bed.

I can't fall asleep because my head starts to tickle again. Tears pool in my eyes then trickle down into my ears. I do my best to swallow my whimpers for fear of waking Frank. Before the accident, I was ready to conquer the world with ambition and brains. Now I'm a broken, foggy-brained junkie wishing some nurse would walk into my room with a blue-capped escape pod.

A low rumble grows in my ear. Bad Gorilla. "What makes you think recovery was going to be easy?" he says. "Your accident destroyed you. The hospital pampered you. You were the center of attention. People fed you, walked you, bathed you, and numbed the complaining out of you. Then they threw you back into a life that passed you by."

He gives me a moment to wallow.

"There's no road back to normal, dude. Time to climb out of recovery on your own and see what's waiting for you on the other side."

I hear another voice, and it takes me a second to realize it's coming from Frank's bed. "Sam, I know what you need. We'll talk tomorrow."

15

Frank tells me a return to the scene of my accident and a walk up Spirit Hill will help me move past my tragedy.

He brings his Polaroid to capture the milestone. It doesn't occur to me I should have considered a solo effort until Frank starts belting out Jimmy Buffet songs as we walk down the street. Frank the Parrothead. While I can sing along when a party enters the sloppy stage, Frank is the only person I know who listens to Jimmy Buffet music in the middle of the day. I find this even more baffling since he no longer drinks.

"Do you realize the irony of singing 'Cheeseburger in Paradise' now that you've given up beef, cheese, and cold draft beer?"

"Abstaining from booze and cheeseburgers while enjoying Jimmy Buffet tunes is a test of my will. And today, *I'm* in control."

"We're in the middle of a walk, Frank. Where's the temptation?"

"Hey, how about a little support?"

"Can you at least sing to yourself so I can concentrate on this climb?"

He tries, without success, but I give him credit for at least singing less loudly.

We get to the base of the hill, and I look to the summit as I've done hundreds of times before. No climb up Spirit Hill is the same, and this afternoon will be as special as any. I try not to, but it's impossible to keep from looking at the spot where I crashed. I expect to see some trace of my flight path into the trees, but the branches sway as they always have, reminding me the tragedy is all my own.

The first two hundred steps to the top breeze by. I pause to catch my breath, then continue for a hundred more before another short break.

A carful of guys from the tennis team shout out their windows as they speed by. They aren't shouting at me. They don't even notice me. They're just coasting downhill in a hurry to get somewhere else.

When I restart, I don't feel rested, and Frank senses what's become clear to me.

"Short steps, Sam."

The effort consumes my lungs and legs—and we haven't yet reached the steepest part of the hill. I start again but can't make it ten steps.

"It's not. Gonna work. Today," I say between heavy breaths.

"Hey, this is the farthest you've made it yet. You can walk home proud." Frank leans in and snaps a picture.

"Get that out of my face!" I swat at the camera and miss, lose my balance on the downhill slope, and end up on my ass. I sit up, pull my knees to my chest, and hang my head in frustration.

As my breath returns, anger at Frank bleeds into self-pity, and I tear up for the second time in twenty-four hours. "God, this sucks."

Frank sits next to me, mirroring my body position. We sit quietly looking at the ground through our knees.

"Define 'this,'" he says.

"Hmmphh." I lift my head and wipe my eyes. "I guess it *all* sucks when you think about it. Doesn't it?"

"I think we've passed peak suck, Sam." He looks up, and his unblinking stare reveals an unusually vulnerable Frank. Set against his otherwise dark Mediterranean features, Frank's green eyes give away more than he likes to share. Today they are asking to be trusted again.

"Think about it," he says. "You're alive, and you haven't puked in a week. I'm sober and working on my own recovery. Dad has a job and is starting to show up again in our lives. Ant'nette's still a pain in the ass, but her heart's in the right place. I think things are looking up."

It's the rare occasion I don't resent Frank's natural ability to charm people into agreeing with him. I extend a hand. "Little help?"

Frank jumps to his feet and pulls me up. "Hey, was that the collarbone you broke?"

I hadn't given it any thought but yes, Frank pulled me up by the arm connected to my formerly broken collarbone without any pain.

"See. The worst is behind us," he says. We brush the dust off our shorts and turn to head back home.

Three girls from the cross-country team glide toward us from the bottom of the hill. They smile at Frank and ignore me as they pass. It's the story of my life, but instead of making me feel sorry for myself, their smiles lift my spirit. Any idiot can drive a car down Spirit Hill, but no one runs up it by accident. Bad Gorilla's rant last night convinced me I'm never going to feel ready to recover from my accident. Better to fail trying than waiting.

"Stay here," I tell Frank when we reach the bottom. Before he has a chance to ask questions, I turn and face the hill. I focus on the first stretch in front of me and start walking, pausing for a short break after a couple hundred steps, no better or worse than my earlier attempt.

Another hundred steps, and I quietly celebrate making it further than my last try. The steepest section is right in front of me, hiding the summit above. I look over to the spot of my crash again. *Fuck you, crash.* I accept life can be messy. My family's been no stranger to tragedy these past few years, but I never expected my own life to get so messy so early. My accident will always be a life-changing event for me, but like the trees that show no trace of it, I need to move on.

I restart my climb and, after another hundred or so steps, pass the steepest part of the hill. There's no need to rest, as the easing slope is like a breeze at my back, pushing me to the summit. I know at this point I'll make it. When I reach the top, I stand fully upright for the first time in weeks. The scars are for life, but my wounds have healed.

Accidents happen, but life doesn't happen by accident—in the same way I didn't get to where I'm standing without choosing to try again. I've made a mess of my life over the past several weeks, but somewhere in that messiness is the stuff that matters. I don't know exactly what that stuff is, but I want to figure it out.

I walk back down the hill so gingerly I'm practically jogging. By the time I high-five Frank at the bottom, I know where to start looking.

1989 Illinois High School Track and Field Regional Finals
3200-meters race, laps six and seven

Self-doubt first appears at the beginning of lap six. Did I miss the move of the race? Coop, Duffy, José and the runner from Ernie Banks High maintain a small gap at the front. Lots of jockeying among my chase group of five leads to no improvement in position relative to the four leaders. One of us works his way to the front only to be overtaken by another runner moments later. This cycle continues until each of us eventually gets spit out the back.

The noise from the crowd builds as we approach the second turn of lap six. The fans sense the real race is about to begin. It may be the onset of runner's delirium, but I hear a voice calling my name. The second time I hear it, I see Summer from the corner of my eye standing alongside the track, fifty meters from the line.

Lap seven. Two to go. I'm wasting valuable energy playing merry-go-round in the chase group. The four tickets to state are three strides ahead, and I need to be up there if I want to be part of the fight in the final stretch. The perfect time to attack will be when I rotate to the front of this chase group.

I'm not the only one with that idea.

The senior from Otis Rush High attacks from the second position in the chase group. He closes half the gap to the four leaders before Duffy and Coop sense the move and pick up their pace. When the Otis Rush kid catches José and the runner from Ernie Banks, they are two meters behind Coop and Duffy and about the same distance ahead of my remaining group of four chasers. All three groups are running faster as a result of Otis Rush's move. Two runners from my chase group fall away, and my breaths are heavy enough I know my body won't be able to outrun the lactic acid about to flood my muscles.

Seven hundred meters—less than two laps—left to race. The senior from William Murray is on my left in lane one. If I'm not in the front four by the start of lap eight, the race is over for me. I pick up my pace as we exit the first turn of lap seven. The William Murray runner matches me, and we catch José and the runners from Ernie Banks and Otis Rush. Assuming Coop and Duffy maintain their lead to the finish, there is room for only two of us five chasers in the top four.

We approach the second turn of lap seven. The runner from Otis Rush falls behind and is out of the race by the time we exit. In the fog of fatigue I weigh the chances my fellow chasers fade in the final lap. I'm not thinking quickly but recognize false hope. The better strategy is a more painful one. Recovery taught me that waiting in the gutter of suffering until I feel ready to act is a losing strategy. I must attack. Six runners, four spots, and one lap to go.

16

"I heard you were dead, dude."

I don't know how to respond to the first words that welcome me back to school, but given my first period is PE, it doesn't matter. I force a smile and count the seconds until Mr. Olczyek shows up.

"Morning, class!" Mr. O says when he enters the gym. "We're going to try something new today. I think you'll like it." He dims the lights, tells us to lie on our backs and guides us through a deep breathing exercise. After the giggles die down, he introduces the concept of positive visualization.

"Picture yourself doing something requiring excellent execution," Mr. O says. "It could be shooting a free throw, delivering a speech, staying focused during an exam—"

"Or taking a massive bong hit," whispers one of the kids usually found in front of the girls' bathroom, loud enough to send another wave of giggles through the crowd.

I picture myself walking. Walking up a hill on a dirt road far from anywhere I recognize. A breeze spreads dried leaves and other debris across the road. My feet lift the instant each shoe touches the ground. My arms swing comfortably behind my body as they help pump my knees. I channel all my energy to my legs, arms, and lungs. I'm a picture of unshakable determination, climbing smoothly as if rolling up the hill, suffering no resistance from gravity or the wind.

We end with another series of deep breaths before Mr. O switches the lights back on. I keep my eyes closed and try to hold the image in my mind—like holding onto a dream while waking. This prompts more jokes at my expense ("Look, he really is dead!") before I give up and walk over to Mr. O.

"Welcome back, Bags."

"Glad to be here."

He asks a few questions about my accident and rehab.

I tell him the visualization exercise was cool. "Where'd you learn that stuff?"

"I started using visualization in my own life this summer. I thought you students could benefit from what I've learned, though it didn't go exactly as I planned."

"Maybe you should stick with shuttle runs up and down the court."

"Ha! The problem is, most of the seniors who haven't opted out of PE never outgrew recess. They'd prefer to be off smoking or testing the odds of conception."

"*Live for the moment*, right?" This was the rallying cry of the kids who made fun of me for taking notes in class freshman year. Whenever I try to live for the moment, however, my tomorrow sucks. Drinking myself sick, blowing off homework, skipping a day of caddying—those things have all tricked me into thinking I'm living boldly until the hangover, bad grades, and empty wallet leave me with nothing but a cliché to blame for a bad decision.

"Hmmm . . ." Mr. O's not convinced either. "I prefer *Every moment counts*."

"Well, I sure found today's class helpful. My mind's always distracted. Your exercise helped me slow things down."

Mr. O offers to pull together information on visualization and relaxation techniques before my calm mind leads me to second period. I make it through AP Physics, AP Calculus, and Latin IV, responding to the sideways glances and covered whispers in the hallways with friendly hellos to let people know I'm neither a ghost nor contagious.

★ ★ ★ ★

I missed six weeks of school and freeze at the entrance to the cafeteria as if it's been six years. The crowd, noise, and random motion are more chaotic than I remember. Before I can turn to flee, Tom Fitzgerald calls me over to a table of the rich, beautiful, and popular. This isn't a normal start to lunch period for me.

"Man, where'd you get that shirt?" Fitz asks a kid in a Smashing Pumpkins T-shirt. I get nervous when I realize I've interrupted a concert brag competition.

"Saw them two weeks ago at the Metro."

"That's cute, but check this out." Chad Jones, pretty boy and all-around cool kid, flashes a ticket stub from Radio City Music Hall. "Dylan. New York City. Last Wednesday."

"Bullshit," the kid in the Pumpkins shirt says. "How'd you get to New York on a Wednesday night?"

"My dad was there for work and flew me out to join him. Best show ever."

I've always struggled to join these sorts of conversations. The topics usually exceed my budget, and I'm as clumsy talking in front of a group as I am playing sports. Competing thoughts fight for space in my head and exit my mouth as gibberish. That's probably why journalism is my favorite class. Writing allows me to work through the noise in my head and revise and revise until I figure out exactly what I'm trying to say.

Charles O'Toole looks me over. It's the first time I've seen him since his party the night of my accident. Unless I find a way to contribute to the discussion, today will be my last meal at this table.

"Have you guys heard the new U2 album, *Rattle and Hum*?" Peter Grayson asks. Grayson is senior class president and one of those teenagers who has it all figured out. He looks like he's ready to start working as a corporate lawyer tomorrow with his Ivy League haircut, Oxford shirt, penny loafers, and khaki pants with too many pleats to count.

"*Rattle and Hum* sucks," a kid wearing an Echo & the Bunnymen

T-shirt says. "It's like they can't figure out how to top *Joshua Tree* so they pretend to slum it as blues musicians."

"Best album of the year in my book?" Hooch says. "*Starfish* by the Church."

"The Church?" Charles says. "I thought you were a tough football jock, Hooch?"

"Morrissey's new album is way better," Chad says.

"Too mopey. Who wants to feel sad and tired?"

"That CD got me laid," Chad says.

"Your dad's beamer got you laid," Charles says.

Chad owns the cafeteria with a confidence that makes him popular for no reason other than being popular. The guy reminds me he's in another league simply by eating potato chips. Instead of arching his head back and shaking the final chip fragments into his mouth, Chad gently tears the bag along one of its side seams. He then delicately picks out the remaining individual pieces—all while avoiding greasy hands and peppering his shirt with crumbs. He even uses napkins, which must be why his jeans remain so clean.

"I've got a vinyl import of *Starfish*," the Echo & the Bunnymen kid says. "The sound quality is way better than the CD."

"What. The. Fuck." Charles says.

"What the what?" Echo & the Bunnymen says.

"I think Charles is trying to say, 'Stop being a music snob,'" Fitz says. "No one wants to hear about your imports and complaints about technology."

Hooch punches the kid in the shoulder, and I join the laughter. For the first time since sitting down, I'm part of the conversation.

"Fitz, you're the biggest music snob here," Charles says. "Always bitching when one of your obscure bands becomes popular with more than a dozen people."

"That's not fair," Fitz says. "I like all kinds of music."

"Then what would you say was the best year for music?" Grayson asks Fitz. I have no idea what brought Grayson to the cafeteria today.

He usually spends lunch period padding his college credentials. My guess is his father sat him down over brandy and cigars and suggested he broaden his network of influence.

"Wow, that's a tough one," Fitz says.

As Fitz contemplates an answer, Hooch chimes in. "What year did *Let it Bleed* come out?"

"Sixty-nine or seventy?" Charles says.

"Close enough," Hooch says. "You can't top a year the Stones, the Beatles, Zeppelin and the Who all put out new albums."

"How do you know those bands all released albums in the same year?" Grayson asks.

"My dad organizes his records by release date."

"He must love having a crazy bastard like you for a son," Charles says. Hooch shrugs his shoulders, as if he never considered the idea.

Fitz weighs in with eighth grade, and a debate over whether the Cure and Talking Heads or Springsteen and Petty made it the best year ever for music.

"You've been awfully quiet, Bags," Grayson says. I'm surprised he knows my name. We're not in any of the same classes, and the only time I see him is when he's campaigning for student government or pushing one of our principal's pet projects. "Not much of a music guy?"

This is finally a cool-kid conversation I know something about, but I don't want to say something that gets me laughed back into obscurity. All I squeak out in response is, "I love music."

Grayson chews his lip, expecting more. "What year gets your vote then?"

I know I should say something cool like Fitz and Hooch did, but the year that sticks in my mind is 1982. I was eleven. Frank was sixteen. That was the first and only summer my parents coughed up the dough for the local pool. Frank was a year from becoming a big football star, which means Dad was still a normal dad. The five years separating Frank and me disappeared when the lights went out. We were partners in mischief, ignoring Mom and Dad's demands to go to sleep and bonding over late-night conversations about superheroes, super models, and galaxies far, far, away. I can't share any of this, but the music from that year preserved plenty of other memories in the wrinkles of my brain.

"Nineteen eighty-two," I say.

"Is this some nerdy Honors English thing?"

"No, Hooch, that would be *1984*," someone says.

"I'll always remember the first time I heard Jack & Diane," I say.

"I had the biggest crush on my tennis instructor that summer," Chad says. "Every time I hear 'Caught Up in You,' I think of her."

"The roller rink played 'Heat of the Moment' and '867-5309' non-stop," Hooch says.

"You hung out at the roller rink?" Charles asks.

"It was a great way to meet girls the summer before sixth grade," Hooch says.

"I spent the summer jumping off the high dive at the pool," I say. "And eating Drumsticks and Snickers bars at the snack shack."

"My parents took me to Washington D.C. for my birthday," Grayson says. "That's when I discovered my passion to become an elected representative of the people."

The table pauses to check if Grayson's serious.

"On our drive home, my mom read me Lou Cannon's biography of Reagan," Grayson says. "He's been my hero ever since."

"I thought this conversation was about music," Fitz says.

"Whenever I hear the J. Geils Band, I remember pretending to shield my eyes from the sun on the pool deck," I say. "Scoping out the first girls to get their boobs."

"Yeah, my sister and her friends turned sixteen that year," Fitz says. "What a beautiful summer!"

"Shit!" Chad says to Fitz. "I don't care *what* you were doing with your sister that summer, but we've got a sweet sixteen minutes to grab a smoke before the bell. Let's go!"

Chad surprises me with another cafeteria first before he leaves. "Hey, Bags, glad you're okay. I'm having a little get-together Thursday night. My parents are out of town. You should come by."

I try to conceal the fact that I've never been invited to a *get-together*. "Sounds cool," I say. "I'll be there."

"Hi, Sam!" My old hospital roommate Marty ambushes me at the trash bins with a full body hug then walks me to his table.

"Marty, you look . . . healthy. How's school going?"

"School's fun. All my friends are here." He gestures to his table of fellow kids with special needs. "But I miss the hospital."

"Why do you say that?"

"I have lots of friends there too, and no one picks on me."

"Who picks on you at school?"

"The mean kids—when no one's looking."

"What do they do?"

"They call me names, like *retard*. This boy named John Hunter says my parents were going to name me *Mistake*, but they were afraid I wouldn't be able to spell it."

"Do your teachers know this?"

"Yeah, but kids still play jokes on me. Do kids pick on you?"

"Uh—I guess so."

"How?" Marty asks.

"They make fun of my last name. They mispronounce it to tease me. They also make fun of my nickname."

"What's your nickname?"

"Bags. Sometimes they chant, 'Just call me Bags!'"

"If that's your nickname, what's the problem?"

"Yeah, you've got a point. They also make fun of me for riding my bike everywhere." I wince at the memory of my bike. "Or at least they used to."

"I love riding my bike! I told you I learned how to balance all by myself this summer, right? Maybe if Mom let me ride my bike to school, kids would stop calling me *retard*."

Before meeting Marty, I never paid much attention to the kids with special needs. On my way to sixth period, I can't stop thinking about the examples of perseverance I've been missing.

Warm welcomes from classmates greet me when I walk into AP US History. The only enthusiasm Mr. Bracovich shows for my return is the speed with which he orders us to take our seats. I haven't read any of the materials covered on today's quiz so circle *C* for all ten questions. After Mr. Bracovich collects the quizzes and starts his lecture, the classroom turns into a battle of raised hands clamoring for class participation points.

My mood improves when I enter the Bullpen, aka the school newspaper's classroom. Mr. King, our journalism teacher and a die-hard baseball fan, came up with the nickname.

If there ever is a werewolf sighting in Linden Grove, Mr. King will be a prime suspect. He has the same sturdy build of the collegiate wrestler he once was, minus the cauliflower ears. His dark eyes match the color of his full beard and thick hood of hair, which he keeps under control with the Yankees cap he wears year-round.

Instead of instructing us to take our seats, Mr. King wheels out a homemade cake on a re-purposed AV projector stand. My teammates burst into a corny rendition of "For He's a Jolly Good Fellow," replacing the last four words of each verse with *but a catheter made him cry*. Like good journalists, nobody gives up the source of the joke. Mr. King lets the party continue for the full period and sends us away with leftover slices of cake.

Exhaustion hits me on the walk home, but today was a big step forward on all the school I've missed. "Here Comes a Regular" by the Replacements plays on the Walkman as I descend Spirit Hill, and Bad Gorilla mocks me for enjoying the special attention I received from Chad and crew in the cafeteria. My conversation with Marty causes me to realize I've always looked around the cafeteria and wished I was sitting at another table. Marty seems to have figured out life is better spent with the people comfortable sitting at his.

17

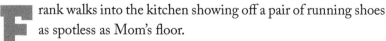

Frank walks into the kitchen showing off a pair of running shoes as spotless as Mom's floor.

"Where'd you get those?" I ask.

"The Runner's Sole."

"Was that girl Summer there?"

"Uh-huh . . ."

This is where I'm supposed to drool in suspense, but I don't want to give him the satisfaction. Since Frank the big talker can't handle silence, the best way to get him to use full sentences is to stop asking questions.

He gives in when I turn to leave. "It turns out her dad owns the shop, and she lives in the apartment above it. She's the real deal when it comes to running. Cross-country state champ in high school. Ran in college. Moved home last year to be a rep for New Balance and work part-time for her dad."

"Why do you look like you're about to start giggling?"

"I asked her if she wanted to go on a run sometime. I got a sort-of yes. She started a local running club and invited me to join her this weekend."

"Any chance I can come?"

"Heck yeah! I mean, really? You want to run?"

"I'm ready to amp up my rehab. Until I get a new bike, I thought I'd try running."

"You got it. Saturday at nine."

★ ★ ★ ★

"I'm glad to see so many of you back for the fourth outing of the Sandy Creek Running Club," Summer says to the crowd outside the Runner's Sole.

The runners span a range of ages, body types, and clothing. Two farty old men brave the crisp autumn air in paper-thin tank tops and slotted running shorts. A group of mom-age women sport similar outfits, each with their own high-visibility color scheme. Three guys in their twenties look as fit and fast as Summer. Spandex covers their toned limbs in warmth and aerodynamics. Then there's Frank and me. Frank flaunts his weight room costume—a worn-out sleeveless Chicago Bears sweatshirt and skin-tight liner shorts under a pair of cut-off sweatpants. I look like a nerd about to get beat up by a jock like Frank. The only quasi-running gear I own is my PE uniform—yellow LGHS shorts, a reversible blue-yellow shirt with the blue side showing, and white tube socks.

This isn't what I expected a running club to look like, which might explain why no one is taking themselves too seriously.

We head out through Sandy Creek Park before the crowd splits into two. I follow Summer's group on a 5K jog at an easy pace. The three young studs are high school friends of Summer's. They take the second group on a 10K run at tempo pace, whatever that means. Frank's libido wants to follow Summer, but pride compels him to stick with the young studs.

My group includes a threesome of feisty middle-aged moms. They remind me of the ladies I caddie for, except they breathe more heavily and smile less.

"So, Summer," a woman clad in an oversize orange-and-purple windbreaker says. "How long until this starts to get easier?" Her fanny pack bulges with a backup outfit and two full water bottles, which seems like overkill for thirty minutes of exercise.

"Yeah, and when will I start losing weight?" asks another. "All this running makes me so hungry, my husband claims I'm the only person he knows who gains weight while working out."

Summer laughs off their complaints and offers patient responses before working her way to me at the back of the group.

"How's the rehab coming, Sam?"

"I started running this week—about forty minutes in total." Since my walk up Spirit Hill, I've run three times. My legs no longer bark in pain, and I can now pace myself for fifteen minutes. This new stimulation fills me with a bliss similar to riding a bike.

"Shoot for eighteen to twenty minutes today," she says. "See how you feel after nine, then turn back shortly after that. We won't be far behind. You can join us for coffee at the White Hen."

Before I find the courage to ask Summer a question, the woman carrying thirty-two ounces of water on her fanny shrieks in terror. "Oh my *God*! *Oh* my God!" She pulls off to the side of the path clutching the back of her leg.

Summer tells the rest of us to keep going and checks on the injured runner. I turn around a couple minutes later and catch them limping toward the Runner's Sole. It takes effort to not stare at the firm curves of Summer's legs while asking if everything's okay when I pass.

I make it to the White Hen in under twenty minutes round-trip, encouraged by a return split thirty seconds faster than the outbound. Summer and her victim join me as I finish stretching out the tightness in my calves.

"I don't think I'll be able to stay for coffee," the lady says. "I better get home and ice my leg." She thanks Summer and hobbles away.

"Well, that leaves the two of us," Summer says to me. We grab two bagels and sit at a picnic table in front of the store.

There's so much I want to know, but I can't think of what to say. I finally ask Summer how she got into running.

"It was the only sport I didn't suck at in middle school, and I got free gear from my dad's shop." She pulls the elastic band from her ponytail, and her hair cascades in a caramel ribbon below her shoulders.

"That's funny. I had the same relationship with cycling. It was the only sport I could do without embarrassing myself."

"Yeah, running and cycling attract a lot of athletes recovering from mainstream sports." Summer shows no resentment for missing out on the cool sports. "Did you ever ride with a club?"

I fill Summer in on my experience with Coach Wolfe's cycling team freshman year.

"How'd you like that?"

"I loved every minute of it. It was the first time I was glad to be born without beach muscles."

"I bet you climbed like a goat."

"Frank got the genes for hand-eye coordination, but we both have healthy lungs."

"Did you ever race?"

"Only once. Our coach drove a few of us up to Wisconsin for a 16-and-Unders road race."

"How'd you do?"

I hesitate, not wanting to sound braggy. "I won."

"Hah! I have a feeling you're going to enjoy running, Sam."

The rest of our 5K group finds their way back. They're tired and sweaty but glow with a sense of accomplishment. They decline Summer's invitation to join us and promise to return next week.

Summer and I keep talking while waiting for Frank's group. Up close I notice a slight kink in Summer's nose and her crooked smile. Like me, her parents must have determined her overbite wasn't bad enough to invest in braces. Her interest in what I have to say and the discovery she's not perfect make her surprisingly easy to talk to.

Frank's hearty laugh precedes the return of the 10K group. "Well, no one said, '*my* left'!" The punchline to the latest of many stories in Frank's repertoire causes his new running buddies to crack up.

"Good ol' Frank," I say. "He was blessed with the ability to make people laugh."

"And you're the serious one, right?" Summer says.

"Yeah, and for some reason that makes everything more difficult."

"Hang in there. Everyone gets their shot."

Summer turns to the returning runners. "Looks like you all had fun."

"Great run," one of them says. "We headed to the mill and ran the trails out there before turning back."

"Frank here played football for Linden Grove," another says. "Do you remember the stories about Bags?"

"Actually, I'm Bags," I say.

"No, I'm Bags, and *you* are Little Bags," Frank says. We act out one of our many sibling rivalries before Frank asks how my run went.

"Twenty minutes. A new record."

"You guys need to join us again next Saturday," someone says.

"Sure thing," Frank says. "By the way, where do you run during the week?"

"All over the 'burbs. We like to mix it up. Sometimes we hit a high school track for speed work."

"Or, like on Monday, we're going to meet at that hill on 19th Street for climbing repeats."

"Uh, we know that hill," I say.

"Spirit Hill," Frank says.

"Spirit Hill? Oh, because of the shop at the top." Summer says. There's no sign inscribed with the name *Spirit Hill.* Frank gave the hill its name on a walk with my parents to the Spirit Soda Shop at the top of the hill before I was born. Our family has referred to it as Spirit Hill ever since.

"Right. We live near the bottom of the hill," Frank says.

"You guys should meet us there. Monday afternoon at four."

The conversation turns into twenty-something talk about college and various mutual friends. It's the first time I've seen Clean Living Frank in a social setting. I admire his natural ease with a crowd, no longer needing to play the obnoxious, boozy football star I hated for so many years.

18

I call 411 to get Marjorie Craven's phone number because she didn't provide one in her note.

"Hi, Sam. So wonderful to hear from you."

I embellish a few details of the update on my recovery, knowing I need to soften her up before my big ask.

"Thank the Lord it all turned out okay," she says.

Instead of telling her being alive doesn't mean it *all* turned out okay, I thank her for offering to cover the cost to fix my bike.

"Oh, right—what do I owe you?"

"The thing is, the bike shop says it will cost more to repair the bike than to replace it. I don't want to be rude, but would you consider covering the cost of a new bike?"

Silence.

"Schwinn doesn't make the Deluxe Varsity anymore, but the closest thing to it sells for about six hundred dollars at the Tourmalet bike shop."

Silence.

"Miss Craven?"

"Let me think it over," she says. "I'll get back to you."

My instinct is to apologize and tell her to forget I asked, but then I remember she technically killed me with her reckless driving.

"Uh . . . sorry if I misread your note," I say. "If that's more than you had in mind, let me know what you're comfortable covering."

"You *were* the one who got the ticket, Sam."

"Well, *you* were the one who drove me into a tree!"

"Sam, you were riding in the middle of the road and under the influence of alcohol."

Nothing she says is untrue, but she's the one who offered to help. Discovering that my recovery has lowered the cost of healing her grief pisses me off.

"And you're a petty bitch," I say.

Dial tone.

"Shit happens." Frank brushes off my story about Marjorie with his rhinoceros skin and Parrothead life philosophy as we walk to Spirit Hill to meet Summer and her friends. After a twenty-minute warm-up jog at the group's easy pace leaves me light-headed, Summer suggests skipping the hill repeats until I have more training in my legs. I hang out at the bottom of the hill when they line up for their intervals.

"Okay, *Big* Bags." Summer cracks a smile while teasing Frank for getting territorial over our shared nickname the other day. "We're shooting for ten repeats up the hill at a sixty-second pace. See how you feel after four or five and push it only if you feel comfortable. You can build up to ten over time by adding one or two repeats a week."

"Gotcha. Any advice on technique?" Frank asks.

"Push yourself, but not so hard you lose your form."

"How do you define 'form'?"

"Make sure to drive your arms back as you run. This will help power you up the hill. You want to stay more or less upright, so don't lean too far forward. And don't look way up to the top. I'd focus on the ground about five yards in front of you."

Frank hangs in for the first two repeats but fades on the third. Summer and her friends make it look easy. They're certainly breathing heavily when they start their fourth repeat, but they remain poised and in control.

Watching them charge up the hill brings back memories of the cycling intervals I buried myself riding freshman year. Despite Summer's advice, I struggle to sit and watch from the sidelines. After they complete their fourth repeat, I line up alongside Frank for the fifth. The steepest part of the hill knocks the wind out of me, and I feel my heart pounding in my throat. Before my body shuts down, the slope eases, and I reach the top a couple steps behind Frank, much slower than the sixty-second reps Summer and her friends keep knocking out.

Frank stops after five. That first run up Spirit Hill motivates me to join the group for a second. They attack the hill hard. I hit the steepest part of the hill, and the call with Marjorie replays in my head. Why couldn't I come up with a better response than to call her a bitch? *Forget about it, lady. If you were only looking to buy yourself a clear conscience, you can keep your money. I don't want to be reminded I owe you a favor every time I ride my bike.* I wish I had said something like that.

I reach the top of the hill several steps behind the others and noticeably more ragged and winded. The air I suck into my lungs cools my anger over Marjorie.

"Nice push, Young Bags!" Summer's new nickname makes me feel welcome, even though I disregarded her advice to hang at the bottom of the hill.

"I had to do it."

"We know the feeling. It's called blowing out the tubes. There's no shame in pushing yourself, as long as you know when to throttle it back."

"I'll throttle it back. After the next one." I chuckle between gasps for air.

I line up alongside Summer and her friends for a third attempt and challenge myself to hang with them to the top. The burn of carbon dioxide fills my lungs, and the sting of lactic acid soaks my legs. Each breath is like a hit of a drug that fills me with energy and purges the numbness from my system. It's no match, however, for the steepest stretch of the hill, which hits me like a wall.

I pull off into the grass alongside the road and drop to all fours. The trees start spinning, and I try to hang onto the earth with my hands and knees before falling over sideways like a dead horse. I cough up a dried, wrinkly wad of something resembling chewed bubble gum the size of my big toe.

Summer hurries over to make sure I'm okay.

"I'm fine . . . fine!" I shout, confirming the opposite and rejecting Sara's advice to begin accepting the help of others.

Lying in bed a few hours later, I accept that recovery is going to be a long and hilly road. Despite ending in failure, today's workout woke me from a long slumber and reminded me how much I love to train. Working hard enough to struggle gives me a chance to get better, and owing Marjorie nothing will help me put my accident behind me.

Bad Gorilla rests quietly. As if whatever I puked onto the side of the hill was the last of my accident's trauma exiting my system, for the first time since leaving the hospital, my bedtime thirst for morphine is gone.

19

Sara strolls into the cafeteria in black jeans and Vans slip-ons. A ratty mustard-brown cardigan I swear must be a hand-me-down from her grandfather covers a white T-shirt and completes her cozy-rocker look.

"How's your week going?" She takes a seat at the table I'm sharing with a few of our AP classmates.

"My brain's finally awake," I say. "But I now know how little I understand."

"That's how I feel about US history," Smitty says. "Only Bracovich could make a subject more boring than calculus." Antoine Smith, aka Smitty, is a sixteen-year-old math and science prodigy who has been in our classes since his freshman year.

"Mr. Paul's AP Physics classes are torture," Jed says. "Why can't he answer questions without the rambling monologues?"

"I suspect he's dealing with inadequacy issues," Sara says. "Did you know he used to be an engineer at GM?"

"That explains why every example involves a car," Smitty says. "I wish he'd spend more time teaching and less time telling stories about his glory days." While Smitty's classmates know he's a whiz kid, most students think of him as a track star. At six foot one and one hundred and forty pounds, he's a live version of the ectomorph poster in the weight room, except the guy in the drawing is yellow, and Smitty's Black.

I see Marty on the far side of the cafeteria, sitting at a table wedged behind the garbage cans with the other kids with special needs. A boy walks up to him and says something. It's Peter Grayson, that future briefcase-toter with a hard-on for Reagan. When Marty responds by turning away, Grayson lifts the bread off Marty's sandwich and spits on it before disappearing around the corner.

Marty replaces the top slice of bread and takes a bite. I can't believe what I'm seeing and hurry over.

"Hey, Sam Bags!" Marty greets me as enthusiastically as always.

"Marty, you can't eat that!"

"Mom says I have to eat my lunch every day."

"But that guy spit on it!"

"The mean kids do that to me."

"That's horseshit."

"No, it's just baloney," Marty says.

"Marty, you need to report this to your teacher."

"Mmhmm," he grunts. Marty's resignation upsets me more than knowing that tassel-wearing, student-body presiding Peter Grayson is also a psychopath. Marty refuses to let me walk him to the special education office and protests when I offer to call his mom. The best I can do is convince him to allow me to buy him a new lunch.

"Thanks—" Marty says when I return with a burger and fries.

"You're welcome."

"For remembering to come back."

20

My brother's journey from Football Jock Frank enters new territory. Two black-and-white portraits of runners from what appears to be the 1970s have replaced his 1986 Super Bowl XX Chicago Bears posters on our bedroom wall.

"It was a matter of time," Frank says. "Too many triggers of bad behavior I'm ready to put behind me."

"What about the helmet?" I point to the gold artifact resting on his stereo.

"That's an exception. I always kept my shit together on the football field."

"Is it hard to erase the memories?"

"I don't think of them as erased. They're earlier chapters of my life I'll reread one day."

"Well, I for one don't miss the old Frank."

I take a closer look at the new posters. "I know the guy on the right is Frank Shorter." Shorter's tall, spindly frame, schoolboy haircut and porn star mustache are easily recognizable. "But who's the one on the left?"

"Steve Prefontaine," Frank says. "Pre was a badass runner in the late sixties and seventies. He was only five foot nine but dominated everything from the two-mile to the 10K. Look at the determination in those eyes."

Stylish isn't a word you think of when describing runners, but Pre is a block of muscle with long hair and sideburns and the obligatory mustache that looks cool, not creepy.

"I love the quote," I say. The bottom corner of the poster reads, *To give anything less than your best is to sacrifice the gift.*

"Pre had a bookful of inspiring lines. Sadly, he died way too young. He was only twenty-four."

"How'd he die?"

"Flipped his car coming down a tight hill late at night."

"Are you kidding me?" I recoil from a flashback of my own accident on a hill.

"Sorry about that." Frank throws his hands up. "You okay?"

"Yeah—Pre sounds like a colorful character. I'll have to read up on him."

I head to the library during study hall and find Smitty explaining electrostatics out loud to himself before our AP Physics quiz tomorrow. He snaps out of it when he sees me, and his eyes grow wide when I tell him I'm looking for a book on Steve Prefontaine.

"Look who's a runner!" Smitty says.

I explain it's a temporary thing to help me recover from my accident until I get a new bike.

"And now you're reading books on Pre? What's next, you gonna hang his poster on your wall?"

I tell Smitty it's too late for that.

"Wow, that's hardcore. You should come out for track in the spring. It'll help you forget about bike riding."

"I'm a little late to the sport, aren't I?"

"It's track, Bags. All you have to do is run, and no one gets cut."

"What sorts of times do you guys run?"

"Depends on the event. I run the middle distances. Last year's winners at state ran the 800 under two minutes and the 1600 a little over four. To be competitive during the season, you'd want to be able to run a mile well under five minutes."

"Feeooo! That's fast."

"Don't let that discourage you. Plenty of guys go out for track to get in shape and have fun with other runners."

"I don't know. I really need to focus on school and my college applications."

"Makes sense. You probably want to take it easy after that accident."

"Probably," I say.

"Hi, Sam Bags!" Marty shouts when I pass his table in the cafeteria. "Did you see the comics in the school newspaper?"

I take the empty seat next to him, and he laughs through a play-by-play commentary about Lucy yanking a football away from Charlie Brown.

I tell Marty I wrote two of the articles in this month's paper.

"No way! Which ones?"

I point to a headline on page two: *Experts Call for Reduction in Fossil Fuels to Slow Greenhouse Effect.* It's the first of a series I plan to write about the Senate Climate Hearing back in June. "See this one? That's my name under the headline."

"Awesome!" Marty says.

"I wrote this one too." The second article is titled, *FCC Remains Opposed to Fairness Doctrine and Requirement Broadcasters Air Balanced Viewpoints.* Mr. King has been railing against the FCC's elimination of the fairness doctrine last year, which he claims opens the door for entertainment companies to pose as news organizations.

"What else do you write?"

"I'm working on something related to the Olympics we watched in the hospital."

"About bike racing?"

"You could say that. It's about cheating in sports."

"Oh, fair play," Marty says.

"Right. I'm trying to make the point that cheating in sports holds lessons beyond elite athletes. It's about playing for the right reasons instead of trying to win at all costs."

"Like my birthday party and the bullies at school," Marty says. "When no adults are in the room, kids do bad things."

I laugh out loud because Marty just gave me a hook to hang my story on. "Marty, you are one in a million."

"That's what Mom says."

21

"Any interest in going out tonight?" I ask.

The Joan Jett poster taped to the inside of Sara's locker door stares me down with the regal eyes of the queen of rock 'n' roll.

"Chad's having a few people over," I say.

"You're going to crash a party at Chad Jones's house?" Sara says.

"He invited me."

"Since when does Sam Bagliarello get invited to a party with the cool kids?"

Leave it to an old friend to question my social credentials. "You wanna join me or not?"

"The last thing I need is to be surrounded by a bunch of people who think I'm a Martian."

"Well, you can show them they've got the wrong planet."

The R-rated scorn in Sara's response surprises me.

"Why are you so grouchy?" I ask.

"My band broke up last night."

"Aww." I reach out and pull her into a hug. "What happened?"

"Our pothead guitarist hooked up with the second hottest chick in the band."

"The one who plays the funky mean bass guitar?"

"Yeah, that one."

"Sex, drugs, and rock 'n' roll, right?"

"She was dating our lead singer."

"Oops. What are you gonna do now?"

"Bands are always looking for drummers. I'll keep my eyes open."

Sara leaves me without a ride to Chad's. Mom took the Beet to celebrate a friend's birthday in the old neighborhood, and Frank gives me a cryptic apology about plans of his own. When I call bullshit on the guy who only leaves the house to workout or buy groceries, he confesses he has a date with Summer.

"You're welcome," I say.

"For what?"

"If it wasn't for me, Summer would be nothing more than a beautiful woman who ran past us in the park."

"Give me a break!" Frank throws his head back, then blinks. "Ahh, you're jealous, aren't you?"

"Well, if she wasn't five years older than me—"

"Yeah, and if you weren't so awkward around women."

"Hey, that's not fair. Who would have guessed she'd be interested in a smooth talker like you?"

"She's definitely out of my league, so I skipped the cheesy one-liners and led with sincerity. It seemed to work."

"I've tried that approach." My failed efforts with Zoe come to mind. "It always blows up in my face."

Frank offers to drop me off at Chad's before his date, and I figure I can hitch a ride home from someone at the party.

Chad's house seems too big for a small party. I worry I have the wrong address until I pass through the empty living room and find, five steps below ground level, a den filled with beanbags, a couch, and a large-screen home theater the size of my bed.

"Bags!" Chad invites me into the cozy pit. "I don't care what everyone says about your 1982 call. I loved it. I've been dreaming about my old tennis instructor all week."

I nod, embarrassed to learn I've been ridiculed by the guys from the lunch table and aware I'm the only person standing. All seats are taken, and I'm like the loser in a game of musical chairs. Everyone sits with crossed legs as if pretending to be their parents. They talk in polite volumes, laugh at each other's words, and use ashtrays for their cigarettes.

Zoe offers a seat on the couch, a long-stemmed wine glass in her hand. I practically leap onto the cushion next to her, but she's up and strutting to the kitchen before I land.

"Vail's the place to go," Chad says to a handful of guys seated around the television with green bottles of imported beer in their hands. Images of extreme skiers screaming down a powdery chute in the Rockies fill the screen.

"My family spent Thanksgiving in Vail last year," Charles O'Toole says. "Epic party scene. Tons of college kids. Count me in."

"Skier, Bags?" Charles's tone makes it obvious he knows the answer, given his father helped me win my scholarship for financially needy golf caddies and gave my dad a job at his car wash.

Dad took Frank and me skiing once when I was eight years old to a pimple of a hill two hours from Chicago. "Does Hidden Valley count?" I say with a smile.

Before I get the chance to recover from a joke nobody laughed at, someone in the kitchen announces "Pizza!" and the pit clears out.

The house has filled up since I arrived. An AP classmate named Ashley Taylor steps out of the crowd forming in the kitchen.

"Hey, Sam. Funny seeing *you* here."

More surprising than meeting Ashley at a party in the middle of the week is noticing her bright round cheeks pulsing like cartoon hearts when she smiles.

"I snuck in," I say. "What's your excuse?"

"Charles and I went to homecoming, and we've been seeing each other since."

I don't know whether to think better of Charles or worse of Ashley upon hearing this, but I can't take my eyes off her hair. It's a shade between red and brown—puffed and wavy, though not distracting.

More Kathy Ireland than Madonna.

"Good . . . for him," I say.

Ashley blushes at my half-assed compliment and offers me a slice of pizza.

"No thanks, I ate before I came over."

"Did you drink at home, too?" She nods at my hands jammed into the pockets of my jeans. Since sarcasm backfired in my conversation about skiing, I try being sincere with Ashley.

"The hospital messed up what I can eat and drink," I say.

"What do you mean?"

"My body hasn't adjusted to normal food since the hospital. I can't keep anything down."

"Like pizza?"

"Anything I used to eat before my accident. Even my mom's homemade pasta sauce."

"What about alcohol?"

"Same thing with beer."

"There's a silver lining to everything, right? You look super fit if you don't mind me saying, and I like the long hair, too—"

"Watch out, nerds conspiring!" Charles taps Ashley's left shoulder while hiding behind her right.

Ashley falls for it and looks left.

"Hah! So much for book smarts!" Charles says.

"Is that one of the big-boy words you're practicing?" Ashley asks.

"Conspiring?"

"No, 'book.'"

Charles's bully confidence dissolves into his usual dopey gaze, and he tells Ashley it's time to go. "You don't want to get grounded for staying out past curfew."

Ashley turns to me, as if obliged to apologize for her boyfriend. "A girl's brains can be an intimidating third wheel. I enjoyed catching up, Bags. See you in calc tomorrow."

"Is that some secret code—*see you in calc*?" Charles asks.

"Yeah, it's code for calculus, a math class you'll never need to take. Let's get out of here before you say something that surprises me."

I take a couple laps around the party after Ashley leaves. Unable to work myself into another conversation, I sneak off to the bathroom for no reason other than to avoid having to stand by myself in a crowd. My reflection stares at me from the mirror while I wash my hands. Despite the weight I've gained since leaving the hospital, the undernourished hollowness in my cheeks remains. My eyes are the one unchanged feature of my face. That is, until the eyes of Bad Gorilla glare back at me.

"What are you doing here?" he asks from the mirror.

A knock on the door sends Bad Gorilla into hiding before I can respond. I return to the kitchen and once again find myself alone in a room full of people. Old Sam is back, the misfit harassed by an imaginary ape inside his head. How often has overthinking how to have a good time prevented me from having a good time? I've been pushing things hard the past several weeks—the healthy eating, lack of socializing, all the running. Haven't I earned the right to enjoy myself a little? I decide to stop thinking so hard and help myself to a beer. A kid leaning against the fridge hands me a can of Rolling Rock. The simple gesture in a shared pursuit of a buzz serves as an easy conversation starter.

"Hey, Bags, welcome back."

"Glad to be here. Cheers." We tap our cans in a hollow sound of belonging.

Unfortunately, my beer lasts longer than the friendly welcome. I've got nothing to add to chatter about fancy clothes, new cars, second homes, and rumors about other kids at the party and get cold-shouldered from one conversation to another.

Charles returns thirty minutes later and announces his girlfriend has gone home. "The Big C is back and free!"

"Hail Charles!" someone replies.

As Charles makes his way through the crowd, I nervously pluck the tab on the top of my beer can. He flinches when he catches my eye.

"Hey Bags, let's keep that one between us men, okay, dude?"

"Yeah, sure."

"Yeah . . . sure . . ." he repeats. "Hey, what's with the long hair? Ashley couldn't stop talking about you the whole ride home. *Did you see Bags? Doesn't he look amazing for all he's been through?* Is there some history between the two of you I should know about?"

"Easy, Charles," one of his buddies says. "We're all friends here."

Charles turns to me. "I remember the last time you showed up at a party." Charles raises his hands and sings in a whiny tone, "Just call me Bags! Just call me Bags!"

"How's it goin', fellas?" Chad inserts himself between Charles and me and reaches into the fridge for a six-pack. "It's heating up at this end of the kitchen."

"It's all good," Charles says. "I was pimping Bags here." He turns to me. "No offense, man. It's my way of showing I care."

"Yeah, sure." I grab another beer from the fridge and walk to the opposite end of the kitchen. The beers are making me hungry, so I reach for a slice of pepperoni pizza. It's cold but tastes better than I expected. The first piece goes down slowly, as I swallow my better judgment with it. Pieces two and three disappear much faster, aided by another beer.

The party thins out, other than a small group that's returned to the pit. By ten o'clock, I'm more buzzed than I've been since August and worry the pizza and beer are going to punish my impulsiveness. Options for bumming a ride home evaporate with the secondhand pot smoke drifting into the kitchen, so I explore the house in search of a phone.

I end up in a large bedroom straight out of *Better Homes and Gardens* and recently ransacked by horny teenagers. I call Frank from the phone on one of the bedside tables (*busy*) and curse my parents for being the last holdouts to pay for call waiting. Five minutes later, I get through.

While I wait for Frank to pick me up, Bad Gorilla chews me out. "You thought you'd be accepted tonight because you were invited?" He chuckles in response to his question. "Charles and Zoe and those kids who boxed you out pay attention to what's loud and shiny. That's not you, mate."

Mom's been right all along. Who am I to think I can be a journalist when I can't get anyone to pay attention to me? I should focus on making money and stop chasing the approval of others.

Fifteen minutes later, I'm sitting next to Frank in the Guinness and nearly fall out of the car trying to pull the two-hundred-pound door of an El Camino closed. "I need to get to bed."

Frank inhales deeply. "Smells like a smart idea."

"Whatever."

"I know the smell of a night of boozing. I also know there's nothing to be gained by preaching. Tell me, though, was it worth it?"

"Not at all. I felt like a loser and tried to make up for it with beer and pizza."

"Of course you did. How's the 'za settling?"

"We'll know by morning."

Morning arrives at seven thirty-eight, according to the radio. A ripping headache, pizza gut, and the sound of sleeting rain make it hard to get out of bed. I stagger to the bathroom and stand under the weeping shower head, holding up the wall with one arm while the other twists the faucet between red and blue in an effort to flush the ache from my body.

Frank wakes up while I get dressed. "What a mess out there! How ya' feelin', Little Bags?"

"Not so hot. Any chance I could bum a lift to school?"

"Sorry buddy. Buy the ticket, take the ride."

Before heading out the door, I pop my head in the bathroom. Frank's belting the chorus to "Is She Really Going Out With Him?"

from somewhere behind the steam of a hot shower.

"Frank, I didn't say it last night, but—"

"No need!" he shouts over the spray of water. "We all mess up. Do yourself a favor and learn from it!"

Fifteen minutes fighting icy sheets of rain on my walk to school clears my head. By three o'clock, the rain and wind have moved on, and I put the week behind me by jogging home.

I come over the top of Spirit Hill and realize Bad Gorilla called it right last night. I tell him I'm done. Done playing dress-up in a costume that doesn't fit. Done trying to keep up with kids on the Advanced Placement track to some make-believe adulthood. Impersonating people I want to accept me isn't the answer. As much as I want to live in their fantasy world, it's time to take my chances with a reality that's all my own.

22

Smitty's suggestion I take it easy after my accident has stuck with me like a cramp. Recovery has been nothing but hard work. I jog every day after school and disappear every Sunday into long runs through the woods along Sandy Creek.

Smitty got me thinking maybe somewhere beyond lonely PT jogs and fun runs with the slow guys is the change for the better Nurse Cooper talked about.

Why shouldn't I go out for track? Bad Gorilla knows. Other than one season of bike racing, the only lesson sports have taught me is I'm no athlete. Coaches instructed me to pass, not shoot, wait for a walk. If I wasn't warming the bench, I was filling water bottles. I don't need another sport to break my heart, so before I decide whether to take Smitty up on his invitation to join the track team, I need to test my body's fitness after all the rehab. Four weeks after my disappointing first session of hill repeats, it's time to return to Spirit Hill.

Frank's making smoothies when I walk into the kitchen and he convinces Mom to try one. "Interesting," she says. "Though I prefer warm drinks on cold days." Mom returns to her newspaper and politely pushes the glass far enough from her scrambled eggs and sausage to avoid contamination.

"What's the forecast, Ant'nette?"

"Let's see . . . sunny, high of thirty-five, windchill in the mid-twenties. Not bad for late November."

"How about the hourly forecast for nine o'clock?" I ask.

"Twenty degrees, cloudy with possible snow, windchill of ten.

Looks like a good day to organize the garage."

"Ugghhh," I say.

"What are you complaining about?" Frank says. "You used to ride your bike in this sort of weather."

"Yeah, but I told myself I'd never again ride when the windchill was less than my age."

"Don't you know there's no bad weather, only bad clothing?"

Coach Wolfe used to bark the same line, first attributed to a quote by Sir Ranulph Fiennes that has inspired athletes around the world to get out of bed when the conditions outdoors suggest otherwise.

My attitude improves when Mom complains about a bunch of old winter cycling gear "taking up space" in the attic. When I get my hands on the box, I rip off the packing tape like I've discovered buried treasure and pull out all the wool and Lycra a winter athlete in the Midwest could need—a thin beanie-style hat, insulated waterproof gloves, a black windproof jacket, full-length bib tights, and various pairs of ski socks. With the weight I've lost, everything fits like it did when I last wore it as a freshman.

The jog to Spirit Hill warms me despite the chilly wind. I line up at the bottom with the goal of hammering ten repeats. The endurance I've gained over the past month gives me the confidence that I can run for hours, and I take the first two climbs at an easy pace.

I power up the third, careful not to push too hard. I survive the increased effort and start to believe I can complete one of these in under a minute like Summer and her friends. During my trip back down the hill, I commit to an all-out effort on the next one.

I hit number four hard from the start. My speed builds as the slope increases. I shorten my stride, and my lungs threaten to burst under the strain of the lighter, quicker steps. The lactic acid seeps into my limbs, scorching my muscles before I get through the steepest section. I'm dizzy by the time I check my watch at the summit, certain I've broken the sixty-second mark. The chronometer on my watch is accurate, but overexertion has distorted my concept of time. Seeing my Ironman ticking 1:13 . . . 1:14 deflates me like the tree branch that punctured my belly.

Bad Gorilla ridicules me for overconfidence, which emboldens me to do better on the fifth interval. It takes all I've got left to fight gravity, and I wobble to the summit in disappointment again. On my return to the bottom of the hill, Bad Gorilla's judgment stands between where I am and where I want to be, and simply willing myself to improve is no match for an ape who's made up his mind. Having lost the motivation to line up for hill repeat number six, I'm left with nothing but another hard lesson in recovery on my cold walk home.

23

Final exams next week are my last chance to salvage the semester. Sara helps by organizing a study session at her house on Saturday afternoon. Jed, Ashley, Smitty, and a girl named Bridget Flynn join us.

"How are you settling into senior year, Bags?" Bridget asks.

I recap the challenges of missing half the semester, and the usual questions about my scars and the surgical wires they hide follow.

"Tell them about the catheter, Bags," Sara says.

I decline like an old maid.

"Please do!" Ashley says. "I've been wondering how you peed without standing up."

After I describe the function of the catheter and its spectacular removal, Sara says, "Speaking of dicks, what's new with Charles?"

"Nothing," Ashley says. "Which is why we're no longer seeing each other."

"Was it one particular thing, or did he finally wear you down?" Sara asks.

"His older sister scared me away. She invited me to brunch at the country club with her friends and introduced me as *Ashley, from a hardworking family,* which is code for *She doesn't play tennis.*"

"How embarrassing," Bridget says. Bridget's a member of the swim team and always looks like she recently climbed out of a pool. The low-maintenance look reveals a natural beauty unspoiled by big hair and too much makeup.

"Then she got sloshed and started complaining about Mr. O'Toole,"

Ashley continues. "Claims he works too hard and nags her and Charles for being lazy and spoiled. When I pointed out we were running up his tab with an afternoon of mimosas, she told me to leave."

"And that changed your view of Charles?"

"No, Charles called later and demanded I apologize. I told him I agreed with their dad. Haven't heard from him since."

Mr. O'Toole never went to college and built his car-wash business out of nothing. I guess helping out caddies who grew up like him is his penance for raising kids like his.

Jed tells a few stories from a party the night before, and Bridget recaps her latest swim meet for Smitty. Sara ends the small talk with a cry of "Bamm-Bamm!" and two whacks of the dining room table with an inflatable club from a *Flintstones* Halloween costume.

Jed, the honor roll student with an allergy to studying, spends most of the next four hours playing Atari with Sara's younger brother, while a semester of calc and physics finally starts to make sense to me. We call time at six o'clock, relocate to the kitchen, and raid Sara's fridge.

A big old Chicago snowstorm rolled in while we were studying, and Smitty points out the window. "Check out the size of those snowflakes."

"It's not often they float straight to the ground," Bridget says. "They're usually blowing sideways."

Sara slides open two glass doors leading to her backyard. The chill clears the brain fog from an afternoon of cramming math and science concepts.

"When's the last time anyone had a snowball fight?" Smitty asks.

"About thirty seconds from now?" Ashley says. She and Smitty are first out the door. The rest of us follow, and Sara brings her Bamm-Bamm club.

It takes six high school seniors less than ten minutes to trample the fresh snow in Sara's backyard. We fall onto our backs, gazing into the night sky from the cold ground. The only sounds are our breaths as we watch fluffy snowflakes float through the blue-gray moonlight.

"When's the last time you stopped what you were doing and stared up at the sky?" Bridget asks.

"When's the last time you could see the stars through the clouds?" Smitty adds.

"I hope the next time is this summer," Ashley says. "I'm freezing!"

"Who's up for a little adventure?" Sara asks. "I've got an idea that will warm us up."

"Orgy?" Jed says.

"Not on your life, nitwit," Sara barks back. "Follow me!"

Sara leads us through the neighboring backyards until we reach a tall wooden fence, three houses down.

"Shit, Sara, it was warmer lying in the snow," Jed says.

"Stop whining, you ninny." Sara whacks Jed's shoulder with her club.

On Sara's command we help each other scale the fence and drop into the yard on the other side.

"My brother shovels snow for this family," Sara says. "They're away until January. Anyone interested in checking out the hot tub?" Sara walks up the steps of the deck, not expecting an answer to her question.

"I don't have a suit," Jed says.

"Why are you being such a wuss tonight?" Sara says from the hot tub. "Drop your trou in the corner and grab a towel out of the box over there. You and your lady friends can lift the cover off this thing."

Jed feigns reluctance to follow Sara's orders but recovers his pride once Smitty and I start undressing. I hustle to the hot tub, self-conscious of my scars, which appear more pronounced than usual as the cold air draws the color from my skin.

The three of us remove the cover and ease our chilled bodies into the water. Jed turns on the jets and cranks up the heat. The girls walk over wrapped in towels.

"Okay, cretins," Sara says. "Show some manners and turn your heads a second."

"One . . ." Jed says. Sara gives him the same *steakhead* look she's directed my way multiple times before.

Bridget and Ashley don't wait for etiquette. They drop their towels and step over the edge of the hot tub in their bras and underpants. My body responds as I'd expect upon seeing Bridget's athletic form descend into the water and Ashley's more voluptuous figure follow. Even Sara's toned drummer arms catch my attention as she lowers herself into the steam.

More cackling than conversation follows as we spend the first few minutes warming up and enjoying the spontaneity of the situation.

"Sara, is that your hairy foot on my balls?" Jed asks.

"No, that's my hand," I say.

The gratuitous *ha-has* from the girls' side of the tub dwindle quickly.

"I've got an idea," Ashley says. She slides into the space between Jed and me, locking her eyes onto mine as she spins around to take a seat. "You boys need to be separated." She puts her hand on my thigh. "Oh, excuse me, is this seat taken?"

I've kissed a few girls and felt the bare breasts of two. I've never been in a hot tub with any of them, let alone felt the buttery smoothness of a girl's thigh against mine.

"Be careful you don't pop one of his wires," Sara says. I laugh a beat later than the others. My throaty *huh, huh, huh* gets an eye roll from Sara. "You've got a real project on your hands, Ashley."

"It feels like it!" Ashley teases, gently brushing my Lord Nelson with the back of her hand and giving me a devilish smile. Her hair looked attractive dry and styled the other night at Chad's, but dripping wet, she's an absolute sex muffin.

"Who's up for some Nordic bathing?" Sara ignores the silence that follows. "Okay, we're gonna jump out, roll in the snow, then jump back in." Nobody volunteers to return to the snow. "Here's how it's going to work. Smitty and I will go first. If we don't die, then Jed and Bridget are next, followed by Westley and Buttercup."

"I'm in," I say. "We'll remember this during our calc exam Wednesday morning."

"Bags is right," Smitty says. "Count of three, Sara?"

The group responds, "One . . . two . . . three!"

Sara and Smitty high-step it to the far end of the yard, run up a small embankment along the fence, then drop to the snow and log-roll down the little hill. When their bodies come to a stop, they sprint back into the hot tub. We repeat the countdown for Jed and Bridget, who cry in whimsical pain in the cold air and fresh snow. I howl like some wild character from a Rudyard Kipling tale. The others join me, as we thank the moon for gifting us a night of unpretentious play.

Jed and Bridget sink back into the hot tub chattering like monkeys, and Smitty starts the countdown for Ashley and me. I extend a hand to help her over the edge. The warm curves of Ashley's cheeks continue down her entire body, giving her the unapologetic figure of another era. A Sophia Loren, a 1968 Corvette, a painting of Aphrodite. She bends forward and shares an eyeful of cleavage separating two full breasts drenched in enough steam and sweat that her bra reveals nipples the size of half-dollar coins.

The frosty air burns my skin as I hold her hand in mine, and we run on pigeon toes into a patch of untouched snow. "Snow angels?" I shout. We drop onto our backs and do a few horizontal jumping jacks until we flatten the snow underneath us. Once back in the hot tub, Ashley and I hyperventilate like Jed and Bridget a minute earlier.

We trot back to Sara's fifteen minutes later. Jed starts a fire, and the group settles into the couches in Sara's living room. Frank and I have an early run tomorrow, so I make my excuses, and Ashley offers me a ride home.

"Wish You Were Here" by Pink Floyd plays on the radio as we drive to my house.

"Great tune," Ashley says.

The slow beat, long bending notes, and vivid lyrics create emotion without the cliché of a love song.

"I think this song is about someone who made bad choices in their life," she says.

"Maybe deliberate choices made for the wrong reasons."

"Yeah, like the pain we've put ourselves through these past four years?"

"I mean, you could have always *chosen* to coast through high school," I say.

"I wonder if I would have been happier."

"You would have had more fun . . . but you also would have pissed away the options in front of you now."

Ashley pulls up to my house and shifts into park.

"Well," she says.

"Ashley, I just want to say—"

"You don't need to say anything. It was a special night, and not just the you-and-me part."

"I might sound like a dork, but that was probably the most fun I've had in high school."

"Yeah, there was something so natural about it. No one was pretending."

I reach in to give her a kiss. The radio continues to the next song—"Hold On to the Nights" by Richard Marx.

"Aah!" Ashley says. "Shut it off!"

"Old boyfriend?"

"No. I just don't want to ruin this very real moment with such a cheeseball song."

With the music off we give our goodbye kiss another try. I get lost in the softness of Ashley's mouth, the tastes of warm fruit and salt, the texture of her tongue, and her moist breath on my upper lip.

Until she leaves me standing at the curb, I forgot how uncomfortable it is to sit on a cold vinyl car seat in wet underwear.

★ ★ ★ ★

The Friday before Christmas provides relief and an uneasy sense of victory. Exams are over, but grades won't be posted until January. There's so much about the semester I want to put behind me, but like recovery, there are no clean starts. Each moment of my life has been the product of the messy events preceding it. This is true of many memories I want to erase on this last day of the semester—my accident, academic struggles, and jerks like Charles O'Toole and Peter Grayson. Marjorie Craven's duplicity is right up there with other uninspiring adults in my life like Mr. Bracovich and Dr. Blakely Moroni.

I end the semester with a seven-mile run home. At the end of my run at the end of the day at the end of this dreadful semester, I look forward to the new beginning that will emerge from the carnage of the past few months.

1989 Illinois High School Track and Field Regional Finals
3200-meter race, final lap

We hit the front stretch of lap seven, and I hear Summer's voice again. "Don't hold back, Bags. Go, go, go!" Like the horn of an approaching train, her cheers dissolve into the louder chaos of the crowd as I pass.

Summer's words confirm what I feared a hundred meters ago. The only option for me is to redline it to the finish before anyone has a chance to lay down a final sprint. The ringing bell announces the passing of Coop and Duffy—and the final lap of the race.

I accelerate around the outside shoulder of the runner from William Murray. He doesn't challenge, so I slot myself in front of him as we exit the first turn of lap eight.

Three hundred meters to the finish. I'm at the front of the chase group. Duffy and Coop are two meters ahead.

My strained breaths force as much air as possible in and out of my mouth. My steps are quick and light, tap-tap-tapping the ground as my glutes and quads propel me forward. I laugh silently in the mayhem of it all when I realize the tempo to the song "No Sleep Till Brooklyn" matches the rhythm of my footsteps. I'll have to thank Sara for planting the song in my head by wearing her Beastie Boys shirt to the meet.

Duffy kicks, and Coop responds. José follows the runner from William Murray, who accelerates in an attempt to bridge the gap to the two leaders. I get left behind with the Ernie Banks runner to my inside in lane one. Three hundred meters would be a long sprint to the finish with more than 2,900 meters in our legs already, but the stakes are too high to wait and see if anyone mistakenly went too early. With six runners closing in on the four spots to state, the race is about to get messy.

24

I recover from the fall semester by immersing myself in running over winter break. Wagonloads of food every few hours break up a daily routine of exercise, sleep, and Ashley. My stomach has grown into a food-burning furnace since those days of starvation in the hospital.

Ashley and I take the train downtown one morning to do Christmasy things and have lunch at a bakery in my parents' old neighborhood.

"So, are you still eating like a bird?" Ashley asks. My hands hoist a bowl of minestrone soup to my mouth so I can guzzle the last of it like a kid finishing his Rice Krispies.

"Yeah. A big bird." I put the bowl back on the table and wipe my mouth with the sleeve of my sweater.

"You must go through a lot of granola."

"It's the breakfast of champions."

"How do you get your protein?"

This is one of the more annoying questions I get since quitting meat and dairy, but I like Ashley a lot and don't want to ruin what's been a beautiful day. "It's easy. I eat foods that have a lot of protein in them. Like beans and nuts and lentils and tofu. And I add soy milk to all that granola."

"I think they call that *vegan*. Are you going to start protesting against fur now, too?"

"I'm not looking to join a crusade. I've simply found the best way to fuel my body."

"Don't you miss the meat?"

"I did for a month or so, then my taste buds adapted. Now I crave rice and beans and vegetables."

We stop to browse the pastry counter on our way out. "The only foods I miss are baked goods," I tell her. "You know, stuff like pastries and cookies."

"Must be the butter."

"Say butter again."

"Butterrr . . ." she repeats in a throaty voice.

"That's it. I'm melting!"

"It's no bean salad, but I'd be happy to share anything you want from this counter," Ashley says.

"I think I can make an exception today. How about a lemon knot?"

"I've never had one."

"Never had one?" I tell Ashley how my great aunt used to make them from scratch every year around the holidays.

The stout older woman working behind the counter stands ready to help us when we look up from the display case. "What can I get you kids?"

"One lemon knot, please," I say.

"Anything else?"

"Uh—make it *two* lemon knots." I turn to Ashley. "They really are the best!"

She gives me a wide smile.

I wait until we're seated on the train before opening the white paper bag and extracting the treasures inside. After unwrapping the protective wax paper, I place one in Ashley's hands with the sort of care reserved for Holy Communion. I let the first bite sit in my mouth and savor the cookie's flaky-chewy texture and the hint of lemon cutting through the buttery richness. Cozy childhood memories welcome the tasty indulgence as it works its way to my belly.

"My God!" Ashley says. "You weren't kidding. It's so rich but not heavy and greasy."

"Must be that butter . . ."

25

Christmas Day. Frank and I spent last night with Dad and this morning with Mom. There's nothing more pathetic than watching your parents try to recreate holiday memories for a broken family. I'd rather be alone on a run than lonely with Mom and Frank, so I sneak out to Spirit Hill and leave Bad Gorilla to deal with the melancholy holly jolly.

Discouraged by my first two hill workouts, I line up for the first climb with no expectations for today and hit the lower stretch at a comfortable pace. Given all my training over the past month, there's no way I can't be getting stronger. I push through the steepest pitch of the hill with high knees and light steps. One down, easy.

I take the next two climbs at seventy percent of an all-out effort. I'm happy to be outside in late December and not puking on the side of the road after three reps like my first experience with hill repeats two months ago.

I push harder on the fourth. My legs know it, and my breathing shows it. Instead of expecting this to get easier, I need to get more comfortable with the pain to come.

Next up is number five, and I celebrate tying my personal record from a month ago with an all-out kick to the top. The burn in the back of my throat cleanses my airways and pumps me with the energy to keep going beyond anything I've achieved before. No matter how many reps I complete today, I'm not quitting until I've drained my body.

I take number six easy to recover. Adrenaline no longer floods my muscles like a trucker slamming the pedal to the floor each time he hits a hill. Instead, the workout becomes one long test of endurance, and my heart beats at a more steady, elevated rate as opposed to violently rising and crashing with each individual climb.

I ditch my jacket and sweats after number seven. My body has become a self-sustaining furnace.

Finishing ten of these won't be a problem today. I hold back on eight and nine so I can give the next one everything and celebrate a new level of fitness when a run up Spirit Hill at eighty percent of all-out effort counts as a recovery interval.

I line up for my tenth repeat and can't resist setting the chronometer on my watch to 0:00. I fly off the line and lean into the incline at the bottom of the steep section with enough momentum to carry me through the first few steps. I'm on my toes and kicking my knees up the hill. The venom of overexertion spreads through my legs, arms, and chest faster than my blood can flush it. My nose leaks like a rusty faucet, and my vision narrows into a long gray tunnel of shadows.

The pain becomes unbearable, and my mouth grows dry like those first few days in the hospital. I get past the bulge in the road but still have to fight through the last thirty steps as the hill flattens. When it's all over, my watch reads 1:07. On the walk down, I tell myself it's not about getting to the top ten times or doing so in sixty seconds. Neither is going to make me a better runner. It's about having the guts to keep going, knowing I might fail on the next one.

So, instead of heading home, I line up for one more.

And another.

Lucky thirteen in the bag, and I walk down for the next one. What makes me want to keep putting myself through the suffering of another repeat? Then it hits me. *Suffering* is the messiness of life. The hard work that leads to greatness. The only way I've ever gotten better at something is to suffer for it. Waking up every summer morning at dawn to get to the caddie shack. Working on my slow reading to show the nuns at Saint Edward's I'm not stupid. Studying harder than my teenage impulses prefer so I can earn more As than Bs.

Sara knows the Messiness helps her drum beautifully when she's onstage. Marty found the Messiness when he endured hours of falling off his bike before he taught himself how to balance on two wheels. A long time ago, Frank embraced the Messiness on the high school football field.

What can the Messiness of running teach me? No clocks or coaches are grading my performance. I'm just a kid who likes to run. Why should I invite more suffering into my life by trying so hard at this most individual of activities? Because by making myself suffer more than anything else can, I know I'll be able to face whatever the world throws at me.

Fourteen and going strong. My legs are pink and numb, my arms are sore, and my face is a palette of spittle and snot. I wipe my nose with the sleeve of my shirt and steel myself for another all-out effort.

I complete number fifteen in sixty-four seconds, a personal record. I could quit now, but one more at this point intimidates me less than the first, despite my heaving ribs, dry tongue, and foggy eyes. While my mouth begs me to soak it in water, the last thing I need is a cramp, so I take a small swig from my bottle, toss it into the grass and line up again.

I give the next three reps all I've got and finish number sixteen in sixty-two seconds. My pace starts to fade on seventeen, which I complete in sixty-four seconds. Eighteen comes in at seventy. My body is past its limit, but my heart has more to give. I spent my first hill repeat session fighting the pain, the second trying to survive it. Today I welcome the pain because on my walk down the hill, I decide to run track in the spring. Running has become something I love to do, and I want to get better at things I love so I never again get distracted by the empty wants of others.

I back off on nineteen and tell myself twenty will be my last of the day. Better to control when I quit than have the hill decide for me. As I work my way up the hill I find inspiration in how far I've come since my failed attempt to walk up Spirit Hill three months ago. I fight as hard as I can to get through the steepest section. Time always slows while ascending Spirit Hill, but this is taking forever. My arms are so sore by the time I reach the top, my right hand struggles to stop my watch. I hear the beep and look down to find the chrono reads 0:59.

Hah.

If I came here today with a goal, I would have stopped after ten because that's how the strongest runners I know do it. I also would have never beaten sixty seconds because it took me twenty tries to find something I didn't know I had.

Hahahaha.

26

Ashley and I skip the Linden Grove High tradition of celebrating New Year's Eve at Doc Riley's and hang out with Summer and Frank. Instead of a buffet dinner, cover charge, and crowd of sweaty underage drinkers fighting for position at an open bar, I enjoy the last hour of 1988 on a couch at Summer's apartment in Ashley's arms.

"I resolve to make no resolutions," Summer says.

Frank tells her to stop talking like a philosophy professor.

Summer tries a second time. "Resolutions are like vacations. You think traveling to an exotic destination will change your life, but you eventually fall back into the same grind when you return home. Unless you move, you're just a tourist."

"Well, do you have any major moves planned for 1989?" Frank says.

"Fair enough," Summer says. "I do have one." After an uncharacteristic hesitation, she adds, "I want to save the Runner's Sole."

Frank and I exchange puzzled looks.

"One of the reasons I moved home is my dad's store is struggling."

"I would have never guessed," Frank says.

"Selling shoes has become a lot tougher since the big sporting goods chains moved into the business," Summer says.

"What ideas do you have?" Frank asks.

"I want to show people how much more you get from your local shop than simply a pair of shoes. Things like the running club are part of this. I'm also trying to differentiate from the big chains by offering expert advice and a highly personalized service. If people can get into the right gear and avoid injury, they'll tell their friends and come back for more."

"Let us know—"

Summer cuts Frank off with a bob of her head and turns to Ashley. "Alrighty, who's next?"

"I'll go," Ashley says. "This sounds trivial compared to what Summer shared, but my goal is to have more fun during our last semester of high school." Frank and Summer cheer in support.

"I know it's silly, but I've worked my butt off while watching other kids enjoy the best years of their lives. I keep promising to treat myself one day and don't want high school to slip by before I get a chance to taste the carefree side of teenage life."

"That's not silly," Summer says. "You've got to loosen that tightly wound coil every now and then, or it'll snap. Better to get some things out of your system before you beer slide into college like Frank-o here."

"Ouch!" Frank says. "Want my take?"

We all respond with groans of "No!" having heard plenty about Frank's one year of college.

"Fine with me, you high achievers," he says. "Since I've got the floor, I'm happy to announce that in ten days, I'll be a student once again." Frank explains he's enrolled in two classes at the local community college and plans to pursue a degree in exercise physiology.

"Congrats," I say. I'm not sure what *exercise physiology* is, so without wanting to sound clueless, I ask what he'll do with his degree.

"You know the health food co-op offering yoga classes and products you can't find at the Jewel?" he says. "It's not going to remain hidden in a rehabbed warehouse ten years from now. The personal health industry is at a tipping point, and I want to help people use exercise and nutrition to live better lives."

"Coach Frank!" I say. "I love it."

"Okay, Bags," Ashley says. "What's on *your* mind for the new year?"

"Hmm." I pause, knowing I won't be able to take this back once I say it out loud. "I'm going out for the track team in the spring . . . and I want to qualify for the state finals in May."

Everyone waits for me to tell them I'm joking.

"That's it? I throw that out there, and you all go quiet?"

Ashley breaks the silence. "I thought you were going to say you want to graduate in June, keep your scholarship, and start college in the fall." It's a decent guess, given that's all I've talked about for the past four months.

"Screw all that," I say. "It's out of my hands at this point."

"So, *this* is where things get interesting!" Frank swings his feet off the couch and leans forward, itching for more.

"I've spent too much time worrying about the wrong things, wanting shit I don't have and taking for granted what I do," I say. "All it's given me is a fat chip on my shoulder. I'm calling time on the self-loathing."

"How will track help you do that?" Summer asks.

I've been trying to figure out what Nurse Cooper meant when she encouraged me to make my accident count for something, other than surviving death. Then I went out and ran those twenty repeats up Spirit Hill on Christmas Day and found myself staring at death a second time. But it wasn't death. It was a glimpse of what I can do when I work really hard at something and stop comparing myself to others.

"I want to do this track thing because I want to become a better runner, but there's something at stake bigger than running. . . It's time for me to stop following others and chase something that's all my own." And scary enough to remind me I'm alive.

"Well, here's a toast to Bags!" Ashley says.

"Here's a toast to all of us," Summer says. "No vacations planned for this group!"

27

"Road or trail?" Summer greets me at her front door after I took advantage of a sunny morning to run to her apartment.

"Trail. From the mill."

"That's your LSD for the week."

"LSD?"

"Long Slow Distance. Sundays are going to be your easy long runs, so you've already knocked out today's session. Come on in."

Three sheets of paper and a plastic binder cover one end of her dining room table. After hearing my plans to join the track team, Summer offered to put together a pre-season training plan for me. The papers are monthly calendars for January, February, and March.

"Let's start with the events I think you should target," she says.

We're sitting close enough I can tell she just took a shower. Her hair smells cool, sweet, and damp—like grass on a spring morning.

"The sprints are the 100-, 200- and 400-meter dashes and the relays and hurdles. One lap around the track is four hundred meters. The 800 and 1600 meters are middle-distance events. In other words, two and four laps around the track. Then there is the longest event in high school track, the 3200 meters. You with me?"

"Yeah, but one question. Is the 1600 meters the same as the mile?"

"Ahh, that's a touchy subject. A mile is 1,609 meters. Tracks in the U.S. converted to four-hundred-meter ovals in the late seventies, making four laps nine meters short of a mile. Purists despise the shortfall because so much history is tied to the mile and the mystique of running it in under four minutes."

"Like Roger Bannister?" I say.

"He was the first. A lot of runners have broken the barrier since, although only a few high schoolers have done so. Guys like Jim Ryun, Tim Danielson, and Marty Liquori."

I thank her for the history lesson.

"Now, let me share how I think your strengths line up with the different distances. The shorter events require explosive speed and power. Based on what I've seen and your experience racing bikes, your secret weapon is the engine you were born with. You've got an exceptional ability to process oxygen and carbon dioxide. In other words, the aerobic capacity of your heart and lungs. Does this make sense?"

"Yep. This reminds me of biology class."

"Excellent. This all means the longer events like the 1600 and 3200 give you the best chance to be competitive. They require solid aerobic endurance for eighty to ninety percent of the race."

"Are you telling me I can win without having to sprint?"

"It's not that simple—and won't be easy. Winning a race will require short bursts of anaerobic sprint energy at the start and finish. Your strategy will be to open your aerobic engine full throttle in the middle of the race and push the field into the red zone before the final, all-out kick to the line."

"So, petrol, diesel, rocket fuel?"

"You got it. Are you ready to move on to the training plan I've put together?"

"Sure, but can I use the bathroom first?"

"Hah—of course. Take a right after the kitchen."

On my walk back from the bathroom, I wander into the open door at the end of the hallway and find myself standing in Summer's bedroom. I've never been in a girl's bedroom, let alone a girl in her twenties. Shades of white and gray soak the room in a clean, bright calm. Framed scenes of seashores, forests, and mountains fill three of the walls, and a montage of small photos forms a large heart on the fourth. I'm a million miles from the ratty blinds, running portraits, and posters of the Clash and R.E.M. tacked to the walls of the room I share with Frank. Neatly arranged pillows not intended for sleeping rest against the bed's headboard. The embroidered message on the one in the middle makes it clear this is Summer's room: *There is no shortcut to running 26.2 miles in 2.6 hours.*

The heart-shaped mosaic of pictures chronicling Summer's life pulls me into the room for a closer look. I take a deep breath, inhaling the scent of fall leaves that fills the room—and wish its occupant had a younger sister.

"Tell me you didn't piss in my closet." Summer's standing in the doorway behind me.

I spin around fast enough to get dizzy, and my face flushes in the absence of an excuse. "Sorry, Summer! I uh . . . I've never umm . . . Everything looked and smelled so . . . dream—y."

Summer laughs. "I'll take that as a compliment and need to remember you're still in high school."

Her forgiveness restarts my breathing, but being reminded I'm a child in her mind stings.

"Let's get back to work," she says. "I'll give you the tour through memory lane on that wall the next time you visit."

We return to the kitchen table, and Summer picks up where we left off as if nothing happened. Thirty minutes later I'm armed with a training plan of long slow days, tempo runs, speed workouts, and strength and flexibility exercises.

"This will give you lots to work on over the next three weeks," Summer says. "I don't believe in looking much beyond that in terms of planning. We'll tailor every few weeks based on how things have gone over the prior week or two. I'll join you for some of the speed workouts and maybe we use the Sunday runs to catch up. So, get used to seeing me a lot."

I want to shout, "Yes!" but instead ask, "Are these weekly totals correct? They're lower than I expected."

"Rest, recovery, and easy miles are as important to becoming a fast runner as the long days and speed work. Too many talented runners have had their love for the sport ruined by a 'run 'til you puke' training philosophy."

"Did you throw up a lot in college?"

"My coach put short-term results ahead of the long-term development of his athletes. He believed every day was a hard training day and winners run through injury."

"No pain no gain, right?"

"Running's not a Jane Fonda workout video. The best coaches know gains come from discipline. It's harder to convince motivated athletes to back off than to keep pushing into burnout and injury. That's why I'm excited to help you. You've got talent, and you haven't been tainted by bad habits. We have three months to ramp up your conditioning for the start of the track season, and the post-season is nearly five months away. With patience and a smart training plan, you should continue to get stronger over the course of your season in order to peak by early May."

"So does this mean you're going to give me a ride home after I ran eight miles to get here?"

"You bet."

"One last question."

"Shoot."

"Any chance I could use your bathroom again?"

28

Grades arrive the second week of winter break. At least that's what I hear from Ashley, Jed, and Sara. All I get is an invitation to meet with the principal and my guidance counselor. Good news wouldn't require a meeting, so I spend the final days of winter break arguing with Bad Gorilla about how bad it could be.

Mom and Dad can't make the meeting because they have to work. I know I did okay in journalism, so I ask Mr. King to join me.

How our principal Dr. Poulet ended up running the public high school in Linden Grove is unclear. He was born in a leafy village in Europe in one of those countries that still has a king, then accumulated an impressive set of academic credentials including boarding school in England, an Ivy League degree and, eventually, a doctorate in education. His prestigious CV and trace of a British accent provide the sensible residents of Linden Grove a connection to the cosmopolitan world outside the Midwest. Despite his status beyond the walls of our high school, the only students he shows interest in are the ass-lickers like Peter Grayson.

Mr. King and I sit across from my guidance counselor in Dr. Poulet's office. I've always assumed Ms. Wolski doesn't like me because up until today, I've never been in trouble at school. Some kids spend more time in their counselor's office than the classroom, and the counselors seem to love them for it.

Dr. Poulet shows up ten minutes late for our thirty-minute meeting. He goes straight to the head of the table and instead of apologizing, thanks us for waiting.

"Before we get started, Sam, let me say I am proud of your ability to overcome such a traumatic series of events last semester. The purpose of today's meeting is to discuss how we can ensure you continue to have an enriching high school experience as you complete your final credits toward graduation."

That doesn't sound so bad. If I bombed my exams, he probably would mention my grades.

I get nervous when Dr. Poulet hands things over to Ms. Wolski, because the only time I've spoken to her was last year when I asked her about college majors. Her advice—after digging out a folder buried deep in her filing cabinet—was something along the lines of: "Let's see . . . you're good at math and science. Why don't you be an engineer?" When I asked what an engineer does, she sent me to the school librarian.

"Let's start with an overview of your grades," Ms. Wolski says. "The *good* news is you have As in journalism and Latin IV, a B in AP Calculus and a C-plus in AP Physics. Any questions before we proceed?"

"Uh—it would be helpful to understand why I got a C in physics."

"I said, 'C-plus,' but we can come back to that after we discuss your grade in U.S. history."

"Okay, but you asked if I have any questions."

Ms. Wolski shifts her bubbly form in the chair and straightens her blouse in some non-verbal attempt to brush away the contradiction. "Well then, let's move on. I fear the situation with AP U.S. History is a little more challenging. Your fall semester grade is—" I know she's enjoying this because she delivers the news like she's unveiling the grand prize on a game show— "an F." She drags out the *efffff* in a way that stings my ears.

"Is this the point where you answer questions?" Mr. King says.

Ms. Wolski turns to Dr. Poulet, who sits up in his chair and straightens his tie. "Why don't I provide some further detail. I don't expect you'll be surprised to hear your history grade was impacted by your absence at the beginning of the semester. Mr. Bracovich applied a score of zero to the quizzes you missed and your class participation score for the first half of the semester."

I knew Bracovich wasn't going to do me any favors, but *zeroes* for the six weeks I wasn't in class? I need some time to think through how to respond, so I ask how I did on my final.

Ms. Wolski shuffles the papers in front of her. "Let's see. You scored a . . . 92."

Mr. King lets out an "Oh boy," and Dr. Poulet takes a turn shifting in his chair. Ms. Wolski busies herself by taking notes about matters unknown.

A ninety-two! I freaking aced it.

"Excuse me," Mr. King says. "I don't understand how a student can fail a class with an A on the final."

"If I may," Dr. Poulet says. "I have spoken with Mr. Bracovich about that same question. You are getting at the concept of *flexibility* versus *objectivity*. Mr. Bracovich believes in the principle of objectivity to ensure fair treatment across all students. Diluting the importance of the individual components of Sam's grade would be unfair to his classmates."

"Does that objectivity assume those classmates were *also* recovering from a tragic accident during the first quarter of the school year?" Mr. King asks.

Dr. Poulet taps the eraser of his pencil on the top of the table as he contemplates Mr. King's question.

Ms. Wolski speaks up. "Sir, should I explain my idea?"

"Uh—certainly, Marge. I mean, Ms. Wolski."

"Samuel," she begins. "We discussed the situation and thought that since you missed so much of last semester, we will allow you to retroactively drop U.S. history and avoid the hit to your GPA."

"But Ms. Wolski, you know if I do that, I won't be able to graduate in June, right?"

Dr. Poulet takes the question. "We discussed that, and the real-world lessons this situation presents—"

"Real world aside, Dr. Poulet"—Mr. King chuffs under his breath—"is there a process for appealing the grade? One teacher's discretion is dictating this kid's senior year."

"That is a fair question, Jacob. I can assure you giving my teachers, including you, discretion to manage their classrooms is preferable to creating the risk of inconsistency and uncertainty by introducing decision making by consensus or an appeals mechanism. Mr. Bracovich came to the conclusion that inconvenience should not overrule the first principles of objectivity and fairness."

"Failing senior year strikes me as an expensive lesson in inconvenience, Dr. Poulet," Mr. King says.

Weird pause.

"So, tell me if I'm missing anything," I say. "My grades are final. I can complete U.S. history this semester and graduate in June, although my GPA will reflect an honors-level F, which means my overall weighted GPA will fall below a B average for the semester. Or I can drop the class but need to make up the missing credits next year as a fifth-year senior?"

"That is the situation." Dr. Poulet leans back in his chair, rolling his pencil along his fingers.

I don't know how to respond. I do know no matter which option I choose, I've lost my scholarship. I also know I busted my ass making up for missing the first six weeks of the semester only to get penalized for doing so in half the time available to my classmates in some warped view of fairness.

"Dr. Poulet, you talk about fairness," I say. "But fairness would have been telling me I was wasting my time with U.S. history when I still had a chance to swap it for another class."

Dr. Poulet sits up, tugs the lapels of his blazer and checks his watch. "I think we've covered everything. Anything else before we conclude?"

"I don't get the principles part," I say. "Objectivity and real world lessons sound like excuses to hide behind instead of dealing with my unusual situation. I guess no matter what you call it, I'm screwed."

Dr. Poulet remains silent, but when he grips the pencil in his hands so tightly it snaps in two, I know I've lost any chance of saving my senior year.

Mr. King exhales a slow looping whistle. "That should do it, Marge. You can probably release us back into the real world now."

I track Sara down after the meeting. Her snooty AP English Lit teacher gives me a chilly look when I pull her out of class.

"You actually said 'screwed'?"

"I think what really burned the boats was calling bullshit on his principles."

"Well, kudos to you for speaking up for yourself. You knew it was going to be a long shot."

"I know, but being proven right doesn't feel so hot."

"Have you considered the positive in all this?"

"It gives me another year to save up for college?"

"Well . . . yes," Sara says. "And since college isn't going anywhere, your prospects are now more attractive. You'll be able to meet the early application deadlines next fall, assuming you stay out of the hospital this summer"—Sara laughs at her own joke—"and you have even more material for an incredible essay about overcoming obstacles this past year."

"Yeah, but how am I going to pay for college without my scholarship?"

"You won't be the first financially needy kid to figure out how to go to college without a caddie scholarship, Bags."

I grumble in the face of Sara's optimism, even though that's why I ran to her.

"Ashley told me about your New Year's resolution," Sara says.

The muscles in my face tighten.

"Don't be embarrassed. It's ballsy—and inspiring. Another upside is those pussies Bracovich and Poulet have handed you a pass to go all out on your training. You'll get a second chance to graduate and apply to college, but you only get one chance to chase your dream."

"Strange, isn't it?" I say. "Death taught me I need to pay more attention to how I'm living my life."

"Some skulls require a heavy hammer, Bags."

29

I jump off the line with a smile on my face. A quick glance catches my knees surging three times per second. My footfalls are so light and quick my body hovers across the surface of the track. My chest, neck, and head are perfectly aligned, slightly tilted and leading my legs forward. Bent arms pump like two cranks driving my body into the final straightaway of the fourth lap with the finish line in sight. The last image I see before leaning across the line is the clock adding hundredths of a second to 3:59:00 as I break the tape.

"Smoke 'em if you got 'em!" Frank rustles me out of my visualized glory. We're meeting Summer this morning for a 1600-meter time trial at the LGHS track. She wants to establish a baseline "race pace" for me, against which she'll set target training zones for my preseason workouts.

Before we line up for our four laps around the track, Summer leads Frank and me through a set of warm-up exercises like arm swings, hip rotations, lunges, and skips. We leave our extra layers at the bleachers, and I ask Summer if she has any advice as we walk to the start line.

"The 1600 is largely aerobic. You want to go out hard for the first eight to ten seconds and keep in contact with the leaders for the first lap. Since there's only three of us, that'll be me. During laps two and three, run the fastest pace you can while controlling your breathing. Don't freak if someone pulls out in front. Try to reel them back without blowing up. At around three hundred meters from the finish, you want to lift the pace. Make sure you're in the second or third lane to avoid getting boxed in. By two hundred meters, kick with all you have left until you pass the finish line."

"Sounds easy," Frank says.

Summer rolls her eyes. "Okay, let's line up, and I'll call it."

We take our positions alongside each other at the start line.

"On your mark. BANG!"

Frank takes Summer's advice and bolts off the line for the first fifty meters. I have no clue what I can sustain for 1600 meters, so I just try to stay close. Frank has ten meters on me when we settle into the first lap. Summer plays rabbit, maintaining a steady pace a couple strides ahead of me.

Frank extends his lead to fifteen meters by the end of the first lap. I increase my cadence, searching for the edge of my aerobic zone. By the time we exit the first turn of lap two, Frank is a few meters closer. I pick up the pace again, probing the edge of my body's ability to process the violent huffs of air scraping the back of my throat with each exhale.

As we begin lap three, my mind gets lost in the rhythm of my breaths. I inhale every two steps, exhale on the third, and wonder if I should breathe through my mouth or nose. After a short experiment with nasal breathing, my body threatens to pass out and forces my mouth back open.

I catch my breath and find Frank close enough that Summer has pulled ahead of him. The pain in my legs, arms, and chest is unbearable. Quitting never enters my mind. I haven't come this far to walk the last lap and a half. My mind wanders again, this time to memories of racing my bike up hills that made similar demands on my body.

I refocus on Frank, and a funny thing happens—he floats back toward me. Summer chugs along a few meters in front of us, and I relax every muscle in my body not responsible for propelling the being known as Sam Bagliarello forward. "Up-up-up," I command my feet each time they hit the ground in a battle with the sensation they're trudging through mud.

I pass Frank when we exit the first bend of lap four. Summer's instruction to "kick" with two hundred meters to go seems masochistic under the circumstances. I pump my arms faster, expecting my legs to follow. Nothing. I have nothing more to give. My arms are burning as hot as my legs. Summer eases up and pulls alongside me.

"Give it. Whatever. You have. NOW," she says.

"Am—" is all I manage in response.

"Okay. Stay. With me." Summer pushes a stride ahead and exits the final turn in lane two. I can almost smell the droplets of perspiration evaporating off the back of her honey-toned neck. I ignore her advice about positioning in the final stretch and stay in lane one. There's no one to box me in, and my body refuses to veer from the shortest path to the finish. I'm a flailing mess of limbs behind Summer's quiet control. I can't find the extra kick she promised and continue to fade. Frank gains back much of my lead. The finish line dances in the air a few meters ahead. I keep pushing with all I've got, slowing despite an increasing rate of exertion, like trying to inflate a punctured balloon.

Crossing the finish line brings no thrill of victory, only relief. Summer walks things off ahead of us, while Frank and I pull onto the grass in the center of the oval. Frank swats me on the hip. "Sweet run, Sam." He then rolls onto his back while I grab the ends of my shorts and strain to catch my breath as if sucking air through a straw.

"You too. Ten more meters. You had me."

"Next time we'll race a proper mile."

A minute later, I pull myself up and cut through the infield to where Summer continues her victory lap. "You want the good news or the bad news?" she asks.

"I'm too shattered for anything but good news."

"Five twenty."

"Five minutes twenty seconds?"

"Actually, twenty seconds and fifteen hundredths."

"That's decent, right?"

"It's rock 'n' roll for a first attempt and more than two months until the season starts."

"Was it supposed to hurt that much?"

"Did you puke?"

"My throat hurts, and I almost lost my vision."

"Sounds about right. You'll get faster as your form improves, and the speed work will condition your body to push itself."

"Any thoughts on breathing?"

"I highly recommend it," she says.

I clarify my question.

"If you can repeat that run with your mouth shut, go for it," she says. "My suggestion is use whatever opening gets the air in as fast as possible."

She goes on to explain the benefits of breathing with my belly instead of my chest and experimenting with different cadences. Discovering an opportunity for improvement adds to the good news.

"Okay, give me the bad news."

"Shaving a minute off your time to make it to state will require a heroic effort. The hurt will become more familiar, but it's never going to feel better."

Her words scrape the inflamed lining of my throat, then I remember I signed up for this.

"So, tell us, Summer," Frank asks when he joins us. "How much were you holding back?"

"Hah! Let's put it this way—the hard part was keeping myself from picking up your brother in the home stretch and leaving you in the dust."

"Dang."

30

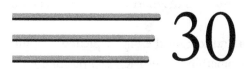

If Mr. Bracovich was a golfer, he'd be the guy holding up play while fishing for lost balls in a water hazard. Forcing students to show curiosity in your classroom is equally petty and self-absorbed. A day after dropping his class, I find Mr. Paul holding Mr. Bracovich's ball retriever. It turns out I scored an 89 on Mr. Paul's AP Physics final, but he gave me a C-plus for the semester because of the labs I missed. Since I'm already signed up for a fifth year of high school, I drop AP Physics too. Not only does this erase the C from my GPA, it also removes another prick from my life.

With only three academic subjects, I no longer need to cut corners in Latin to keep up with an overloaded schedule of core classes. In the luxury of time, I find the patience to explore the relevance of the ancient Greeks and Romans to a teenage boy two thousand years in the future.

"Did you know Sisyphus cheated death?" Sara says. "Twice in fact." Sara and I are in the library selecting stories for our independent mythology projects due at the end of the semester.

"Sounds like Sisyphus and I have lots in common."

"Except he was a king."

"I'll keep researching."

Sara selects Athena's role in *The Odyssey*, intrigued by the goddess of wisdom and war's efforts to help Odysseus find his way home and reunite with his family.

"I'm going to stick with Sisyphus," I say fifteen minutes later. It seems like a simple enough story: Zeus punishes Sisyphus by forcing him to push a boulder up a hill, only for it to keep rolling back to the ground before reaching the top.

"I'm not sure a story about futility is the most inspiring theme for a senior project." Sara says.

"I'm trying to be like you and look at the bigger picture. My life is like Sisyphus's boulder—something I need to keep pushing up a hill in the hopes optimism and persistence will free me from Linden Grove."

"Don't forget, Zeus punished Sisyphus for eternity," Sara says. "Unless you discover a sequel to the story, optimism and persistence didn't help him much."

"Glad I've got all semester to work on it."

31

I return from school to an empty house most days. Mom is increasingly absent, spending more nights out with friends in the old neighborhood than at home. I can't tell if her detachment is due to disappointment with my grades, or if Frank's return provides a sense of freedom from life as a single parent. Regardless of what she tells herself, Frank isn't around much either, since he spends most evenings at the community college library.

I quickly figure out that if I want to eat, I need to feed myself. Given my Big Bird diet, this doesn't require more than chopping vegetables, boiling rice or pasta, opening a can of beans, and heating up bottles of sauce or salsa to top everything off. The more I prepare my own meals, the more I notice what goes into my body, and nutrition becomes as important as rest and recovery to the quality of the miles I log running.

Each day's workout is manageable on its own, but the persistent exertion, day after day, drains me. My weary body soaks up the rest and recovery Summer so strongly advocates when I climb into bed each evening. I wake from deep sleep refreshed and oblivious to the radio reminders that morning is ticking away. I begin most runs stiff and tired but within a few minutes, my body reemerges stronger than the day before.

I invite Ashley over for dinner one night and plan to impress her with a meat- and dairy-free version of Mom's famous gravy. Mom refused to share the recipe when I told her I wanted to exclude the ground sausage and beef, butter, parmesan cheese, and "neck bones," but lightened up when I assured her Ashley eats meat, loves lemon knots, and the silly idea is all mine. Two hours into simmering my version on the stove, I discover the family secret is the greasy animal fat from all the ingredients I cut out and abandon my culinary experiment minutes before Ashley arrives.

"Your mom's sauce is amazing!" Ashley says once we sit down to eat.

When I fess up and show her the generic bottle of pasta sauce, we laugh at the suggestive power of the pot of tomatoes and spices left cooling on the stove.

Ashley has been taking her New Year's resolution seriously. The many opportunities to party during the school week surprise us both, and Ashley applies her honors student work ethic to seeking them out. This works fine for our relationship, since I'm knackered most nights after hours of training and studying.

"What are we going to do with this big old house to ourselves?" Ashley says. We're sitting on the couch reciting lines from *Fletch* playing on "Chicago's Very Own" WGN.

"It's not that big a house," I say. The movie cuts to a commercial advertising no installment payments for sixty days from Empire carpets. "And believe me, it feels even smaller when my mom yells at you to stay out of the clean areas."

"We don't need much room, Bags." Ashley drapes her leg across my lap, straddles my hips, then pins me to the couch with her hands on my shoulders. With mischief in her eyes, she pulls her hair behind her ears and dives in for a deep kiss that fills my mouth with the soft warmth of her tongue.

We work our shirts off each other without much trouble. She surprises me when she grabs my belt buckle. "We're still in *let's wait* mode, right?" I ask. Over winter break we agreed neither of us is ready for sex.

"Sure, Sam," she says. "That doesn't mean we can't get creative with all the other parts of our bodies."

For the first time since learning the truth about Santa Claus, I'm bursting in anticipation of unwrapping presents—in this case, the clothes on Ashley's body. Ashley makes up a game she calls Treasure Hunt. The basic idea is one person hides, leaving a trail of clothing for the other to find. Ashley volunteers to go first while I count to ten. She fortunately takes it easy on me. I find her socks in the kitchen, jeans in the hallway, bra in front of the bathroom Frank and I share, and underpants inside the door to my bedroom. That leaves nothing but my blanket covering her body when I discover her in my bed. "Please, Please, Please, Let Me Get What I Want" by the Smiths plays from the tape deck on Frank's stereo.

"Can I borrow your blanket?" I pick up where we left off on the *Fletch* quotes. "My car just hit a water buffalo . . ."

"You've got to be kidding. Lose those clothes and come keep me warm."

I'm learning a lot about the female body this semester, and Ashley is really into it tonight. She keeps letting out these steamy moans that aren't noises you hear people make in the normal course of a day. Her enjoyment elevates the adventure beyond the physical, and I try to make up for my inexperience with naked girls by responding with horny sounds of my own. There's something erotic and romantic about exploring these different paths to pleasure together and knowing so much more lies ahead of us.

32

By late February daylight remains in short supply, and the temperature becomes meaningless unless measured in terms of windchill. Restless for the end of winter and a chance to put my off-season conditioning to use, I drop in on a late-season indoor track practice.

The LGHS fieldhouse is nicknamed the House of Blues and Gold in a nod to our school colors and Chicago's musical heritage. The stocky six-foot frame of LGHS's running coach, Robert "Rip" Ipswitch, is easy to spot, alone in the center of the indoor track with a whistle around his neck. His blue-and-gold sweatsuit looks so thoroughly faded it could be the only one he's ever worn since joining the LGHS track and cross-country coaching staff twenty-five years ago. Practice hasn't started, but a sense of perpetual purpose drives the man, already at work adjusting lighting, arranging hurdles, and picking up pom-poms and frisbees left behind by less conscientious users.

Coach Rip's presence in the center of the House of Blues and Gold mirrors the understated command Father Pierce wielded over recess at Saint Edward's. Our pastor's quiet authority terrified us kids in the school yard. He maintained order with a discreet word and an iron grip of a shoulder before arguments, teasing, or foul language escalated. I tell myself if I could survive Father Pierce, there's no reason to be intimidated by Coach Rip. Nevertheless, I approach cautiously.

Standing toe to toe with the man, the vigor and youth in his weathered face surprise me. "Excuse me. Coach Rip? My name's

Sam Bagliarello . . ."

His eyes lock onto mine as if I'm the most important person in his world at the moment. His full attention and gregarious response put me at ease. "It's a pleasure to meet the famous Bags," he says in a gravelly voice. "You've had one heck of a year. How ya' feelin' these days?"

I explain my reason for standing in front of him.

"I'd be honored to have you join the team. Outdoor practice starts the week after next."

"Thanks, Coach."

"What sort of running have you done?"

I ramble through my rehab and training over the winter. I also mention my stint with the cycling club.

"Coach Wolfe was one of the good guys. It was a shame to lose him. Have you given any thought to the events you want to run?"

"I think I'm best suited for the middle-distance events. Maybe the 1600 meters?"

"Everyone wants to be a miler, ya' know? We only have one or two strong runners at the 800 and 3200 meters, so keep those in mind, too."

I ask if I can join today's workout.

"Sorry. This being the last week of the indoor season, I want to make sure the team takes things easy before we ramp up again in March. I'm not comfortable with some new guy coming in hot and pushing the pace. Besides, I like to walk everyone through the same initiation on the first day to make sure we're all clear about expectations."

"Okay, Coach. I'll be there in two weeks and ready to go."

We shake on it, and I turn to leave.

"Hey, Bags. What sort of pace have you been running the mile?"

"I've only run it once. I did it in five twenty." I detect the slightest grin on Coach's face. Sensing the same regard for precision Father Pierce would have demanded, I add, "And fifteen hundredths."

Coach Rip's grin eases into a full smile. "Well now, that gives us something to work on, doesn't it?"

33

March might be associated with spring, but the first full week of the month refuses to let go of winter. A hefty wind hammers my walk to the bleachers to join the rest of the track team for the first practice of the outdoor season. An unseen boom box softens the bite of the cold air with the familiar guitar chords of an AC/DC song that never gets old.

The upperclassmen dish out a mix of trash talk and sandbagging with references to eating too much over the two-week break, the lingering effects of colds, and exaggerated descriptions of niggling injuries.

"Dude, what's with the shammy?" The team's senior captain, Dirk Anker, calls attention to the chamois pad in the crotch area of my cycling tights.

"These are just some old cycling pants." Other than a few pimply freshmen, I'm the only person not suiting up in LGHS-branded gear.

"Where's the velodrome?" he persists. I let out a soft laugh, more to reassure myself than react to a guy referred to by his teammates as "last name's Anker, the *W* is silent." Dirk Anker-Wanker has been touted as a future state champ in the 1600 meters since freshman year. After taking second place last year, this season is his last chance to live up to those expectations.

"Pay attention, Dirk," Smitty says. "Bags is gonna show us how to race track this season."

I thought Smitty was on my side until he pegs me for a

presumptuous outsider with his comment.

"Aren't you a senior, Bags?" a fellow senior named Billy asks.

"I am."

"What have you been waiting for?" It's a simple question I don't have a short answer to.

Billy Perry was known by his given name, William Perry, up until eighth grade when the Chicago Bears drafted another William Perry—aka "the Refrigerator"—in the 1985 NFL draft. Other than sharing the same name, the two athletes couldn't be more different. Billy is five nine, one hundred forty pounds, compared to the Fridge at six two and more than three hundred thirty pounds. In order to shake the nickname "Mini-Fridge" before freshman year, the younger William Perry started referring to himself as Billy, which mostly works unless he gives someone a reason to tease him.

"How many layers you starting with?" I ask Dirk.

"One under this." He pinches the insulated wind jacket zipped snugly up to his neck.

"Is it okay if mine has jersey pockets on it?" I hold up my jacket and display the three cycling pockets stitched across the back. The laughs from the upper rows of the bleachers restore enough of my confidence to respond to Mini-Fridge.

"I started running after an accident I had last August."

"Oh yeah. I heard you died. Glad to see the rumor wasn't true."

"Me too."

Coach Rip's whistle calls practice to order.

"Alright, men. Circle up!" Coach Rip greets the thirty or so boys gathered around him with a few pleasantries and housekeeping items. He adopts a more serious tone when he transitions to his prepared remarks.

"I want to talk about goals."

Backs straighten.

"I know you all have goals. For example, we know Dirk wants to win state this year in the 1600 meters, Smitty's working to qualify for state in the 800, and Billy's looking to make it onto the podium in the 3200. Apologies for not covering everyone's goals, but you get the idea."

Coach paces back and forth, never taking his eyes off his audience.

"Here's what I want you to do with your goals." Coach captures the attention of a group of boys who, for a few minutes, left their giggles and chatter back at the bleachers. "Write them down, stick 'em in a drawer and forget about those goals until the season's over."

The audience waits for the catch like a hungry pack of dogs.

"My point is, you each have everything you need to accomplish your goals. Focus instead on what you're going to do to perform your best when it matters. You need to *own* your training. You need to act like a winner *every day*. You need to *take responsibility* for how you live your life off the track. What are you eating? How much sleep are you getting? Are you avoiding booze and drugs?"

Coach's words draw adolescent snickers.

"Because track is the sport of *truth*. There's nowhere to hide on the oval. You can't blame a missed block or a bad shot for a disappointing outcome. *You alone* are responsible for your performance. What you do every day is the only thing you control. You can't control the weather, the state of the track surface, or the talent and training of your competitors. This means you can't control whether you *win* your event. But you *can* control whether you show up and deliver the best possible version of yourself. And that's what will make you a winner on *and off* the track."

I try to make sense of the contradiction in Coach's words. I've always set goals to motivate myself to accomplish things. Then again, I showed up for those Christmas Day hill repeats with nothing more than a commitment to leave everything I had on Spirit Hill. Likewise, I signed up for track to pursue something that's all my own, but what would be more *my own*: focusing on a specific goal—like making it to state—shared by hundreds of other runners—or working every day to become the best runner I can be?

Coach Rip tugs the waistline of his sweatpants before continuing, and I hang on every word.

"Let me share two goals I've tucked into *my* sock drawer. First, I want to use running as a vehicle to teach you men life lessons bigger than this beautiful sport we love. Over the course of your life, you'll face many challenges in your personal and professional lives. You'll find success, and you'll encounter failure. My hope is the hard work, victories, *and* failures you endure on the Linden Grove track team provide the lessons and self-confidence to navigate the ups and downs of life.

"Second, before I retire, or die along the way, I want to coach a state champion. We've won our share of silver and bronze medals over the years, but I'd like to see one of my men on the top step of the podium before I leave the sport." Coach Rip allows the wave of enthusiastic hoots and claps to rise from the crowd before quieting everyone down with a gesture of his hands.

"One last thing before we get to some actual running today. Allow me to review my ground rules for the season. If you want to run in an LGHS uniform, you will adhere to the following.

"Rule number one: no assholes. We are a team, your teammates need you, and you will find at different points of the season you'll need them. When you are respected, trusted, and valued, you are more happy and confident. This will enable you to train—and ultimately race—better. Only a fraction of the time you spend running over the next three months will be in a race. The support of your teammates the other ninety-nine percent of the time will ensure that while you may race *on* your own, you will never race *a*lone.

"Rule number two: no booze or drugs. I not only want you to avoid limiting your performance on the track, but I refuse to be a passive bystander to young adults adopting habits that risk harming their future lives off the track.

"Rule number three: show up. This means you need to attend every practice the week before a meet. No one gets to ride their reputation and past performance. Race slots go to those who've done the work to earn the right to compete. If you miss a practice because of injury or illness, then the rest will make you stronger. If you miss for any other reason, that's your fault.

"That's all I've got, men. Thanks for listening. Now, let's warm up with a few easy laps."

As we settle into our first lap around the track, the conversation turns to the upcoming season. I learn the boys' field events and the girls' track and field teams have their own head coaches. Each week follows a similar pattern of two meets per week, four days of training and one rest day. Weekly practice consists of a long run on Monday, one speed workout, a medium distance day of five or six miles, a day of strength work peppered with some form drills, then an easy jog with a few strides on pre-meet days.

"The Invitational is early this year," Billy says as the pace picks up during our second lap. The Invitational is a meet our school hosts each year. We invite three other teams to compete, making it a "quad" event. "Only three weeks away."

"Early is better," another senior says. "Makes it more likely Mayflower's not yet in peak form."

This leads to a heated discussion about Mayflower Academy, winner of the team title at last year's state finals. Fancy private schools are easy to root against, and Mayflower's dominant track and field program makes them the team everyone hates.

"Who's returning from last year?" Smitty asks.

"Their sprinter, who cleaned up in the 100 and 200," Dirk says.

"And, of course, their distance man, Cooper," Billy says.

"Cooper?" I ask. A pleasant memory of Nurse Cooper pops into my head, and I wonder if there's a connection. "What's his first name?"

"That *is* his first name. Cooper Assel."

"ASS-el is his last name? He'd break Coach's first rule." The response to my attempt at humor indicates it's an old joke.

"Any intel on Coop this year, Dirk?" someone asks.

"He had a light indoor season," Dirk says. "Probably a sign of overconfidence."

Coop has been an open wound for Dirk for the past three years. Dirk took second in state last year behind Coop, which was the last time the two competed. Coop also took silver in the 3200 meters against a senior last year, which makes him the favorite in that event this year as well.

"Yeah, but he won every 1600- and 3200-meter race he ran indoors," Billy says. "I'm not looking forward to running against him."

"Well, he hasn't run the mile as fast as he did last year in the state finals, and I've gotten faster, so I guess we'll know more in three weeks' time," Dirk says.

"How fast did he run it last year?" I ask.

"Four thirteen flat," Billy says.

"How fast did you guys run it?"

Before anyone answers, Dirk accelerates away in an imitation of a toddler throwing his toys out of his crib. I turn to Smitty. "Is Coop that good?"

"Four thirteen isn't unbeatable. Plenty of state champs have run faster, but there hasn't been anyone at that level these past three years to push Coop. I think Dirk has come to believe no matter how fast he gets, Coop will always be able to shave a few seconds off his pace to beat him."

The next day's practice is the speed workout for the week. During our warm-up, I ask Dirk how Coach Rip will select the team for Saturday's "triangular" meet.

"It's the first meet of the season, so the guys who raced indoors have the most miles in their legs and will get first dibs."

"How many runners get to race?"

"We'll field three from our side for each event."

"What would I need to do to earn a spot?"

"Keep up today and get Coach's attention during the intervals."

"Thanks, I'll let my legs know."

After the warm-up we split into sprint and distance groups. The distance group runs "ladder" intervals: two sets each of 1200, 400, and 200 meters designed to target the high-power requirements of an 800- to 3200-meter event. The idea is you can run these shorter distances at a faster pace than race speed, thereby improving your explosive power for the all-out anaerobic portions of a longer event.

I make a point of staying close to Dirk, Billy, Smitty, and a junior named José Rodriguez. José earned the nickname "Hot Rod" based on his last name and speed on the football field. He's a nineteen-year-old junior because his parents held him back three years before sending him to kindergarten. José claims his dad wanted him to have an advantage in sports. His teammates, however, joke that leaving all his speed on the field leaves him slow in the classroom. While José's no honors student, his dad got what he wanted. José has been a first-string wide receiver on the varsity football team since his freshman year, and he's our number two man in the 3200 meters, behind Billy.

Coach instructs us to run the 1200-meter intervals at seventy-five seconds per lap. This equates to a five-minute mile, twenty seconds faster than the mile time trial I ran with Summer and Frank. The time trial, however, was four laps instead of three, so two additional months of training and one less lap today give me a chance to hang on.

In a sign of early season marking of territory, the first lap starts fast, and Coach Rip flaps his arms in a fit when we cross the line in sixty-five seconds. I hang with the front group of four without any major issues.

Everyone looks to Dirk to set the pace for lap two closer to Coach's target. Senior Captain Dirk, however, refuses to signal weakness, and we complete the second lap only two seconds slower than the first. I'm still with the leaders and retain enough brain function to realize we're running close to a four-and-a-half-minute mile pace—almost a minute faster than my mile time trial.

Lap three gets underway, and Dirk, Billy, and Smitty push each other, taking turns holding a hair's breadth lead during the final lap. José and I stay close to the front three, and we complete the third lap in sixty-five seconds again. Instead of pulling over to suck wind, we recover by jogging easy for six hundred meters. No one says a word, but the sideways glances suggest my pace surprised my teammates as much as me.

After regaining his breath, Smitty says, "Hey fellas, glad to see everyone's ready for the season, but I don't want to burn out before Saturday." The subsequent grunts confirm agreement to dial things back without anyone losing face.

Coach articulates Smitty's point more colorfully. "You guys were on fire! Too bad I didn't want you to burn all those matches. I want to see you hit this second 1200 at a seventy-five-second lap pace, or you can show off with a third set. Got it?"

My body hums through the three laps of the second set, and we rest with another six-hundred-meter easy jog.

My strong showing on the first two intervals unravels on the first 400. Midway through the one-lap interval, my legs turn over as quickly as before, but there's a slack in my form, as my body steals tiny breaks from each stride with a fractionally heavier footfall, an extra millimeter of heel drop, one less degree of arc in each pump of my arms.

I can't tell if the runners around me feel any worse themselves until we exit the second turn. Someone picks up the pace, and I lose contact with the front group. I finish four seconds behind the leaders. They didn't smoke me, but the gap is noticeable. We jog two hundred meters easy before starting the second 400-meter interval.

I'm cooked and unable to fake it beyond the first hundred meters so stick to a speed I can sustain the entire lap. Dirk, Billy, and Smitty complete the interval at their same minute-plus pace, a few steps ahead of José and Mark Cornell, a chunky senior nicknamed

"Cornbread" whose mom makes him run track and cross-country to get him away from the television and Ho-Hos. Despite finishing sixth, my form held up much better running within my limits instead of trying to keep up.

During the easy jog before our first of two 200s, Coach shouts, "All out on this one, gents!"

Curiosity and fear shoot through me because I used my "all out" gear on the 400s. I hold nothing back on the first 200. Smitty takes first, followed by Dirk and Billy, all within a stride of each other. José finishes two steps behind Billy, and Cornbread and I finish right behind him. I can't believe how hard a half lap can feel.

José senses my frustration. "It's not about one half lap. You need to respect the eight laps that came before it," he says.

Smitty, Dirk, and Billy finish the second 200—our last interval of the day—in a tight bunch once again, while Cornbread and I stumble across the line well behind José in fourth.

"Bags!" Coach Rip calls from his impromptu office on the bottom two rows of the bleachers. I jog over, worried I got his attention as Dirk advised but not for the reasons intended.

"Yeah, Coach?"

"How'd those intervals feel?"

"Pretty good. I need to work on my speed in the shorter distances."

Coach raises an eyebrow, which stops me bobbing my head and shoulders in false confidence. "Yeah, you started to fade in the 400s and struggled with the 200s."

"I'm not a sprinter." My hands search for nonexistent pockets in my cycling pants.

"No one considers Dirk and Billy sprinters either. The difference is, you're still building up an ability to deliver peak efforts."

"I could go out and run 1600 or 3200 meters right now against anyone."

Coach Rip winces at my bravado. "Maybe, but here's why I called you over. We've got a full squad for the 1600 on Saturday. Based on what I saw tonight, I'm going to let Billy, José, and Cornbread race the 3200. Now, we only have one legitimate 800-meter man, Smitty. Frankly, I'd prefer to hold you back from racing until you get more training miles in your legs, ya' know?"

"Yes, sir." I shoot for deference over eagerness, this being the second track practice of my life and all.

"You may indeed have potential for the 1600- and 3200-meter distances, but if I'm gonna let you compete, the 800 will get you some race experience and develop your speed. We have nearly three months of racing ahead of us, so I'd prefer to ease you into things."

"I'll take whatever spot you've got for me, Coach."

"Well then, plan on running the 800 meters on Saturday."

I rush home to tell Frank and Mom about Saturday's race. The absence of the Beet and the Guinness remind me I'll need to wait to share my news. Mom's out smoking at Bingo Night in some VFW hall with old high school friends, and Frank is studying late at school as usual. I call Summer to share the news and ask her thoughts on the 800-meter event.

"Coach Rip is right to question your ability to survive a longer-distance race at this stage. You saw tonight you need to keep building your endurance and speed. Don't put too much pressure on yourself Saturday. View it as an extreme interval session and an opportunity to learn what racing's all about."

34

Life after graduation begins to take shape for seniors *not* returning for a fifth year, and I get caught in a discussion about college plans over lunch. Ashley accepted an offer from Purdue University to major in industrial engineering, Jed's attending the University of Illinois to pursue a degree in mechanical engineering, and Sara is headed to Charlotte College to study philosophy.

"Isn't that an all-girls school?" Jed says to Sara.

"What's your point, Bobby Brady?" Jed makes an easy target for Sara in the red-and-blue-striped T-shirt his mom dressed him in today. "The school's in this coed town called *New York City*?"

"I still don't understand why you need to go to an all-girls school," Jed says. "I mean, it's not like the guys around here are lining up to harass you."

"Easy, Jed," I say. "Visiting Sara in New York sounds a lot more interesting than a weekend of cow tipping in a cornfield with you."

"So, what's new with you, Bags"—Sara takes the opportunity to redirect the conversation—"other than your hair continues to grow out of control?"

"I'm taking your advice and making the most of my five-year plan."

"I keep telling Bags he makes me jealous," Ashley says. "He's living a charmed life while the rest of us spend the last semester of high school stressed about overloaded schedules and AP exams."

"No one's forcing you to party five days a week, Ash."

Ashley shoots me a look as pleasant as a knuckle sandwich. Marty helps me dodge the punch by tapping my shoulder with the March issue of the school newspaper.

"Hey, Sam Bags!" he says. "Great job on today's paper!"

"Thanks, Marty."

"Did you see this article with your name on it?" He points to the headline *Food Industry Promotes Kentucky Fried Fraud.* Inspired by my NewTrition shakes, the McDonald's in the hospital and Coca-Cola's sponsorship of the Olympics, the article criticizes the food industry for its questionable healthy marketing messages.

"I did see that, thanks for noticing."

"It also says you're on the track team. Way to go!"

"My first meet's on Saturday. Wish me luck."

"Ah—if you want a little luck, take this."

Marty pulls a *Star Wars* figure from his pocket.

"Cool, Chewbacca!" The Wookiee Marty hands me has clearly seen its fair share of action.

"He's a gentle giant. Strong and fast."

"Thanks, but I can't accept this."

"No problem. That's the one I carry because he's missing an arm and right foot. Take it."

"Okay, Marty. Thanks—"

"Oh boy! Sorry, Sam." A screaming girl back at Marty's table distracts him. "I need to hop. Someone needs me at the special needs table."

During an easy road run the day before Saturday's meet, I ask Smitty for advice on the 800-meter race.

"Your first race is gonna be rough, Bags," Smitty says. "Try not to freak out about it."

"How'd your first one go?" I ask.

"I had everything under control until the starter called us up. Then I took off my warm-up gear and barfed all over the bleachers."

"Ouch."

"Yeah, I got blown away, but I learned a lot."

"Like what?"

"Try to keep your cool and focus on the meter you're running. Don't worry about the lap ahead."

"How do you keep your cool?"

"I race with my head, because you don't win by running fastest. You win by falling apart slowest. There's no way to hide from the hurt, so you gotta tell yourself, 'I feel you, pain. You are nothing but a signal my legs are sending to my brain. I can hang with you for another stride.' Then I repeat it. 'Okay, one more. And another. Another . . .'"

"I never took you to be so mental, Smitty."

"Mental. I like it. Better than crazy."

Coach Rip's face is one big smile when we get back to the track. A box of new uniforms sits beside him on the bottom row of the bleachers. His enthusiasm spreads quickly, as my teammates discover the gaudy yellow and blue uniforms last updated five years ago have been redesigned in a sleek, simple style that looks light and fast.

I get all weepy when Coach Rip calls me to collect mine. Cycling was an intramural sport, so we never got team kits. I hide my moist eyes from my teammates by inspecting the bag holding my first team uniform—proud to have earned the sense of belonging contained within.

35

Hello, pain. Join me for one more step. One more step. One more.

Before getting out of bed I visualize the morning ahead, from boarding the team bus to crossing the finish line. I picture the nearly eight hundred steps it will take to finish today's race, from the starter's gun to breaking the tape with my chest at the finish.

"WBBM Newsradio. It's six fourteen. Sports is up next . . ."

The sky is gray and soupy when our bus arrives at Oak Forest High. A temperature in the upper thirties works for running but isn't the sort of weather you want to spend a lot of time standing around in. Our big yellow school bus serves as a warming hut and mobile locker room, safe from the elements outside. PA announcements, cheers from spectators, and intermittent shots from the starter's gun seep into the bus as little more than white noise.

A football team might get fired up before charging onto the field by blasting hard thumping music and feeding off the medieval energy of their teammates, but I try to slow things down during the anxious moments before my race. Coach Rip makes this easier by declaring the bus a quiet zone. The prerace rituals I picked up in cycling are likely to appear eccentric to otherwise normal people. Fortunately, they look a lot like those of the runners around me. I stretch out across the bench seat in comfortable warm-up gear and take refuge behind my headphones. The bluesy-rock tracks of Big Head Todd and the Monsters help me slow my thoughts and conserve energy. I keep my legs loose and in constant motion, as if they'll atrophy if allowed to rest. Every few minutes I knead the sore spots, picturing fresh, oxygen-rich blood saturating my precious muscles.

The 800-meter race is one of the last on the meet's schedule. The girls race each event first, followed by the boys. I plan to leave the bus to watch the 1600-meter race, then join Smitty to warm up for the 800. My last few minutes on the bus are spent listening to a couple songs from *Nothing's Shocking* by Jane's Addiction. Time to pick things up.

The announcer calls up the runners for the 1600-meter race. I join Coach Rip on the infield near the finish line and notice Mom and Frank in the bleachers.

I cross the track and wave to them. "I didn't expect to see you guys here!"

"I didn't expect we'd spend so much time waiting to see you race."

I disregard Mom's inability to appreciate the human drama playing out in front of her and climb up to join them. "Keep your eyes on this next race," I say. "It's the first of the three distance events."

I preview what to look for over the course of the four laps. Mom observes the race on the surface of what it is: nine guys trying to complete four laps around the track faster than anyone else. Frank, on the other hand, is on the edge of his seat. He understands winning a race requires strategy and tactics and doesn't mean simply running as fast as possible from the gun. His cheers for the LGHS runners rally the other fans around us.

The crowd is on its feet for the final kick over the last two hundred meters, cheering Dirk to victory. Smitty takes fourth, and Billy sixth, both appearing to hold a little back for their priority events later in the day. Dirk's expression at the tape is more relief than joy—and I wonder who he's running for.

"Dad's not coming, is he?" I say.

"Sorry, Samuel," Mom says. "I don't think he's ready for another athlete in the family."

Before my resentment of the once and only athlete in the family sets in, Frank surprises me when I get up to leave for my warm-up.

"Go get 'em, Bags!"

Lending me the nickname for the day is like letting me borrow his lucky socks.

I trot across the track to congratulate the 1600 squad and change into my spikes. Smitty and I head to the warm-up area—nothing more than a lumpy grass field behind the bleachers. Cornbread joins us. He'll be using the 800 as a warm-up for his priority race, the 3200 meters.

We start with an easy jog through the grass. "Who are the top runners from Oak Forest and River Park?" I ask.

"I only recognized one name on the sheet," Smitty says. "Tony Vittorini."

"Is he any good?"

"Vito's solid. He runs all three distance events and made it to regionals last year in the 800. He's a senior, so he'll be looking to prove something his final year."

After fifteen minutes of jogging, we end with a set of 100-meter strides. Strides are a short and fast interval designed to fire up the engine and reinforce proper form before a race. The idea is to accelerate quickly while exaggerating your running stride over one to two hundred meters.

The announcer calls up the 800-meter runners as soon as we finish—just like I visualized this morning.

The starter sorts us into our lanes and runs through a few instructions. As the guy with no racing history, I get the outermost position in lane eight. Smitty and Vito take the more preferable third and fourth lanes. Lane eight is the least desirable starting position because you have to cover the most ground to get to the inside lanes, and the staggered start format of the 800 meters offers me no one to serve as a rabbit to chase at the beginning of the race, since the start line for the outside lane is ahead of all the others.

We shake loose the last few butterflies in the start area, and Vito asks, "Who's the new guy, Smitty?"

"Sam Bags," Smitty says. "I can't pronounce his real last name. He's got one of those funny Dago ones like you." Vito has the short and wide build of a fullback, which makes him look uncomfortable in the narrow cut of his singlet.

I offer Vito a handshake. "Hi, Sam Bagliarello."

Vito ignores my hand, making me feel like a schmuck when I pull it back. He sizes me up with the squinty look of a small person with a big ego, unsure if I'm filling a charity slot or a serious competitor. If he asks, I don't know how I'd answer.

"You a transfer or something?"

"No. I just got a late start."

"Well, make sure you stay in your lane, if you know what I mean. I don't want some JV go-getter getting in my way."

Vito turns away, and Smitty whispers in my ear, "Don't worry about him. He's just messing with you."

"Is everyone like that?"

"No, most guys just elbow your ribs in the turns."

"Great." I wonder if Smitty might be starting to like me. "Hope to see you at the finish."

The starter waves us up to the line. Once we get into position, he calls out, "On your mark!"

I lower my body, lean forward, and wait a long second for the gun.

The staggered start gives me room to run my own race, although Smitty and Vito waste no time passing me from their positions in the middle lanes. The 800 meters requires you to stay in your lane until after the first turn, so as soon as I exit the bend, I angle my body toward the inside lanes. Smitty wasn't kidding about the sharp elbows. He failed to warn me, however, about the exaggerated knee kicks that find the meaty parts of my left leg as I try to merge into the pack clogging the first two lanes. I back off and remain in lane three as we head into the second turn. I find a spot in lane one after the bend and scold myself for running half the race in an outer lane and wasting so much energy fighting for position. Vito and Smitty cross the line, and the bell signals the second and final lap. I cross a few seconds later, trailing Cornbread and two runners from River Park.

I need to make up lost ground during the first half of lap two to have a chance in the final stretch. I increase my pace gently to avoid wasting unnecessary energy in the acceleration and pass the outside shoulder of the fifth-place runner from River Park. When I pull level with Cornbread in lane one, my upper body is way too tense—my fists are clenched, shoulders raised tightly around my ears, and my arms weigh me down as if I'm carrying two buckets of rocks. *Loosen up, man.*

I work my way up to Smitty in lane two. He's in his own little world, running smooth and easy alongside Vito in lane one.

I move to lane three in an attempt to pull even with Smitty. Gritted teeth turn my breaths into gasps for air until I unclench my jaw, once again frustrated with an inability to follow my own simple instructions.

Vito turns his head and kicks into a higher gear when he sees me approaching Smitty's outside shoulder. Smitty matches the acceleration. We're still three hundred meters from the finish. My legs and lungs are on fire. I try to urge them on: *One more step, breathe.* They couldn't care less, and things fall apart quickly.

Smitty and Vito pull away as we enter the final turn. The lead runner from River Park passes me on the inside. The last two hundred meters are so hard. My form suffers as my body tightens up again. More bodies blow by, and even Cornbread passes me in the final meters. I turn my head when I cross the finish line and see no one behind me. Last place. My shoulders drop to my knees, crushed by the weight of disappointment and depleted muscles, and I let the cold air revive my shattered lungs.

Coach Rip and my teammates celebrate Smitty's victory. Vito took second, and the runner from River Park took third. Smitty thanks me for helping him win.

"How'd I help?"

"Your push from three hundred meters out spooked Vito into running faster than either of us would have from that far to go. He blew up before we got to the finish, and I kicked past him at the end."

"Glad it helped. I ran out of juice after six hundred meters and fell apart at the line."

"Like I said yesterday, use your first few races to teach your body you're not trying to kill it."

Coach holds "office hours" with individual runners on the bus ride home and shares his take on my race during our one-on-one. "You lost the race when you tried to cut over to lane one too early, Bags. You took geometry, right?"

I don't respond.

"Instead of cutting hard after the first turn, enjoy the lack of traffic for a little while and take the tangent instead. You know what I mean?"

I don't respond, but this time it's because I don't have an answer for him.

"Aim for the spot where the first lane begins its second turn. By doing that you'll run a straighter line, it will be shorter than cutting across eight lanes all at once, and you'll avoid the hand-to-hand combat."

"Okay, I'll give it a try."

"You also started out too slow and buried yourself catching back up to the front on the second lap. The idea of a negative split doesn't apply in the 800. It's too short a race for you to run the second lap faster than the first. The first lap is always going to be fast, so there's no chance to pace yourself. Your body will be tired during the second lap and will naturally slow down. If you want to run your fastest 800, you need to jump on the first lap a little faster than your overall pace for the race. Then in lap two, when everyone's fighting to hold on, do all you can to hold on a little longer."

"Thanks Coach. I'll keep that in mind."

I stand and turn back toward my seat. "Hey, Bags, one last thing," Coach Rip says. "Don't look so defeated. You were at the front with three hundred meters to go."

"Mmm-hmmh."

"If that was really your first race, you fooled everyone."

36

Dual meets are the cornerstone of the midweek track and field calendar. They avoid long-distance travel on school nights by matching two teams from the same conference and are kept simple and short by hosting the girls at one school and the boys at the other. Although duals attract fewer spectators than a Saturday invitational involving multiple teams from a large geographic area, they play an important role in developing younger track and field athletes because more athletes can compete in a two-team matchup and get a chance to experience multiple events.

Our second meet is a dual at home against Otis Rush High. A gangly sophomore named Peter Papatonis, aka "Pops," joins Smitty, Cornbread, and me for the 800 meters. Pops has a gift of raw speed, which Coach Rip is trying to wrangle into a coordinated racing form.

Rush is one of the stronger teams in our conference. One of their junior 800-meter runners made it to regionals last year, and a senior 3200-meter runner made it to state. They also have a solid squad of young milers—all sophomores and juniors—one of whom made it to state last year.

"We got smoked by two sophomores," Smitty reports when he joins our warm-up following the 1600-meter race.

"Ouch," Cornbread says. "How did the team points shake out?"

"Rush took first and second. Dirk came in third. I got fourth, but who cares? Only the top three places earn points in a dual."

"What happened to Dirk?" I ask.

"The Invitational against Coop is messing with him. Instead of taking it easy yesterday, he snuck in an interval session after practice. I think he's tired, and I didn't get the feeling his head was in it today."

The announcer's first call for the 800 meters cuts our conversation short. I get lane eight again, which is fine given it's the lane I visualized earlier today. My presence at the start line goes unnoticed, in contrast to our last meet. Word must have gotten around there's no reason to fear me.

I go out hard from the gun and maintain my staggered-start advantage through the first turn. My eyes lock in on the far end of the straightaway, and I tack smoothly toward the spot where the second turn begins, taking as flat an angle as possible. Four runners hug the inside of the track across lanes one and two. I stay in lane three until midway through the turn then uneventfully slot myself into lane one when a gap opens. Everything's going to plan.

I cross the line of the first lap two strides behind Smitty and the junior from Rush. A fourth runner hovers behind my outside shoulder, but I don't have the energy to turn and see who it is. My breaths are too shallow to push the pace, and I start to lose the feeling in my legs as the first turn approaches. Staying loose to avoid sliding backward is a constant battle with the individual muscles running from my fingers to my jaw. Halfway through the back stretch I move into lane two. The runner on my outside shoulder follows, taking lane three, and from the corner of my eye I see it's Pops. I jump with two hundred meters to go in an attempt to catch up to Smitty and the kid from Rush before they put down their final kicks. My legs are merely along for the ride at this point, so I pump my arms, imagining blood and power flooding my lower limbs. *One more step. One more. Another. Another.*

I catch up to Smitty when we exit the last turn—the kid from Rush is a stride ahead. My limbs thrash frantically as if I'm falling from a building, and Smitty hasn't broken a sweat. Smitty initiates his kick and blows past the junior from Rush, who reacts but can't match his acceleration. I'm unable to hang with the Rush runner.

Another runner from Rush pimps me at the line, and I take fourth. Pops finishes right behind me in fifth. Smitty's time is nearly the same as Saturday's race. Although I once again faded at the end, my time improved by five seconds thanks to better tactics, less wasted energy, and a body beginning to understand I'm not trying to kill it.

We have two more meets over the next week. I continue to make mistakes, learn, and build my "race wheels"—the power, fluidity, and mental focus I can unleash at an intensity so fragile it can only be called upon during those few minutes each week when competing.

37

For one day each March, track is a big deal in Linden Grove. Dirk's four-year rivalry with Cooper Assel has created plenty of hype around this year's Invitational, but no individual competition can outshine the spectacle the event has become since it started in 1971. The meet's official name is the Shamrock and Roll Invitational because it falls on the Saturday closest to Saint Patrick's Day. This rallies a loyal following from the heavy Irish Catholic population of Linden Grove. The two Catholic high schools invited to the race, from the proudly Irish American South Side of Chicago, add to the enthusiasm.

A more civilized noon start time and the sale of green beer at the concession stand amplify the festival atmosphere. While a mousy minority of voices object each year to the sale of beer at a high school function, prudence is no match for the school's finances and the cultural norms of a city known worldwide for dyeing its eponymous river green every March 17.

Coach Rip helps his young athletes avoid the distractions surrounding the Invitational by hosting a team feed the night before the meet. Asking about menu options never crosses my mind. In the days leading up to the dinner, my teammates can't stop talking about the Irish comfort food Mrs. Ipswitch serves every year: Irish stew, corned beef and cabbage, Irish soda bread, and something I've never heard of called a Dublin coddle—layers of stewed sausage, bacon, potato, onion, and spinach topped with gravy.

All that would send me back to the ICU, but I keep my thoughts to myself. Knocking tradition would only add to the ridicule when I pull out my Tupperware dinner: a can of black bean chili, rice, and lettuce topped with guacamole, cilantro, and a dollop of hot salsa.

The questions follow the sneers as soon as I sit down. "Rice has carbs? How does one bowl fill you up? What's an avocado? Don't the beans give you gas?" And, of course, "Where do you get your protein?"

Mrs. Ipswitch's perspective reminds me of something Mom would say. "If you ask me, you runners all need a little more meat on your bones. Good luck getting fat on a bowl of vegetables."

After dinner I pass through the kitchen and find Dirk pecking away at a second helping of corned beef.

"Ready for tomorrow?" I ask.

"What's that supposed to mean?"

"Uh, it means are you ready for tomorrow? You know, the meet and all."

"Yeah, I'm ready. Ready for people to stop doubting me."

"Ah, got it," I say. "It wasn't a loaded question. I know you've been working your ass off. I was wondering if you're ready to beat Coop."

"I've been ready to beat Cooper Assel for four years now."

Even small talk with Wanker-man requires endurance, so I ditch the pep talk. "Hey, can I ask you a question?"

"Sure, happy to help the new guy." Dirk straightens his spine. This causes his chest to thrust forward like a rooster about to crow.

"Right. . . Well, how do you manage your nerves before a big meet?"

"I cut out all the bullshit thoughts that could slow me down and focus on winning."

"Yeah, but this isn't basketball where half the teams playing win. Ninety percent of the runners who line up are going to lose. How do you stay optimistic week after week?"

"I wouldn't get out of bed if I thought I'd lose."

"I've lost every race I've run, but I keep improving," I say. "Getting closer to the podium every race is what gets me out of bed. Does that count for anything?"

"That's a healthy attitude when you're learning the sport. At this point, I'm too close to the top of my game to be playing for self-improvement."

"Who are you trying to impress?"

"I'm the son of two collegiate All-Americans. That comes with big expectations to live up to."

"Were your parents runners?" I'm intrigued by the idea of growing up knowing you have exceptional genes.

"My dad ran cross-country. Mom was a swimmer."

"Did they compete after college?"

"No, they got married when they graduated from Michigan and started the construction company."

Anker Construction is a household name among Linden Grove students. It's a major booster of the school's athletic program and sponsors various student clubs and events.

"Well, good luck tomorrow," I say. "I'll be rooting for you. If I can do anything to help, let me know."

"Thanks, but at this point I think I know how to prepare for a race, mate." If Dirk wasn't such a dick, I'd almost feel sorry for him. There's something tragic about having loads of talent and ambition, only to be laughed at by the people he's trying so hard to impress.

Dirk and I aren't all that different. No one's going to wake up one day and start admiring Dirk because he won state, just like people aren't going to accept me because I show up to a party with the cool kids. People will have accepted or rejected us well before then. We've both made the mistake of chasing other people's goals, and I hope my pursuit of something that's all my own is where our similarities end.

"What a beautiful day to crush it!" Frank raises the blinds on our bedroom window with a game-day energy he struggles to manage every morning.

I adjust my eyes to the cloudy light filtering in. "What's it like out there?"

"About thirty degrees with flurries, and it's expected to snow later."

Like the native Alaskan languages with forty-seven words for snow, a flurry is one of the many flavors of precipitation known to Chicagoans. Flurries are the gnats of the Chicago winter—visible, annoying, yet not really threatening.

Frank drives me to the track. The temperature nudges thirty-two degrees, and the flurries stop.

"Maybe the snow will miss us!" Frank says.

I pretend I didn't hear Frank's reckless optimism.

The visitors' buses idle in their reserved spots outside the stadium. Running engines power the heat that keeps skinny athletes warm in their mobile locker rooms. The only noticeable activity inside the gates to the track are the volunteers setting up the announcer booth, officials' table, concession stand, and beer trailer.

The parking lot fills with fans. The cars from Mayflower Academy are easy to spot because they're new, large, and have bumper stickers proclaiming *We're better than you.*

Sprinters shuffle to the warm-up area before the noon start. The darkening sky triggers the sensors on the stadium lights. The frost on the oval glistens in the artificial sunlight as if Mother Nature is laughing at us humans for declaring tomorrow the first day of spring. By eleven forty-five, our school's marching band attempts to warm the place up with a mix of fight songs and Irish folk tunes.

Five minutes before the first race of the day, the skies open and unleash a gush of icy rain. Fans scramble to cars, and the sprinters hustle back to their buses.

The announcer mercifully pushes the start back fifteen minutes.

My teammates and I look out of the bus for a break in the clouds. Dirk paces the center aisle, and Mother Nature shows her dark sense of humor once more by flogging the windows with a gust of wind whenever he peers outside. Dirk grimaces in agony each time, like a kid about to get a tooth pulled.

The rain complies with the delayed start by dying down a minute before twelve fifteen. The announcer recalls the 3200-meter relay runners, and the fans return, now dressed in a rainbow of colorful winter gear.

As a Shamrock and Roll newbie, I want to soak up the stadium's festive energy. It's also clear that Dirk needs to get moving before he self-destructs.

"Dirk, Smitty, what do you say we head out for an early warm-up?" I say.

They don't seem too eager, though when I catch Smitty's eye he falls in line and persuades Dirk to join us.

"Don't you have anything to wear besides shorts?" I ask Dirk. I'm fully layered up and as waterproofed as possible, while Dirk's legs are covered in nothing more than goose bumps. When he blames his mom for forgetting to pack his thermal gear, I toss him an extra pair of padded cycling tights and a hat.

The other three 1600-meter teams opt for an early warm-up too, and Dirk isn't alone in failing to prepare for the weather. Not one of the other 1600-meter runners wears leggings, a hat, or gloves. They look miserable and on the verge of hypothermia.

"Glad I've got all this winter cycling gear!"

Smitty and Dirk ignore my gloat three weeks after ridiculing me on our first day of practice.

The dire expressions of the other runners energize me. This is my kind of adversity. I've been training for this sort of weather since I was a kid delivering newspapers on subzero winter mornings—any snowfall a welcome distraction from the cold darkness. I left my paper route for a job on a golf course, carrying bags through all conditions during the spring, summer, and fall—even if it meant walking hours in waterlogged gym shoes. Until I crashed my bike, it served as my year-round mode of transportation, and while my competition spent the past winter training on dry indoor tracks, I suffered through the depths of a Chicago winter running outdoors on icy roads in repurposed cycling gear.

A gusty crosswind interrupts my thoughts by knocking me a step sideways. A moment later I notice Dirk on the ground. He's clutching his left calf, and his wail suggests bad things.

I bolt to get Coach Rip. By the time we return, Dirk's hopping alongside Smitty on their way back to the bus.

"This doesn't look good," Coach Rip says.

"I think I tore my calf, Coach."

"How the hell did you injure yourself during a warm-up?"

"These guys convinced me to come out early in the cold. I knew I should have stayed on the bus." Smitty and I glance at each other, while Coach Rip ignores the comment and points at me.

"Bags! You're running the 1600 today."

Coach senses my internal processing of the situation and cuts me off before I outthink myself. "You've been asking for the opportunity, here it is. I'd suggest you take it before I go back to the bus and ask for volunteers."

I swallow the lump in my throat and respond, "Okay, Coach. I can do it."

We change into our racing spikes back at the bus, and the sky opens again. This time, the precipitation comes in the form of snowflakes the size of a leprechaun's gold coins. The announcer sees no reason to delay the start a second time, and I blame Frank for jinxing the weather.

Smitty and I join the other 1600-meter runners behind the bleachers for our final warm-ups. Coach Rip calls me to the side of the track.

"Bags, don't let this snow distract you."

"Uh-huh."

"You know, twenty-five years since my last race, I don't remember the sunny, warm days. I do, however, remember all the miserable ones in vivid detail. Those are the days me and my buddies still talk about. The runs when the wind howled, the rain pissed down sideways, and my waterlogged sneakers pickled my feet. Catch my drift?"

I smile, recalling the fun of riding my bike through the snow as a kid.

"There's no doubt today will be *memorable* for everyone here. I want *you* to make it *unforgettable*."

We shake hands, and he calls Smitty over. I turn back to the track and see Summer walking my way.

"Warming up early, Young Bags?"

She cracks a smile after I explain.

"Be careful what you wish for, right?"

"I wish I had more time to prepare."

"Sam, you are sooo ready for this. You've been working toward these four minutes for months. Don't overthink it. Just let your body run."

She tops off her words with a bear hug that warms me all over.

I pass friendly faces on my way to the start line. Frank and Mom are standing with Summer. Jed, Sara, and Ashley are hanging out with a group of classmates. Right before I enter the starting area, Marty surprises me with his standard "Hey, Sam Bags!"

I turn and wave.

"Run like a Wookiee!"

The announcer introduces the eight runners by name. Shared religion, genealogy, and class means the fans of LGHS, Mother Mary High, and Father Hagan Academy cheer every runner that isn't from Mayflower. Despite the friendly crowd, however, my substitution for Dirk turns the cheers into a groan bordering on a boo.

I get Dirk's placement in lane four, next to Coop in lane three. A runner from Mother Mary stands to my right in lane five. Smitty has lane two. Unlike the 800 meters, the 1600- and 3200-meter events don't utilize a staggered start. The start line in these longer races is a single white stripe with a gentle arc, providing a slight compensation to the runners in the outer lanes. As a result, there's no requirement to stay in your lane until after the first turn.

The snow continues to fall, leaving the track a mess. It's not cold enough for any accumulation, so the flakes liquify when they hit the ground. Imperfections in the surface create little pools of water that will be impossible to avoid during the race. A peek left and right glimpses seven bodies that would prefer to be anywhere else. I breathe in one last dose of inspiration with a glance to the south. The far end of the oval is covered in snow and low clouds, but somewhere beyond is the origin of my seven-month journey to this spot. The leaves are gone, and snow has replaced the rain, but Spirit Hill and the tree that nearly ended my life are still there.

"On your mark!"

Bang.

Coop jumps to the front, his upper body motionless save for two pumping arms. He cuts to the second lane, smooth and efficient. So different from the hurly-burly I typically encounter when choosing a lane.

I take the diagonal that places me in lane two at the start of the first turn without wasting a meter of track. The field plays things cautiously given the conditions and Coop's presence. Coop maintains a slight lead, with all seven chasers packed tightly behind him. Leading from the front is a dubious strategy, fully exposed to the wind and an attack from behind, but Coop suffers from being feared by everyone else. A race with one marked man simplifies tactics: stay close to Coop. His predicament has its advantages—Coop avoids the scrum behind him and sees the obstacles ahead, while the rest of us waste energy jockeying for position and splashing through the puddles littering the track. This game of Pied Piper leads to a sluggish first lap, and we cross the line with one minute twenty seconds on the clock.

The green-beer-drinking gallery crowding the outside lane of the track doesn't seem bothered by the pace. They go completely bonkers as we pass, and the roar from the second turn to the finish line is deafening. The Mayflower fans rally their hero as he faces down a threat they are certain he will overcome. Everyone else cheers for a pack of underdogs sticking it to the unbeatable three-time state champ. It dawns on me as we pass the crowd that I'm one of the underdogs they're rooting for.

Two runners from Mother Mary and Father Hagan get antsy and test Coop at the start of the second lap. Coop matches their half-committed attacks with zero drama. I take a page from criterium racing in a tight pack of cyclists and keep my eyes focused a meter past the rotating race leader, avoiding the individual brakes and surges I hope are quietly sapping energy from Coop's hyperactive challengers.

As we round the second turn of lap two, random shouts of my name escape the rumble of noise at the edge of the track. We complete the second split in a more impressive seventy-two seconds. *The race is on!*

The conditions begin to snatch their prey during lap three. The Hagan runner up front falls off the pace, and Smitty has been absent from the lead group since the start. Seeing one of the leaders struggle boosts my confidence, and I run with the same fluidity as if spinning on the tops of my bike pedals on the early stages of a climb. Coop shows no weakness, still polished and businesslike. Letting Coop control the race will never allow me to test my fitness or shitty-weather resilience, so I pick up the pace when we hit the second turn of lap three. Coop and the lead runner from Mother Mary match me with little struggle. We settle into this elevated pace until halfway through the turn. I breathe in the energy of the crowd and push the pace again. Coop and the guy from Mother Mary follow. Where's Smitty?

The sporadic calls of my name grow into a distinct chant of "Bags! Bags! Bags!" and the hairs on the back of my neck rise. The support of the crowd lifts me like a tailwind, and I have no intention of falling off the pace. No matter how this race ends, I will make today one of those sweet memories Coach Rip described, frozen forever by the ice and snow in which it was created.

We cross the line a third time. Seventy seconds, a personal best. Four hundred meters left. A minute to go. I know I can sprint for a minute up Spirit Hill. Shit, I survived death for nearly a minute. I can do this, but I also know if I don't drain Coop's more explosive kick out of him, I'll get smoked in the final straightaway.

So, I turn the dial up another notch.

We enter the first bend, cold and lonely after leaving the energy of the crowd behind us. The cumulative effort of the last thirteen hundred meters becomes impossible to ignore.

You've got this, I tell myself. *One more stride. Make it unforgettable.* The self-talk gets me to the back straightaway. The crowd becomes visible once again through the snowfall. For the first time in the race, I hear Coop breathing. Just a single inhale. Have I been huffing so hard I didn't hear him earlier? His form remains solid, but then it happens. A little thing that might be nothing. Coop puts his left foot into a puddle. The icy water won't affect his running this late in the race, but it's the first puddle he hasn't stepped over. Is this it? Is Cooper Assel vincible?

Midway through the back straightaway, I hear the rhythmic chants of the crowd—my tribe calling me home. I glance south toward Spirit Hill, and it stares back through the gray sky and falling snow. I pump my arms and, for the first time in my short track career, my legs respond. Coop does too. Have I tragically misread the situation? Months ago I would have backed off in the face of self-doubt and a fear of embarrassment. But today, at this moment, on my turf, all I want to do is drop this fucker.

Halfway through the final turn, Coop leads me by a half stride. If the three-time state champ felt good, he would have left me behind. There's only one reason he'd let an unknown like me make him fight for it.

I keep breathing and pumping and breathing and kicking. The strain on my lungs is excruciating. My legs drown in acid. These are mere sensations wanting to be noticed—uncomfortable but nothing that can hurt me. I tell my body the 800-meter races hurt more.

The crowd has lost its marbles. Arms flail, beer spills. The fans creep onto the track, leaning forward and blocking our path. The sea of bodies pulls back in a rolling wave the instant before collision with the runners passing through.

One hundred meters to go. The runner from Mother Mary is a stride behind on my outside shoulder. I continue to dig, searching for something, anything that will put me a hair in front of Coop. In reality I work harder to run more slowly, torching all I have left to keep from getting dropped. Where is Smitty? Is he hanging back, waiting to pounce? Panic fuels me. When will Coop and the runner from Mother Mary blow me away? I keep pushing, pushing, pushing, running for my life. Then, paranoid I'm about to be passed, I lean forward ever so slightly and snap the tape.

The engines shut down, and my legs take another ten meters to slow to a stop. I roll onto my back and stretch my arms out wide, sucking in air as I sink into the cold, wet surface of the track. A crowd circles around—a dozen faces screaming at me. Warm breath, spit, beer, and snot pepper my face. I can't open my eyes wide enough to recognize anyone but hear Coach Rip clear the scene. He pulls me up and supports me with his shoulder. I regain my breath as we walk, and my face becomes one effortless smile.

Frank slams into me, grabs my shoulders, and shakes me like a rag doll. "Holy shit! You won. You won!"

Smitty slaps me on the back, knocking the wind out of me again. "I knew you had it in you, Bags. Way to go!" Smitty's selfless congratulation, after showing little confidence in me prior to today, makes my victory official.

"How'd you do?" I ask him.

"Fourth."

"Who took third?"

"A kid named Rich Duffy from Mother Mary. He's a badass. Took third in the 3200 meters at state last year."

"Glad no one told me he was racing today."

An official shuffles us off the track to allow the 400-meter dash to start on time. I walk as if my bones have softened into cartilage—half stepping, half stumbling.

Summer appears and wraps me in a second hug today.

I return the gesture with all the force I can direct to my arms. "Thanks, Summer. I love you."

She sniffles, and I can't tell if her runny nose and moist eyes are from the wind or her heart. I keep my arms wrapped tightly around her, well past the socially acceptable duration for a hug. She's so warm, and all Summer. Frank finally steps between us. "Sam, you've got to let go."

Frank and Summer lead me back to the bus where I dry off and warm up. Before I leave to race the 800 meters, Marty and his mom stop by to say hello. He gets a kick out of seeing the inside of the team bus and chuffs when I pull his Chewbacca figure out of my track bag. I thank him for sharing his good luck with me.

Marty tells me he never doubted my chances. "The Wookiee would have won in the snow, too."

38

Something's strange. The hallway feels more narrow and crowded than normal. Kids flash puzzled looks at me like on my first day back from the hospital. People I know only by name or reputation say hello. David Boardman, captain of the diving team, acknowledges me for what may be the first time with a nod. "Way to go, Bags."

Mr. O solves the mystery with a pat on the back. "Nice job, Bags! I didn't think that kid from Mayflower was beatable." This is particularly generous of Mr. O given I dropped PE two weeks ago now that I'm playing a varsity sport.

I see Dirk in study hall, an orthopedic boot wrapped around his left foot. "The doc says two weeks 'til I can run again."

"You'll be back before conference finals." I try to sound encouraging.

"Yeah, so enjoy the spotlight while you've got it." What would count as friendly shit-blowing from any other member of the team reeks of spite and envy coming from Dirk.

"I think I prefer being the underdog." This is more confession than self-deprecation. Dread kept me awake last night until I offloaded the fear of having to repeat Saturday's performance to Bad Gorilla.

"With luck like yours, what do you have to worry about?"

Dirk's not done venting, so I let him continue.

"I've raced Coop nine times over the past three years. Nine times out of nine he showed up in peak form. You come along and get him on an off day."

"He didn't feel off his game to me."

"You guys ran a nearly five-minute mile—and you had the help of shitty weather."

"We all raced in the same weather. Those of us who made it to the start, that is." My sarcasm fails to lighten his mood.

"I'd tread carefully, Bags. One race in the snow doesn't make a season. One day you'll appreciate your luck of the Irish."

"Dirk, it's going to be a long season for sure, but your theory about luck on Saturday is bullshit. For one thing, I'm not Irish."

Our next meet is at home against conference rival Major Taylor High. While I've earned a spot on the 1600-meter squad, Coach Rip wants me to keep racing the 800 meters to build my sprint power. Major Taylor has several runners who made it past conference finals last year, but according to Smitty, we have something they can't match: "FoMo."

Victory comes more easily when you're already winning, due to what Smitty calls the power of Forward Momentum. It's like a bicycle wheel in motion, a runner leaning into the tape at the finish, or the positive mental attitude of thirty young men who believe they are winners. Momentum is fluid, however, and the challenge is to ride in the slipstream separating confidence and hunger from hubris and entitlement.

FoMo is rocking as we warm up for the 1600-meter race. A sunny early spring afternoon draws an unusually large crowd for a midweek dual meet. Frank is unable to make it, offering his usual excuse of needing to study.

In the middle of our jog around the practice fields, I ask Smitty how he got into running.

"I started running in middle school and fell in love with the simplicity of racing. You know, sport-of-truth stuff. Fastest kid wins. Whenever I start worrying about the post-season or running in college, I try to remember being a kid running my ass off."

It's comforting to hear someone else admit they suffer from overcomplicating simple things. "How do you remember to run like a kid?"

"Running has become a personal act of defiance for me. Society has some messed-up stories it tells itself about minorities. Every time I stand on the podium, I defy one of those stories, and I like to think I'm inspiring some kid like me to go out and write their own."

Smitty places first in the 800 meters with a time of one minute fifty-five seconds, five seconds faster than his win against Vito in our first race of the season. I take fourth in the 800 meters after putting everything I have into the 1600-meter race, which pays off with another win.

My first win changed my life. Today's win convinces me I had something to do with it. And Smitty inspires me to find a reason to run beyond myself.

39

"Whatcha readin'?" Zoe looks like she stepped straight out of an Esprit catalog. The weighty fabric of her yellow sweater exaggerates the gentle curves underneath. A gray leather skirt hugs her subtle hips, while black tights tie it all together in a comfortably sexy style appropriate for April in Chicago.

"'The Myth of Sisyphus.'" As if it will help, I add, "It's for a Latin project."

"Huh . . ." Zoe's shrug beats rejection for reading a dead French philosopher's essay about the absurdity of life.

"What brings you to the library?" If it was possible to kick my own ass for dropping such a lame line, I would.

"Study hall. I usually ditch and grab a smoke, but I've got a paper due for AP U.S. History."

"Ahh—" I restrain myself from venting about Mr. Bracovich. "What's the paper about?"

"We need to analyze three works from a major American author. Something that ties the author's themes into events that shaped our country at the time the stories took place."

"Who'd you pick?"

"John Steinbeck."

"Steinbeck? He's one of my favorites." I say this way too enthusiastically.

"I've already read *Of Mice and Men* and *Travels with Charley*. Mr. Bracovich suggested *East of Eden*, but I don't have the time to read seven hundred pages over the next three weeks."

"What about *The Pearl*? It's an easy read and a relevant commentary on America. You know, greed, evil, inequality, and the illusion of happiness."

"Sounds depressing." Zoe drops into the chair next to mine. A reading lamp sits on the small table between us. She leans on her inside elbow to face me, crossing the toned legs that travel for miles before disappearing into her skirt.

"You could say the same about *Of Mice and Men*, and it's not like the theme at the end of *Travels with Charley* is full of optimism."

"When did you read John Steinbeck?" she asks.

"Sophomore year English. We had a similar assignment. One author each semester. I chose Steinbeck and Thoreau."

"The anarchist tree hugger?"

"I described him as a fan of responsible individualism."

"He lived alone in the woods and gave up all his possessions."

"He was making a case for simplicity and self-reliance."

We continue like this for the rest of the period. The bell snaps me back to reality, and I wonder how I spent the past half hour discussing books with the girl I've never managed to utter a full sentence to in nearly four years.

"Wow, I lost track of time," Zoe says. "Is this where I can find you during study hall?"

"I'm usually right here, four periods every day."

40

The phone rings as I enter the kitchen after a two-hour bus ride and disappointing day on the track.

"Suit yourself, but you're going to miss an epic bash," Ashley says.

Coach Rip tried to reassure me that sixth in the 1600 meters was my body telling me it needs a break.

"Sorry, Ash, I'm beat and need to lay low tonight." It's hard to hear with her hair dryer blowing in the background. "You wanna stop by before you head out?"

"Hang with your mom on a Saturday night?" She's shouting loud enough it's no longer a conversation. "Barf me out. Let me know when you've figured out your priorities."

I tell her again my priority tonight is to chill out. She either can't hear me over all the hot air or isn't listening, because she hangs up without saying goodbye.

Mom comes home with dinner from a local Italian restaurant. It's the rare Saturday night she's not out doing God knows what with her friends. Although I miss Ashley, no *epic bash* can beat nerding out with Mom tonight over pasta primavera and *Saturday Night Live*.

Mom's magic spell wears off by morning, when I find her pacing at the front window, asking if I know why Frank never came home last night. She keeps poking her head through the drapes, willing him to return.

When the Guinness pulls to the curb, Mom stares Frank down with her darkest Sicilian glare, punctuated by a quivering lower jaw and hands on her hips. She rebuffs Frank's gregarious "Happy Sunday, Ant'nette!" with a harsher than usual "Go around the back!" then slams the door hard enough the outside knocker strikes a beat after she turns back toward the kitchen.

Frank cools Mom's anger with an apology for staying out all night without a phone call. He then tells us Summer's moving. Her dad sold the Runner's Sole to one of the large sporting-goods chains. A forty-something fat guy in a branded golf shirt takes over next week and will start selling a full selection of sporting goods ranging from footballs and basketballs to hunting gear.

Summer's shocked and disgusted her dad gave up without a fight and screwed over the shop's employees, customers, and Summer herself. She's decided to return to Boston for a graduate assistant position, which will allow her to coach while restarting her master's degree. Over the course of their all-nighter, Frank failed to persuade Summer to reconsider, and they decided to break up. Their independent lives don't need the burden of a thousand miles separating a young relationship. Or at least Summer's doesn't.

Mom's frustration turns to sympathy, and she listens to Frank without her usual judgment. When Mom pats Frank's hand and says, "There, there," I feel left out, alone at the kiddie table. I want to shout, "What about me?" but instead sneak off to my bedroom to process the hurt with Bad Gorilla.

Don't these guys recognize Summer has become a big part of my life, too? It's always about Frank. He sweats drama and conflict wherever he goes.

"When you're not a problem, you get to watch the people who can't do anything for themselves burn up all the oxygen in the room," Bad Gorilla says.

Frank's been hogging the oxygen his whole life. Even when he went away to college, I remained the invisible younger brother because

Frank failed so remarkably he dragged my parents down with him.

FoMo is fragile, and by Monday the momentum in my life has shifted to a headwind.

"Sorry to hear the news about our mutual friend," Charles O'Toole says. He looks like he's been waiting for me at the entrance to the cafeteria.

"Who are you talking about?" I'll have to rethink the laws of nature if he's referring to Summer as a mutual friend.

"Ashley," he says.

"What happened to Ashley?"

His eyes flare faintly. "You don't know, do you?"

My confusion answers his question.

"She hooked up with Hooch this weekend at Beth's party." He pats me on the shoulder and cracks a *now-we're-even* smile. Before disappearing through the double doors, he adds, "I heard he fucked her."

The only place I can think to hide from the shitstorm Charles unleashes in my head is the library. I find Jed asleep at a table. Instead of giving him a hard time for using his physics book as a pillow, I want to thank him for the first predictable event in my life since Friday.

"What's the special occasion?" he says after I shake him awake.

"What do you mean?"

"I haven't seen you in weeks. Ever since you became a track star, you've started hanging with the cool kids and studying with the hot girls."

"Lighten up, you have no idea what you're talking about."

I fill him in on what Charles told me about Ashley.

"You didn't know?"

"Didn't know? This happened two days ago at a party I wasn't at. How would I know?"

"I figured you guys broke up. I didn't realize she cheated on you."

"I don't get why she insisted we wait to have sex. Maybe she thinks I'm boring."

"Says the guy who's been living like a monk since Christmas," Jed says. "I'm sure she was bored, but I doubt it was sex that drove her away. You know she wants to expand her horizons before we head off to college."

"Well, if Dan Hooch and his tobacco-chewing muscle-head friends are what she considers expansive, she's not the same girl I fell for."

"Maybe this setback will help you be more sensitive to the needs of the women in your life."

"Oh, yeah? How's sensitivity working for you?"

"You know that idea I had to book a boat cruise on Lake Michigan for prom night?"

"Yeah," I whimper. "Ashley and I were looking forward to it."

"Whatever, man. Word got around, and I now have about a hundred people interested. This morning I booked a luxury yacht with a dance room, pool, diving board, and hot tub. This is going to be my own personal ChicagoFest, and I won't even need to trash my parents' house."

"Have you found anyone looking for a date?" I ask.

"That's the part I haven't worked out yet."

41

Summer leaving and Ashley cheating are tough problems to force onto an imaginary primate, and Bad Gorilla pushes back a fair amount of the anger, rejection, and jealousy I've been sending his way. Finding Frank lying in bed listening to "She's Got a Way" by Billy Joel only deepens my gloom.

"Clocked off early tonight, huh?" I say.

"Yeah. Tough week to motivate."

"Tell me about it."

"Thanks, man, but don't worry about me. I'll get over it." Frank plays for pity like a pimply middle-schooler who lost his sweetheart.

"Who's worried *you'll* get over it?" I say. "You're a pro at moving on."

"Come again?"

"I'm just saying . . . Summer left me too, but no one seems to care how I feel about it."

"Is that right?"

"Summer left when I needed her most, and as usual, you get all the sympathy for a problem you created."

"Hey, don't forget who got you into running. And what do you mean by *as usual*?"

"No offense, Frank. You got me into running, but Summer helped me become a runner."

"No offense? Now you're a runner? You've been running less than a year, pal. Get over yourself!"

"Get over myself? Who disappeared when they started taking

classes again?"

"I thought you'd be impressed. I'm enjoying school for the first time in my life."

"It's a good thing, given how much time you spend studying for two classes at a community college."

"Listen, you pretentious twerp, not everyone can get straight As in their sleep. Last I heard, it's going to take you five years to graduate high school. Be careful who you shit on."

"I missed half a semester, you know." Frank knows good grades don't come naturally to me. He also knows how to push my buttons.

"If you want sympathy, stop being so self-righteous." Frank gets up from his bed and heads for the door. This is where our arguments normally end: Frank walks out, and I'm relieved the confrontation has passed.

I'm done accepting normal.

"How am I being self-righteous?" I say.

He stops and turns. "You walk into my room, act like a martyr, then insult me."

"*Your* room? That's classic." I step toward him, and years of anger boils in my bones. "You know, all you've ever been All-American at is taking what you want and leaving a mess behind."

"I now see why you don't get invited to many parties," Frank says. "And I have no idea what you're talking about."

"You piss away everything that matters. When's the last time one of your high school buddies called? College, your football scholarship, our relationship with Dad." I point a finger at Frank to emphasize my point. "You let him down so hard it tore our family apart. Now Mom doesn't even come home anymore. And did Summer move across the country to show how important your relationship is to her?"

Frank shoves me, and I stumble backward. His stereo breaks my fall, and I find myself staring into the facemask of his helmet. I rip it off the turntable and take a swing.

He dodges my lunge. "PUT THAT DOWN!" he yells.

I'm not trying to hurt Frank. I'm just channeling years of sibling resentment through the golden relic of his past glory clenched between my fingers. So, when Frank commands me to return the helmet to his stereo, I give him what he wants with the weight of all the little brother shit I've shoveled into Bad Gorilla's cage since I was a kid.

"I'm sick of your bullshit!" *Slam.*

"Sick of news radio!" *Smash.*

"All your crappy music!" *Crack.*

"I'm done losing another relationship because of you!" *Crash.*

"I want them back. I WANT THEM BACK!" *Whack. Whack. Whack.*

His stereo is in pieces, the helmet's fine, my arm is spent, and Frank stands in the doorway staring. He walks over and gently pries the helmet from my fingers before leaving our room and closing the door behind him. It's the first argument in our lives he allows to end without the last word.

The screen door slams, and I hear the Guinness peel away from the curb.

42

"I guess you already know," Ashley says.

I'm not interested in including Mom in this conversation, so I pull the telephone cord as far as it will stretch from the kitchen into the hallway leading to my room. No matter. Mom's preoccupied with the latest cigarette she claims is helping calm her nerves two days after Frank disappeared.

"I might have been the last person to find out, but Charles made sure to let me know you cheated on me." After Jed confirmed the news, I wanted to track down Ashley so she could tell me it wasn't true. When I passed Hooch gloating in the hallway, all I wanted was to find a way to show her she made a mistake taking me for granted.

"Who cheated on who? You've blown me off for the last three parties I invited you to."

"That's not cheating, Ashley."

"Maybe I was looking to have some fun and got caught up in the moment. You know, we're only going to be seniors once in our lives."

"Speak for yourself. I get to do it twice."

"Oh yeah. Sorry, Bags."

The team bus rambles along after a non-conference invitational at George Halas High. Saying I raced the 800 and 1600 meters is an exaggeration. I ran both but placed poorly and recorded my slowest times yet in each event.

"What's going on up here?" Coach Rip taps his index finger

against the side of his head. "Is it a girl? Problems on the home front?"

The understanding stare from a serious man deserves a straight answer. "It's three girls, one brother, a friend and, I guess you could say, a fucked-up home front."

"That bad, huh?"

"Uh-huh."

"Hmm . . ." Coach Rip rubs his jawline as if caressing some nonexistent beard. "Do the three—you said three, right?" I nod. "Do the three girls, friend, and your family know how you feel?"

"Not exactly—" I lower my head and speak to my shoes as they scrape the floor of the bus. "No."

"Okay, well, here's the deal, Bags. Remember our conversation before you raced the 1600 at the Invitational?"

"I do, but I've lost whatever I had that day."

"You haven't lost a thing," Coach Rip says. "It's what you've gained that's your problem. You knew nothing about running a year ago. Since then, you've learned how to train, what it takes to win, and the feeling of being a winner. Think about what led you to win that first race—you beat Cooper Assel and Rich Duffy, for chrissakes! You had a fearlessness you could do anything. Since then you've learned the fear of losing can be stronger than the hunger of never having won. Any idea how you can get that rookie spirit back?"

"I've been thinking a lot about momentum, Coach." His look suggests I keep this short. "When everything was going well, the relationships in my life were moving in the right direction. Unfortunately, I've lost the forward momentum in my personal life and that's knocked everything off balance."

"Makes sense to me. And if you don't mind me saying, having the tough conversations with the important people in your life is best for everyone, especially the demons in your head."

"Mine's a gorilla."

"Huh?"

"The demon in my head. It's actually a gorilla. But never mind, it's sort of an inside joke."

"I'm sure it is." Coach chuckles.

43

Zoe strides over like a Botticelli in Keds. I'm halfway through my third study hall of the day, lost in Edward Abbey's wildfire of modern civilization, the environment, and government policy. I bookmark *Desert Solitaire*, shake the stale air out of my shirt, and pull two handfuls of hair behind my ears.

"Hey, Bags. What brings you back from the woods?"

"Thoreau never mentioned the poison ivy." The fact she remembers our last conversation is a good sign, though Ashley paid attention at the beginning, too. "Where've *you* been hiding?"

"Distracted by bad habits, I'm afraid." She takes a two-finger drag on an invisible cigarette. "Thanks again for the advice on my assignment."

"How's it coming?"

"I finished *The Pearl*. Working on my outline now."

"Good luck." My mind races to remember my script. "Hey, Zoe, can you help me find a book?"

"What are you looking for?"

"*Walden* by Henry David Thoreau."

"Ugh—you're pimping me, right?" she says.

"No, I want to get your thoughts on a passage."

"Fine. You got a Dewey Decimal number or something?"

"It's supposed to be in section 818."

We walk to the Literature racks, and Zoe turns down the 810–820 aisle. When we hit the Middle Nineteenth-Century American Authors section, Zoe runs her fingers along the top of each book.

"Emerson . . . Poe . . . Thoreau!" she says. "And here's *Walden.*"

"Open it to page four thirty-six."

Zoe fans through the pages, and a small envelope falls to the ground. *Read Me* is handwritten on the outside.

"Oooh . . . mysterious!" she says.

"Open it!"

"I'm kind of afraid to."

"Okay, I'll open it, but you read what's inside."

She agrees and hands the envelope to me. I work the seal open and look over her shoulder as she reads:

Want to go to prom with me?
—Sam Bags

She must be reading it more than once because it takes her several seconds to look up. "I've never been hit on in the library."

"I didn't want to interrupt you in the bathroom."

"You know, you're sorta weird . . . but, okay, why not?"

It's not exactly a *yes*, but it gets me what I want. I can't wait to tell Jed—and let Ashley find out—I'll be going to prom with the hottest girl in school.

44

Dirk returns for our meet against Bethlehem Catholic with a fully recovered opinion of himself. "I've been running for two weeks now," he boasts. "I'm right where I want to be, especially against these coal miners from Bethlehem." Four weeks off due to injury deserves humility, but Dirk is Dirk, and Bethlehem isn't known for track and field, as evidenced by having one of the last cinder tracks in the state.

I'm running much better since my one-on-one with Coach Rip and asking Zoe to prom. Finishing in the top three today will be a big boost to my confidence before conference finals in three weeks. Looking out at the charcoal-colored oval from our team bus, however, I shiver. Runners return from earlier races resembling chimney sweeps—their shoes, white singlets, and faces caked in the black soot kicked up from the track's cinders.

The Bethlehem runners wear long, needle-tipped spikes designed to bore into the dusty, loose surface. Dirk is the only member of our 1600-meter squad equipped with similar weaponry. Smitty, Pops, and I will try not to get swallowed by the rubble in our shorter pyramid-shaped spikes.

The race starts hot, as a Bethlehem runner jumps ahead before we hit the first turn. While he chews up the track in front of us, I adjust my stride to run on what sound like Fruity Pebbles crunching under my feet. Debris flies in all directions, and every few steps a chunky cinder stabs through the bottom of one of my shoes.

Smitty and I settle into a steady pace, drafting behind the Bethlehem runner and waiting for an opportunity to attack. Dirk moves toward the inside lanes after the first turn. The right spot for Dirk to insert himself is behind us, but trailing Smitty and me is not part of Dirk's playbook. I greet his attempt to squeeze into the tight space between me and the Bethlehem runner with a flick of my outside elbow, blunt enough to send him back to lane three. After a second attempt and rebuff, he takes his place behind us. In the meantime, the Bethlehem runner leads us through the first lap.

Track may appear to be an individual sport, but a coordinated team can inflict plenty of pain on a rival over the few minutes it takes to complete a middle-distance event. The Bethlehem runner is in a bind. Separated from his teammates, he can't simply pull off the front and slip behind us to recover before the final stretch. Any change in his pace will be matched by us in an effort to keep him isolated up front. Smitty and I are happy to remain patient and let him lead us to the final stretch. We can then fan out across the track and sprint to the finish. May the best runner win.

Dirk, however, is more concerned about his position behind Smitty and me than the greater goal of making sure our team takes all the points for the top three places. When we hit the first turn of the second lap, Dirk accelerates past my outside shoulder with no intention of being denied the spot ahead of me a third time. He pulls level with the Bethlehem runner by the middle of the turn, then cuts hard to the inside, essentially falling into my lap. Unlike his earlier lateral attacks, I can't deflect his frontal assault. When he squeezes ahead of me, he plants the hypodermic spikes of his left foot on the laces of my right. My body goes horizontal like tripping over a curb at fourteen miles an hour, and I fly toward the outside lane before the track surface swallows me in a cloud of crushed rock and iron shavings.

I peel my body out of the crud while assessing the damage along the way. Chin? Skinned and bloody. Hands? Palms scraped raw. Shoulders and legs? Dripping with blood. I stand, relieved to have avoided disaster, when a flash of pain shoots through the arch of my right foot, dropping me back to the ground. The only way to get out of the path of the race is to crab-walk past the edge of the track and lie in the grass, shielding my eyes from the sun as I wait for Coach Rip to rescue me.

A familiar shape steps between me and the sun's glare. I recognize the dark outline of the head against the brightness behind. "Frank . . . thanks for coming. I've really messed things up, eh?"

"It's not Frank, Sam. It's Dad."

"Dad? What are you doing here?"

"I've been here all along," he says. He kneels down, helps me sit up, then begins to wipe the blood and grit from my skin with a handkerchief.

"What are you talking about?" The crash must have knocked me unconscious. Coach Rip should wake me at any moment.

"Sam, I've been to all your races. I was at your first meet at Oak Forest, stood in the snow when you got your first win, and I've watched the good and bad since."

"I can't believe it!" I haven't seen him since Frank and I celebrated Christmas Eve at his apartment. "I mean, why didn't you let me know?"

"Good question. I guess I wasn't sure you were ready for me to get involved again in your life."

"Seriously? I've been ready for four years!"

Coach Rip and Smitty join us. Smitty tells me he won, Dirk took second, and Pops took third.

"Just like we planned, right?" I say.

"Except for the part where you go dirt surfing," Smitty says.

"Track didn't feel like the sport of truth today," I say.

"How about it?" Smitty says. "I told Coach about the Wanker's move."

"Alright, men, we'll cover that later. Bags, you look awful. Are you able to stand?"

Dad helps me up and holds me steady. He offers to take me home, and I hobble alongside him toward the parking lot. He opens the passenger door to a silver Honda Civic. The fresh scent of glue and plastic hits me when I settle into the bucket seat.

"What's this—a new car?" I ask.

"Yeah, I bought it this winter. The front-wheel drive gets great traction in the snow. High gas mileage, no maintenance issues. Best car I've ever owned."

"We're still driving that piece of shit Skylark."

"Buick makes a good car."

"Whatever, Dad."

He responds with a soft laugh, and I smile back at him.

"Let's get you home," he says. "We need to clean you up and ice that foot."

"My foot . . ." I reach down and rub the sore spot. "Just what I need!"

"Mom filled me in. Sorry about your girlfriend."

"Argh, Ashley. I was actually thinking about school, college, my losing streak on the track—and Frank."

"Mom told me about that, too. I'm worried no one has heard from him."

"Everybody's always worried about Frank," I say. "How many second chances does one guy get?"

Dad's face suggests he has a response, but he keeps it to himself.

A minute passes, and I say, "You know, Frank isn't the only one who's had a rough four years."

"I know, and I'm sorry you've suffered for my problems."

I blame my family for a lot. I resent Mom and Frank for always looking for a fight and Dad for running away.

"I'm ready to start over, Sam," Dad says. "Will you give some thought to how we can do that together?"

I haven't given any thought to how I want Dad to reenter my life. All I know is it's time we stop taking each other for granted. The years since he left are gone for good, so starting over means starting as soon as possible.

"You know where I'd like to start, Dad?"

"Hmm?"

"A walk up Spirit Hill sometime. Maybe get an ice cream at the soda shop."

"You got it."

"Yeah?"

"I'll make you a deal," he says. "When your track season's over, we'll go get that ice cream and celebrate."

"Will you keep coming to watch me run?"

"Why would I stop now? I think the best is still to come."

I ice my foot over the weekend and apply my world-class wound-treatment skills gained after leaving the hospital. By Monday I can jog without pain, but Coach Rip forces me to lay off it.

"There's no upside to testing that foot this week," he says. "Another few days of rest will leave you two weeks to get ready for conference finals."

I want to get back on the track, but when Coach benches Dirk for the reckless move that led to my injury, I trust he has my best interests in mind.

Dirk's parents show up the next day to protest Coach's decision. According to Billy—who was in Coach Rip's office at the time—Dirk's parents threatened to use their influence as the school's biggest financial boosters to get Coach fired. Coach Rip launched into an animated recap of every violation of the no-assholes policy by their son. He dared them to invite him to rethink the scope of the penalty, pointing out that Dirk's track career hinges on the next few weeks of the season. The conversation ended shortly thereafter, and Dirk's parents exited Coach's office with less bluster than they entered.

As if I didn't respect Coach enough already, putting the interests of his athletes ahead of his own provides me an Advanced Placement lesson in sticking to your principles.

45

Teddy Lincoln stops by the house to let me know Frank spent the last two nights at the caddie shack.

I thank him for the good news.

"I wouldn't call it good." Teddy's eyes wander before continuing. "He's been drinking again."

I kick the ground, knowing Mom's going to blame me for this. Part of me feels responsible, and part of me fears if Frank can't be saved, neither can our family.

"I tried to talk to him, but it got ugly," Teddy says. "He needs to clear out, or I'll have to call the police."

"I get it. Thanks for the heads up."

"Your brother . . . He's always running full speed ahead, even when he's pointing in the wrong direction."

"You're telling me. I'll go get him tomorrow."

"Is it me, or is it strange you never eat lunch with your prom date?" Jed asks. Zoe's sitting with a group of cool kids at a table in the back corner of the cafeteria.

"She's not the clingy type." I say it like I believe it.

"Have you ever gone on a date with her?" Jed asks.

"How are *your* prom plans coming, Lothario?" Sara lays into Jed before I have a chance to get defensive.

"I'm keeping my options open," Jed says.

"Which means you've got butkus," Sara says.

"It's *bupkus*—no relation to Dick *Butkus*, the toughest linebacker in Chicago Bears and NFL history," Jed says. "Anyway, how many offers are *you* sorting through, City Girl?"

"Hah!" Sara responds.

"Not everyone's going with a date," I say. "A lot of people are going as groups of friends."

"Thanks for the charity, Bags," Sara says. "The truth is, there's not a long line of guys looking to ask out girl drummers."

"I think girl drummers are sexy," I say. "I mean, in general. I'm not talking specifically about you."

"You've proven once again you're a moron, Bags," Sara says. "The usual response I get when I tell guys I'm a drummer is a laugh."

"Does it get better after they see you play?" Jed asks.

"No. That scares them away."

"You could join our group," I say. "Zoe's parents are hosting a party before the dance, and we're all taking limos from there."

"Sorry, Bags, but I don't think you want to push your luck. It's not like I pass notes in class with Zoe and her friends, you know."

"There are a ton of people going. I don't see why it would be an issue. Let me ask her."

"You missed your opportunity, Bagman." Jed points his nose toward the cafeteria doors. "Your prom date just snuck off with her real friends to smoke a joint."

I catch Zoe when she slips back into the building through the side door across from my locker.

"Hey, Bags. See you at study hall?"

"Yep, I'll see you there." Before she walks away I ask, "Hey, Zoe, you got a minute?"

I mention the idea of including Sara in our prom plans.

"Oooo . . . I don't know if she'll enjoy herself," Zoe says.

"Why do you say that?"

"The other girls can be a little—what's the word? Cliquey. I don't want her to feel left out."

"She's not that sensitive. We can invite her and let her figure out if she wants to accept."

Zoe sighs. "To be honest, Bags, I've never felt comfortable around Sara. I mean, what's with the green hair and the punk-rock T-shirts?"

"The Velvet Underground is *not* punk rock," I say.

"Well, flying her freak flag all the time only draws more attention to how she looks."

"What's wrong with her looks? She's just not into all the makeup and hairspray. Have you ever noticed her freckles?"

"Since when did freckles become hot?"

I figure it's a Catholic school thing. "Forget it. Can you do me a favor and keep me posted on the plans? If there's a spot in the limo, I'd like to offer it to her."

"I'll let you know, but I'm not sure the other girls will want to parade She-Hulk in front of their parents."

Zoe's hostility reminds me I'm playing one of those sports I've never been any good at. I decide to skip today's study hall to avoid blowing my lead.

46

"Three meets stand between us and conference finals . . ." Coach Rip begins his pep talk after our Monday recovery workout. The miles, strain, and a long Midwestern winter show in the slack expressions hanging on Coach's words of assurance. Like an individual race, no one pulls ahead in the final stretch of the season. Victory goes to the runner who fades the least. I'm counting on my forced rest over the past week to help me hang on.

Coach Rip announces the lineups for our Wednesday meet. "Smitty, Papatonis, Cornell, and Bags. You've got the 800. Welcome back, Bags."

"Glad to be here, Coach."

"Dirk, Billy, Pinot, and Bosko will run the 1600. Welcome back, Dirk."

"Uh-huh."

I dodge the curious glances after Coach leaves my name off the 1600-meter squad.

"And Billy, José, Cornell, and a runner to-be-named will cover the 3200."

Coach calls me over after dismissing the rest of the team. "I can tell you're not happy with the lineup for the 1600," he says.

"My foot's fully healed, Coach, and my body's rested after a week off."

He waves me over to the bleachers, where he unrolls a large rectangle of paper that looks like some ancient scroll with grid lines. "Bags, I've spent hours reviewing everyone's race results and captured every lap time of the season here." Each runner is listed down the side of the sheet and every meet of this season across. Hundreds of numbers are neatly scrawled where the rows and columns intersect. "I call this my *split sheet*."

"You should call it a *spread sheet*," I say. "Because it could cover a bed."

"Right. Well, if we look at your numbers, two things stand out. In every race you've run this season, regardless of the distance, you've put up strong, consistent times. That is, until the final kick." He slides his finger across my row of split times. "Take a look. You've run multiple sixty-second laps throughout the season, but the 1600s you've lost were due to getting beat in the final kick, and you've never finished better than third place in an 800, even after keeping up with the leaders for the first six hundred meters."

"Then why do you have me running the 800?"

"I'll get to that. First, your numbers tell me that you can hang with anyone for most of a race. The problem is you're no kicker."

"How do I get faster?"

"Oh, we can sharpen your top-end speed over the next few weeks, but I don't think we'll find the best runner you can be in the 800 or 1600. I believe your competitive advantage will be in the 3200 meters."

"3200! Isn't that a stretch this late in the season?"

"Bags, thanks to genetics and all the miles you've logged riding your bike over the years, you're built to go long. You can use your advantage of endurance to tire your competition out over seven laps and remove their punch in the final lap."

Coach's information validates Summer's observations and the training plan she developed for me months ago, and neither of them have given me bad advice yet.

"How do I make the jump to 3200 meters?"

"I want you to keep racing the 800 to continue building your speed, but we need to get you running the 3200 meters so you can learn what it takes to race eight laps."

"How confident are you I can make the leap?"

"Bags, I think you could beat Coop and Duffy in the 3200—without the snow."

47

I get to the caddie shack after practice. Despite Linden Grove Country Club's Members Only sign and fancy driveway, the area behind the parking lot is a different story. "Shack" is an overstatement. It's more a leaky roof supported by two plywood walls with a long wooden bench stretched across each. A rusty basketball rim hangs off a chain-link fence in the caddie yard out back, but the potholes in the concrete make the space useful for little more than games of H-O-R-S-E, throwing dice, and smoking.

I find Frank asleep on one of the wooden benches, a copy of the *Chicago Sun-Times* spread across his face, suggesting he's been here since it was light outside. The shack has always provided an unofficial community service as a safe house for caddies trying to catch some *z*'s before their next loop, high school kids too wasted to face their parents, and even the occasional member hiding out after a bust-up at home. A few years ago, Frank could have been mistaken for any old caddie waiting for an early morning loop.

"I'll be gone tomorrow," Frank slurs, which explains the empty Jim Beam bottle underneath the bench and the eighty-proof stench infesting the confined space.

"Frank, it's me, Sam."

He lets out a heavy sigh.

"I came here to say I'm sorry."

"Fuck off!" The newspaper remains on his face.

"I want to help. I said some terrible things the other day. It's the least I can do to pay you back."

"For what, helping you buy a new pair of shoes?"

"For being my brother. For showing me we can learn from our mistakes."

I hear him breathing under the newspaper, unsure if he passed out again.

"Frank?"

He pulls the newspaper off his face and, with the struggle of a man twice his age, sits upright. Those green eyes that inspired me to get off my ass so many months ago on Spirit Hill look too distant to care if anyone trusts them. "I'd suggest you head home before I give you the ass-kicking you deserved the other day."

"Frank, don't do this to yourself again. The people you love are ready to give you whatever help you need. Let us in, and we can put this all behind us."

Frank reaches under the bench, and disappointment colors his face when he shakes the empty whiskey bottle.

I ask him again to give it some thought, then turn to leave. Before I get to the end of the caddie shack, the empty glass bottle whizzes past my head, shattering on the ground in front of me. I spin around to look at Frank and see wasted potential trapped in an adult body.

"Don't worry," he hisses. "You know I could have completed the pass if I wanted."

48

"Laps five and six got you," Coach Rip says. We're riding home from conference rival Ray Meyer High where I placed a discouraging sixth in my first 3200-meter race. "Those laps are a no-man's-land between celebrating the mile behind you and dreading the one ahead."

"The weird thing is, I started feeling better by lap seven, but it was too late to catch back up."

"Look at it this way. Your body now knows that if Sam Bags is going to win a 3200, you need to make the competition suffer in the second half of the race so they can't out-kick you on the bell lap."

"Tell me about the Dodgy Knickers." Sara's audition last night is all she's talked about for the past two weeks.

"They're the real deal. They've got a punkish classic-rock sound. Definitely louder and heavier than alternative music. Moved here from the UK to produce a record and build their following, but their drummer got homesick and moved back to London."

"How'd the tryout go?"

"I played my heart out and should hear back soon."

"Apologies for interrupting, Mister *Bag-roll-lee-oh*, but I don't think the rest of the class heard what has you all excited." Math teacher and self-proclaimed smart person Mr. Jones fails basic phonics trying to pronounce a last name with five syllables. "Feel free to share—or you can join my discussion of the mean value theorem."

"Okay, Mr. Jones. I'm back." *Okay-okay-okay.*

"How wonderful." He clears his throat loud enough to make it clear he believes he's in charge, then returns to scratching the blackboard.

Sara tosses me a tightly folded note that cuts through the air like a Jart. The note reads: *What's the latest re prom plans?*

My stomach churns as I weigh telling Sara everything against protecting her feelings. I convince myself I'm doing the right thing by sticking to her specific question and write: *Zoe + friends finalizing details.*

Again from Sara: *So I'm joining you?*

Ugh. I squeeze *Plan on it* into the bottom corner of Sara's note, relieved no space remains.

Sara tears another sheet from her spiral notebook, scribbles something and sends it my way. *What did Zoe say about me?*

I think carefully about my response before writing: *She doesn't want you to feel left out. Something about freckles being hot.*

Surprised but happy!!! Sara replies.

Me too! I respond, and jump from my desk more quickly than usual when the bell rings.

49

My second opportunity to race the 3200 meters is against Ernie Banks High on the North Side of Chicago. Our journey takes us past suburban fields of chain stores, franchise restaurants, and expressways before traveling through time across the Chicago River to a neighborhood of hundred-year-old brick storefronts housing the world in two-story buildings separated not by lawns and fences but by shared walls. We announce our arrival by laying a trail of branches and leaves ripped by our bus from the low-hanging trees lining historic Armitage Avenue.

Ernie Banks High has a strong sprint-distance team but only one solid middle-distance runner. That runner, however, is a junior who made it to regionals last year in the 3200 meters.

I'm determined to stay focused for the entire race and stick my neck out in the no-man's-land of laps five, six, and seven as Coach Rip suggested. Like the Meyer race, the first mile feels like a warm-up. The clock reads four-fifty at 1600 meters. I pick up my pace into the first turn of lap five. No one responds, and I find myself in front of the pack on the back straightaway.

The junior from Ernie Banks and one of his teammates join me in the second turn. Billy and José catch us as we cross the line and start our sixth lap. I feel strong. I'm exhaling out my mouth, steady and controlled. Time to tighten the screw once more. Again, no one responds immediately, but by the middle of the back straightaway, the Ernie Banks junior and Billy catch me. I knew this wasn't going to be easy, but what does it take to break free?

Another surge, and I'm first across the line after six laps with two to go. No one challenges my lead as we circle the track a seventh time. Hearing the bell signal the start of lap eight, alone at the front, is a victory in itself.

I don't need to turn my head to check on my pursuers because the *tut-tut-tut* of footsteps soon becomes all I hear. I fight back with a little extra effort but run harder to move slower. The junior from Ernie Banks pulls alongside me in lane two as we exit the first turn. Billy hangs tight on his heels. I expect them to lay down their final kicks and leave me behind, but that doesn't happen. The three of us stick together for the next fifty meters. After successfully pushing the pace over laps five through seven, I've got nothing to lose and put down a final kick with two hundred meters to go.

The footsteps come roaring back, along with a draft of air as Billy and the Ernie Banks runner blow past me. Exhaustion and humiliation leave me wobbling into the final straightaway. The only thing I recognize in my field of vision is the finish line, which appears to creep further away the closer I get. The arms of the Ernie Banks runner rise into the air before he drops to his knees. Billy veers to the outside of the track. The four additional seconds it takes me to reach them feel like a minute. I'm glad the race is over but gutted with the result.

"What were you doing pushing the pace, Bags?" Billy launches in while I'm hunched over gasping for air. "If you don't have what it takes to win, don't make us all suffer by showboating. No wonder I got beat in the final kick."

"It's called racing, Mini-Fridge," José says.

"And you, Hot Rod . . . you did the same thing against Meyer High. You two need to start racing smart before conference finals, or I'll be lucky to qualify for regionals."

Billy's criticism stings and exposes the foolishness of thinking a nobody like me can make it to state his rookie year.

Coach Rip jogs up and puts his arm around me during my lonely recovery walk around the track. "Now that's what I'm talking about, Bags!"

"Blowing a lead?"

"Playing to your strengths and making the competition suffer."

"But if I suffered more, how is that success?"

"You had them beat, Bags, but you hesitated too long to go for the kill. You waited for the final kick to attack and lost a sprint. You're *always* going to lose the sprint. Replay the last two laps in your head. What if you attacked with four hundred or even six hundred meters to go? It wouldn't have been a sprint at the end."

"It would have been suicide."

"Painful yes, but more painful than the runner from Ernie Banks could have sustained. We have one meet left before conference finals. Do exactly what you did today through the first six and a half laps. But instead of inviting a sprint in the final stretch, turn it into a six-hundred-meter interval. I can't guarantee you'll win, but you're likely to post your fastest 3200-meter time yet."

I find Dad at the far end of the bleachers after the race and flinch when I see Frank standing next to him. He looks smaller than usual but more human than the last time I saw him. He catches my stutter-step, so I continue walking toward them, wondering who'll speak first.

"Nice race, Bags," Frank says.

"Thanks." It's generous of him to say that, since he knows enough about track to know I'm disappointed with the outcome.

"I'll let the two of you catch up," Dad says. "Meet me at the concession stand when you're ready to leave."

"You look better, Frank," I say. "Sorry, I mean you look good."

"No need. I know what I looked like—and how I acted."

"Frank—"

"Please, Sam. You tried to help, and I was too ashamed to listen."

"You also threw a bottle at my head—"

"And . . . I could have seriously hurt you by throwing that bottle at you."

"Where does that leave us?"

"I could tell you I'm sorry—"

"Nobody needs another apology from Frank Bagliarello," I say.

"I've been afraid of letting people down if I ask for their help."

"Bullshit," I say. "You've never been afraid of letting people down. You wanted the glory of staying sober without anyone's help."

Frank and I have something in common besides our parents. Until I got over my morphine cravings, I always thought quitting was the hardest part of recovery. The real suffering, however, is living with the uncomfortable clarity of sobriety day after day.

"You're right," Frank says. "Asking for sympathy is easy because no one expects anything back from you. Asking for help creates an obligation, but I'm ready to sign up for it. The only way I'm going to stop cheating myself is to stop doing this just for me."

Frank needs a new addiction. I thought it was his healthy lifestyle. Maybe it could have been Summer. Maybe it will be school and his career. I hope he lets his family be part of it.

I'm a jerk for judging his commitment to all these things.

"Frank, I meant it when I said you showed me we can learn from our mistakes."

"I believe you."

"Does this mean we're even?"

"Assuming you buy me a new stereo, yes."

"Deal."

50

"This prom thing is a mess!" I say to Jed. We're shooting hoops in the school gym. He was the star of the Saint Edward's basketball team but a palm too short to make it at the high school level. He still plays pickup games at the Y, so I offered to shoot around during lunch in exchange for his help with my bizarre prom triangle with Sara and Zoe.

"I don't want to tell you I told you so," he says.

I dribble the ball twice then take a shot from the high post on the left. The ball floats well short of the net—just like in grade school. "This isn't Zoe's fault," I say. "It's her friends."

Jed grabs another ball from the rack and drills a shot from the opposite high post. "If Zoe wanted Sara there, she could make it happen. She told you herself she doesn't like Sara."

"I didn't come here to get reminded of your opinion of Zoe."

"You're the one who asked to play with the mean kids." He dribbles three times then passes to me.

I don't want to embarrass myself further, so stick to dribbling without kicking the ball with my toe. "What I'm looking for are some creative ideas."

"Dude, you've sold Sara out for a night of cheap thrills. You don't need creativity to fix that."

I drive to the net for a layup and brick it off the backboard straight to Jed. It took me years to figure out what makes Jed tick. It all started with his first prank in sixth grade. The rope trick. Loop kite string between two trees on opposite sides of the road after dark then wait for an unsuspecting driver to slam their brakes right before breaking through the barrier. For a little extra fun, Jed started throwing snowballs at the cars when they stopped.

Whether forcing a homecoming queen to smile and wave with AC/DC's "Big Balls" playing in the background, advertising sex to the family mass on Christmas Eve, or causing a weary father to shit his pants before driving into a wall of string, Jed's pranks have always been about more than giving the finger to authority and milking a laugh at someone else's expense. Jed figured out long before me that we're all Sisyphus, pushing our personal rocks up a hill. Consumed with our own bullshit, we miss what's going on right in front of us. Jed strikes when we're walking back down the hill, when we have a chance to realize the absurdity of our expectations, lost in the futile pursuit of some TV commercial version of a good life. Who better to take on such a challenge than the son of two perfectionist parents?

"This isn't about Zoe, is it?" I ask.

"No."

"It's about me, right?"

"Yep."

"I'm next on your prank list, aren't I?"

"Show me you learned something when your head hit that tree."

I put all my concentration into one last shot from the free throw line, dribble three times, take a deep breath and deliver a textbook release and follow through. The ball falls a foot short of the rim and rolls under the bleachers. I'm not cut out for this game, and that ball is gone for good.

51

Coach Rip offers our starting runners the option to sit out the final meet of the regular season to rest for conference finals. This gives a number of younger runners the chance to get some varsity race experience. The coach at William Murray High takes the same approach, so both schools essentially field JV teams. I ignore the derisive comments from Dirk and Billy about racing against a group of B-teamers and see today's race as one last chance to work on my speed in the 800 meters and race tactics in the 3200.

I win my first 800-meter race of the season with my fastest time yet. When Smitty asks my secret, I tell him I finally chilled out like he suggested. "I didn't think about it as a race. I just thought about running two laps as fast as I could."

"That's the secret, Bags. It's good to see you all, like, really just chilling for real."

Emboldened by my performance in the 800 and keen to put the frustration of my last 3200-meter race behind me, I tell myself anything is possible today. It takes me six laps to start believing it.

I hold nothing back from the crack of the gun and blaze through the first 1600 meters. After that first mile, I'm alone at the front, meters ahead of Cornbread and two runners from Murray High, so I keep going. The crowd loves it. I soak up the energy of the fans and build a five-meter gap by the end of lap six. It feels so good to be in the lead. I smile through the pain with the rookie spirit Coach Rip challenged me to rediscover after my disastrous race against George Halas High weeks ago.

Coach Rip runs across the infield and meets me at the middle of the far straightaway of lap seven. One-and-a-half laps to the finish. "Now, Bags! Pick it up and bring it home!" I do as instructed and run the final six hundred meters at a sixty-nine-second-lap pace. No one kicks past me today.

52

Zoe showers me with affection as prom approaches. She weaves me a friendship bracelet, speaks to me in the cafeteria, shows up for my track meets and starts wearing an LGHS Track and Field T-shirt (with the sleeves fashionably rolled up to her shoulders). I welcome the attention of the girl I've lusted after for so long, and her public acknowledgment I exist—beyond our conversations in the library—makes us an official couple.

The sight of Sara standing in front of my locker reminds me all is not perfect in Promville, and I have less than a week to figure out a solution.

"I've got a problem with prom," she says.

My heart sinks, expecting Sara to call me out for being a coward.

"I got a call back from the Dodgy Knickers."

"Yeah . . . ?"

"It's down to me and a dude. They want us each to play a gig before making a final decision. I drew this Saturday at the Hideaway."

"The Hideaway?" Part dive bar, part dusty music hall, the Hideaway has launched several musical legends to fame. "That's the big time!"

"It's also prom night," Sara says.

"Who gives a shit about prom?" I couldn't be more conflicted, but my enthusiasm for Sara's big break is sincere. "All the drama and fancy dresses? You'll hate it. This is your chance to celebrate everything you've worked for during high school."

"But prom is supposed to be our last hurrah and all that. I'll be spending the night alone instead of with my friends."

"You're not going to be alone, Sara. You're going to be . . . you'll be with your people."

She drops her gaze as if she's about to cry. When she lifts her head, the shimmer in her eyes turns to a smile. "I know," she says.

She gives me a hug, and I tell myself protecting Sara's feelings was the right thing to do as her friend.

53

"I worry I'm about to be exposed as the great Illinois track imposter." Frank and I are enjoying his new stereo system. I splurged on a model with a three-disc CD changer. My caddie savings took a hit, but I have an extra summer to earn it back before college. The first CD Frank purchased was *Born to Run* by Bruce Springsteen. "Thunder Road" muscles through the new Sony speakers while I look to Frank to help me get over the fear of embarrassing myself at conference finals this weekend.

"I've never said this before, but you need to stop oversimplifying things, Sam."

"What does that mean?"

"This is the rare situation where your tendency to obsess and overanalyze will help you."

"You mean the fact I'll be competing against kids who have thousands of more miles in their legs than me?"

"Have you considered the fact you've been competing with those same kids all season long?"

"Yeah, but this isn't a single meet with one or two strong runners. The best runners from all the schools in our conference will be in the same race."

"You've put up times that place you among the fastest in the state. And keep in mind, you don't need to *win* Friday's race. You only need to finish in the top four."

"The problem with your math is the same four runners that made it to regionals last year are returning this year."

"Listen, you have two other things going for you. First, you're coming off a rest week and have only gotten stronger over the past month. Second, you have the advantage of surprise. No one's going to be focused on you when there are four marked men on the track."

Frank switches on the radio after the final track, and I try to put things into perspective while WBBM Newsradio lulls me to sleep. It's been nine months since my last bike ride ended in tragedy, seven months since my first run with Frank, and nearly three months since my first high school track race. Conference finals are in five days, and I'm two races away from my goal of making it to the state finals. To Frank's point, my win against William Murray High may have been against a JV field, but I did it in a time that would have put me within a second of qualifying for state in the 3200 meters last year. Frank is right. It's time to stop worrying about the competition and run my own race.

54

Bodies crowd the hallway, blocking my path to the library. I ask a girl standing on her toes if she can see what's going on.

"One of the retards locked himself in the utility closet," she says. "He keeps crying for his mom."

The spectacle has captured everyone's attention, though the crowd hasn't decided whether to laugh or help.

I push my way to the front and try unsuccessfully to jiggle the door open. "Who's in there?" I shout.

"Sam, is that you?" Marty says from behind the door.

"It's me, Marty. Hold on. I'll get you out."

"I can't see anything," Marty cries. "It's scary in here!"

Before I get to work on the door, a hand falls on my shoulder and spins me around. "How'd your dick-holding friend manage to lock himself in a closet?" Peter Grayson. Winner of the student body popularity contest, magna cum laude ass-kisser, and spitter on baloney sandwiches. I pull away but can't shake his grip. He's an inch shorter than me but spends a lot more time in the weight room. "I don't think you want to do that, Bags." He whispers through a face of concern, smooth enough he won't blow his cover in front of his constituents. "You might excite Dumbo and cause him to hurt himself."

"Let go of me, you prick!"

Marty bangs on the door.

"Hang in there Marty. Gimme a—"

Grayson's knee lands a direct hit to my sternum—and the knot of surgical wires underneath my skin. The blow knocks the wind out of me, and I fall to the ground.

"Sam? What's wrong, Sam?"

Before I catch my breath, a repetitive thud sounds from behind the door. Ms. Manley, one of the school's narcs, shows up with a janitor. The thuds continue for another four beats as the janitor fiddles with the ring of keys on his belt before all goes silent. A girl in the crowd shrieks. Grayson worms his way through a crack in the crescent of onlookers. When the janitor finally opens the door, Marty is on the ground, his head resting in a halo of blood. Groans and screams wail from behind me.

"It was Bags and Grayson!"

Ms. Manley speaks into her walkie-talkie, then orders the crowd to disperse. I walk up to her and Marty.

"I told you to clear out!" she says.

"He's my friend." I take off my shirt and offer it to her.

She grudgingly accepts, wipes the blood off Marty's head and face then lowers her cheek to his mouth. "He's breathing. The ambulance is on its way."

Thirty minutes later, Grayson and I stand in the principal's office. Dr. Poulet sits behind his desk, with Ms. Manley in a chair against the wall to our right. I'm wearing a PE shirt borrowed from Mr. O that is two sizes too big for me. Grayson looks dressed for a regatta in a pastel polo shirt, seersucker shorts, and Top-Siders.

Ms. Manley confirms my explanation of everything that took place after she arrived. She's not willing to speculate on my allegation Grayson is the reason Marty got locked in the closet.

Grayson follows with his version of events. "I think this is all a misunderstanding, Dr. Poulet. I noticed a kid was locked in the closet. The first thing I did was ask a freshman to find a narc."

"Bullshit, Grayson!" I say. "You've bullied Marty in the past, and you sucker punched me when I tried to help. Then you snuck away from the scene like a coward."

Grayson gives Dr. Poulet a look suggesting someone needs to restrain the maniac in the room. Dr. Poulet nods, reassuring his chief flunky he has things under control. "I think I have heard enough. I will reflect on this and let the three of you know if we need to reconvene."

I have zero interest in losing a fight over Dr. Poulet's policies a second time this semester. His fancy credentials may entitle him to a position of authority, but he's more comfortable sitting behind his fat desk, staring at certificates on the wall, than walking the halls of the school. The adults I admire lead by example and give a shit about people not procedures.

"This is a joke, Dr. Poulet," I say. "When are you going to stop reflecting and start acting like you run this place?"

"Mr. Bagliarello—" The only thing left to respect about Dr. Poulet is his multilingual pedigree and ability to pronounce my last name correctly— "I would tread very carefully if I were you. You haven't had the most stellar semester, and if I'm not mistaken, this would be a bad week for you to get suspended and become ineligible to play sports."

That shuts me up, and Dr. Poulet dismisses us after repeating his plans to do nothing. Ms. Manley shows Grayson and me the door, while she stays behind.

"Wow, we got lucky there," Grayson says back in the hallway. "Don't feel so bad. It's not like your friend broke something he needs."

I take a swing, but Grayson expects it. He deflects my punch and once again leaves me on the ground sucking air. He turns to slither away and walks straight into the Godzillian mass of Charles O'Toole. Charles tosses him aside like a car blocking his path and continues toward me without missing a step.

"What do you want?" I hate myself for backing down from Dr. Poulet and looking vulnerable in front of Charles.

Charles looks down at me and extends a hand. I hesitate to take it until he cracks a smile and says, "I only pick on people I respect, and that kid's not worth the trouble."

He pulls me up and pats me on the shoulder. I give him a reluctant "thanks," then watch him lumber away.

Bad Gorilla pounds his chest in a fury that makes my head throb.

"Where were you?" I say to myself, as if it were possible to release Bad Gorilla into the world outside my imagination.

Mom's at the kitchen table when I walk in after practice.

"Newspaper day?"

"Yeah."

"How'd your article turn out?"

"You can read it yourself." I drop the paper on the table and head for the shower.

My article about last year's Summer Olympics expanded beyond the topic of cheating in sports. Prompted by the front-row seat my accident provided to a profit-maximizing healthcare industry, a misguided food system, and a school's prioritization of rules over common sense, the article became a plea for more responsible leadership across all areas of society. Marty got it right when he said kids do bad things when the adults leave the room.

I'm starving and too discouraged to make dinner, so I grab a half-empty jar of salsa and a bag of Tostitos. Mom puts the paper down when I join her at the kitchen table. To reach the salsa, I have to hold a chip between two fingers and dig deep into the jar.

"I never knew you felt so strongly about McDonald's," she says.

I wasn't expecting irony from the woman who hasn't cracked a joke since 1985.

"What else is bothering you, Sam?"

I tell her about the incident with Marty. "He was banging his head against the door, and I was completely powerless to do anything about it." I can no longer reach the salsa with my fingers, so I shake some out of the jar onto a chip. Mom doesn't even nag me when a chunk of tomato falls onto the table.

"I'm so sorry to hear about Marty. What a terrible thing to do to someone." She reaches for her wrinkled pack of Kents and surprises me by retracting her hand before shaking one out. The situation seems like an easy excuse to calm her nerves with a smoke. "You know, you're not as powerless as you think."

I huff at her for not realizing what a wimp I am. Mom gets up, pulls a cereal bowl out of the cupboard, and casually slides it in front of me, along with a napkin.

"What do you think this article is?" she continues. "If you want to call out the phonies and the cowards, you can do that right here"—she waves the newspaper in the air— "and a lot more effectively than playing ass-grab with some punk in the school hallway."

I pause to admire Mom's language before sharing how I acted like a coward myself in Dr. Poulet's office.

"Avoiding a senseless battle is not cowardice, Samuel. You've got all next year to fight back by exposing the bullies and a spineless school administration." Having Mom's fiery passion on my side for the first time in a while causes me to smile.

She takes my hand. "Listen, Sam. You know those conversations we've had about college?"

She senses my reluctance to get into it right now and beams. "I want to show you something."

I keep tossing Tostitos into my mouth even though the salsa's gone.

Mom walks to the fridge, reaches for the junk basket on top, then hands me a piece of paper. It's a letter from Loyola University dated March 19, 1965. Three short paragraphs explain Antoinette Gimignano has been accepted to the accounting program within the university's business school.

"I never knew," I say.

"At the time it was easy to trade a silly dream for the safety of marriage and a family. Years later I started to second-guess the decision. I was proud to leave the old neighborhood but spent the rest of my life uncomfortable with where I came from."

"Maybe you should apply to college with me in the fall."

Instead of scolding me for being a smartass, Mom laughs. A real laugh that twists her face in a pleasant way. I wrap up the half-full bag of chips and put them back in the cupboard.

"Sam, I've wanted you to have a comfortable, predictable life because your dad and I couldn't give you one—"

"Mom. That's not—"

She waves me off. "Listen, Sam. You figure out what you want to do about college when you're ready, and I'll be your biggest fan, whatever path you pursue."

"Thanks for that, Mom."

"Just do me a favor and don't end up back home like your brother."

55

LGHS's creaky old school bus carries us to Memorial High, "Home of the Mascots"—an appropriately dull team name for a town created from a cornfield and given the name Pleasant Estates. While Memorial High lacks the timeless character of Ernie Banks High, it boasts a state-of-the-art running track, and the town's six-lane Main Street enables school buses to avoid the typical congestion upon exiting the tollway.

The atmosphere at the track is electric, supercharged by the high stakes of the conference finals meet and the first short-sleeve day of 1989. It reminds me of the St. Patty's Day Invitational, minus the green beer and snow. I walk to the warm-up area behind the bleachers and wave hello to Sara and Mom, sitting together about four rows up from the finish line. Dad and Frank stand among the dozens of overflow fans lining the final straightaway. Zoe called last night to apologize for not being able to attend. Prom is tomorrow, and she has too many last-minute details to finalize with her friends and their mothers.

Each of the eight teams in our conference fields three runners per event. To accommodate twenty-four runners on an eight-lane track, we'll be using a second start line in what's called a "dual-alley start." One set of twelve runners squeezes onto the normal start line in lanes one through four. The second twelve start about ten meters ahead in lanes five through eight.

I'm in the first group, along with the four runners who made it to regionals last year: Billy, the seniors from Otis Rush and Ray Meyer, and a junior from William Murray who sat out our meet last Saturday. Billy and the junior from William Murray get the two inside starting positions in our group of twelve since they made it to state last year. I get the twelfth spot at the outside of lane four. José is in the second start group along with Tony Vittorini, the loud little man I met in my first 800-meter race from Oak Forest High.

Vito walks over as we're waiting for the starter to call us to the line. "Congrats on surviving the season, Bags. I wouldn't have pegged you for a two-miler."

José puts a hand on Vito's shoulder and flexes his wide-receiver arms. "Who walks around calling themselves a two-miler, Vito? Stop yapping and line up for the 3200."

Vito's trash talk would normally intimidate me, but there's not enough time to be bothered. In less than ten minutes I'll know whether this track thing is for real.

The race gets off fast, and the senior from William Murray breaks away early. Runners cut over to the inside two lanes before the first turn, at which point Billy is in second position, two strides behind the guy from William Murray. The second group of twelve runners crashes the inside lanes as soon as they exit the first turn, finding open positions with no more than the usual hokery-pokery.

The William Murray runner's aggressiveness would be dismissed as careless were he not a returning state qualifier. Instead of leaving him to self-combust off the front, the pack pushes the pace to keep him close. I risk foolishness and jump ahead to join him at the front, breathing in the confidence gained from my last race. The two of us lead the field through an uncomfortably fast sixty-five-second first lap. Murray slows things down a bit, and I do the same. The front of the pursuit group remains within a few strides as we complete the first 1600 meters in four thirty-five, a new personal record.

Things get more exciting when Billy chases us down after the second turn of lap five, bringing four runners with him: José, the senior from Otis Rush, a runner from Major Taylor I haven't seen before, and

Vito. This prompts the William Murray runner to press ahead in the hope of avoiding a dogfight with more than three laps to go.

He keeps a three-meter lead through lap six. The runner from Major Taylor blows up, and us five remaining chasers keep in close contact with each other. If the William Murray runner holds his lead, only three of us five chasers will make it to regionals. José leads the chase group from lane one. Six laps in, and José's stride remains smooth and efficient. I'm directly behind him, and the senior from Otis Rush is on my right in lane two. Billy and Vito are directly behind us. Everyone around me runs with a natural finesse that makes me look like a donkey among a troop of thoroughbreds. Donkey or not, I'm still in this race and trotting faster than last weekend.

I notice a serious problem when we exit the first turn of lap seven: I'm boxed in. If Billy and Vito come around the Otis Rush runner to my right, I'll have no way to respond. I need to get out of lane one, and my best chance is to shoot through an alley created during the next turn.

José takes the second bend of lap seven wide in an attempt to attack the William Murray runner from lane two. The runner from Otis Rush on my right cuts to the inside to fill José's vacated spot in front of me. This causes Billy and Vito to fill the hole left by the Otis Rush runner, and both end up on my right. The move I feared. Everyone improves their position while I remain boxed in.

I'm hanging with the five best runners in the conference. For once my challenge isn't speed or fitness. Ignorance and inexperience are beating me today. Dropping back and pulling around the two guys on my right is not an option—that would take time and energy I can't spare. Before I have a chance to freak out, the anxiousness of the group presents a solution.

José pulls alongside the William Murray runner, creating a path for one of us remaining four chasers to follow him to the finish line for a comfortable third place while avoiding being one of three left behind to fight it out for fourth.

I'm not the only one to see the opportunity, as all four of us chasers attack the hole at the same time.

Now, I don't know if Isaac Newton was a runner, but he figured out in the seventeenth century that when four bodies collide at thirteen miles an hour, the heaviest wins. Three hundred years later, Smitty reimagined Newton's laws of motion in his theory of forward momentum. As it turns out, the four of us chasers aren't all traveling at the same speed. I'm the farthest from the gap behind José, so the only way to beat the others to the same spot is to travel faster. My advantage of velocity causes me to absorb less force at the point of collision. While the other three runners scatter upon impact, Vito bumps me forward. I clumsily regain my stride and exit the final turn of lap seven directly behind José. Along with the William Murray runner, we have a five-meter lead over Billy, Vito, and the Otis Rush runner.

Boosted by a flood of collision adrenaline and terrified of getting beat in a straight-up sprint, I launch an attack from five hundred meters to the finish. William Murray and José stick with me, and the chasers never catch us. In the end, William Murray beats José by a hair, I take third, and Otis Rush takes fourth. Vito and Billy's outrage at getting beat by a donkey sweetens the victory.

I get goosebumps each time I replay the last two laps of the race in my mind and the gamble that separated third and sixth place. Track is the sport of truth, and today was proof tactics and experience matter. But if the truth isn't going your way, FoMo fueled by a burst of speed, the natural laws of physics, and a jolt of adrenaline can make up for a lot.

I go to bed happy. I'm headed to regionals next Saturday—the last race standing between me and state. Sara's going to live out her rock 'n' roll fantasy at the Hideaway, and her good fortune freed me from the dilemma I created by messing with the cool kids' social order. Everything is coming together the night before prom, and I fall asleep knowing in twenty-four hours I'll be wrapped in the arms of the hottest girl at school.

Bad Gorilla wakes me early the next morning, chucking self-doubt like rotten bananas. I want to believe he's channeling strain and fatigue from yesterday's race, but by the time I get into the shower, I accept why he's acting so ornery.

Not hurting Sara isn't enough.

"Playing along with Zoe's prom charade makes you part of her shitty behavior," he says.

I tell him I tried to get Sara an invite to the prom party.

"Not as hard as you've tried to hang onto the validation Zoe provides you."

"That's not the only reason I'm interested in Zoe," I say. "Remember those stimulating conversations we had in the library?"

He tells me a good banana in a barrel of garbage still stinks, then laughs at his own joke. By the time I get out of the shower, I've worked out a plan to make peace with my hairy conscience.

The only way to speak to Zoe on the day of prom is by telephone. Even then, I have to tell her dad it's an emergency.

"Hey Bags," she says. "I hope it's not bad luck to call your date the day of prom."

"Yeah, sorry for stalking you. I needed to talk one-on-one."

"You're not calling to ask again about the Green Goblin, are you?"

"Eh . . . actually, I am. And her name's Sara."

"My God, Bags, what now?"

"Well, it's kind of funny, you know—"

"Spit it out, Bags. I owe the florist a final decision in ten minutes."

"Okay. Uh . . . so . . . I know you and your friends booked the limo to take us to the boat cruise after the dance . . ." I picture Zoe's arms crossed as I tug the strings of her tightly wound plans. "I wondered if you have any interest in stopping by a show Sara's playing downtown on the way."

The plan sounds even more half-baked than when I rehearsed it in the shower, and her silence jams my ears like a No. 2 pencil.

"Zoe? Are you there?"

"What the fuck, Bags. Are you stoned?"

"Let me tell you why—"

"I don't give a shit why. Are you trying to back out of prom on the *morning of* prom, dumbass?"

"No, no! That's the last thing I want to do. It's just that Sara—"

"Do you have any idea how many people thought I was crazy for letting you take me to prom?"

"I know, Zoe. I just figured maybe we could mix up the traditional prom routine tonight."

"Oh, shove it! Do you think I'm someone who *needs* to mix up the traditional prom routine?"

I guess that's the difference between us. Zoe needs prom more than she needs me. After straining the closest relationships in my life by chasing ideas of what's important, I've accepted all I really need are people happy to be with me, whether we're at sixth-period study hall, a bench at the top of a hill, or a dumpy little kitchen table. Maybe I knew asking Zoe the impossible would leave me no option but the right one, because my next words bring the sort of relief I get after crossing the finish line of a race.

"Well, I can't believe I'm saying this, Zoe, but I'm not going to be able to go to prom with you."

"You smug little dweeb. Beth was right when she said if you aren't afraid your friends are going to fuck your boyfriend, you can do better."

"I'm sorry. Maybe we'll both do better next time."

"You think you're gonna get a next time? You're torched, dude. You don't get second chances with girls like me."

"It's okay, Zoe. Once was plenty."

Dial tone.

56

Sara's backing out of her driveway when I pull up in the Guinness, ten minutes after Zoe slammed the phone in my ear. She rolls down the window when I walk over to her car.

"What's up?" Sara says.

"Where you goin'?"

"U-Haul."

"Moving?"

Her frown tells me she's in a hurry. "I need to rent a van to get my drums downtown."

"No you don't." I lean into the open window. "I'll take you."

She cocks her head.

"I want to be your friend in the crowd," I say.

"What about— What about prom and everything?"

"Screw prom. How could I miss the biggest show of your life?"

"Uh . . . okay," she says. "You want to tell me what happened?"

"Yeah, but let's pack up your shit first."

It takes an hour to get to the Hideaway, tucked between two old warehouses on the industrial outskirts of the city. While Sara warms up with the band, I play groupie and explore the hallowed halls of this former Prohibition-era boarding house. The walls sweat a hundred years of booze, gambling, and dancing that made the place a venue where obscure bands catch breaks and established musicians test new material.

The doors open at eight o'clock, and the DKs take the stage at nine. Actually, no one takes the stage. The bar's owner walks up to the mic and introduces the band. The room goes dark and a minute later, Sara's silhouette settles into the cockpit of her drum set. All remains silent as her three bandmates take their places onstage.

From the darkness, Sara drills her snare drum five times followed by a 4/4 thump of the bass drum and a simultaneous *te-te-te-te* off the high-hat cymbal as she launches into a cover of "Sunday Bloody Sunday" by U2. It's a kick-ass opening, and the darkness intensifies the machine-gun drum groove before the stage lights explode with the first notes of the song's iconic guitar riff. The crowd responds to the lights and music with equal energy, and the room shakes.

The band follows its cracking opener with one of their own songs. Sara bangs away, her beefy triceps and shoulders pumping under her sweat-soaked T-shirt.

The DKs rip through their playlist, mixing original material with British rock covers. It's a fireworks show of pulsing lights, thumping Kevlar, crashing cymbals, and the occasional cowbell—and that's just Sara's contribution.

Forty-five minutes later, the stage goes silent, and the house lights switch on, as if the show never happened. The crowd remains in place—a silent protest for more—while a few opportunists forfeit their spots to hit the bar for refills. Minutes later the room falls into darkness, and shadows become active again onstage. Red backlight bathes the stage in a mysterious glow, and a smoke machine coughs up clouds of fog. A single spotlight shines down on Sara seated at the drums, her head tipped in a solemn bow. She raises her sticks in the air, pauses, then throws down two short, violent beats of the floor tom and snare drum followed by three quarter-notes on the high-hat cymbals in the unmistakable intro to "Good Times Bad Times" by Led Zeppelin. The room comes to life once again, and Sara carries us up a roller coaster that breaks into the song's opening lyrics.

I shout, sing, and bounce along with the crowd. Sara pummels the drums and flicks sweat off her head in all directions, as if her body triggered its release valve. Through the pulsing lights I see Sara as never before. Underneath her percussive power is the girl I've known since kindergarten, the one with the smiling eyes and delicate freckles who teared up when I told her I'd drive her to her show tonight. I know she cares about me because she always points out how I can be better. She sees through my mistakes and makes sense of my thoughts and fears and desires before I do. I feel as close to Sara in this smoky bar as if I held her in my arms. After years of confusion, I finally get it. Sara loves me, and I love her. I don't want this song to end, yet can hardly wait to be alone with the beautiful girl in the black T-shirt and phosphorescent hair—no matter what the girls with spray tans and perms say.

I've never driven down Lake Shore Drive in the dark. The absence of traffic in the middle of the night makes it look like we're flying through space. Lake Michigan hovers like a black hole to our left, and the streetlights cast a starry glow as we cruise through twelve lanes of emptiness.

"Was it everything you hoped it would be?" I ask.

"Mm-hmm." Sara nods with a straw in her mouth. I stopped at 7-Eleven for a Slurpee to top up the bucketful of sweat she shed during the show. "I've never been in a band that counted both U2 and Led Zeppelin as influences."

"Maybe they don't feel the need to choose sides like the high school bands you've been playing with."

"Thanks for being there, Bags. I hope you don't regret it when we're back at school Monday."

"Why do you say that?"

"You traded a night with the girl of your dreams to haul me and my shit downtown."

"Sara, tonight was about much more than hauling you around."

"Hmm?" Sara asks through a mouthful of fruit-flavored slush.

"Well, I bet you didn't hear me yell, 'I love you!' in the middle of your encore."

"Uh . . . my ears are still ringing. Give me that one more time?"

I repeat it and add, "I'm sorry it's taken me so long to figure it out."

"Bags—"

"Yeah?"

"Uhh . . . I don't know how to say this—"

"I know the feeling. Something about watching you play tonight—everything finally fell into place."

"That's um . . . well . . . this is going to be awkward, Bags, but I need to say it."

"Go for it!"

"I—I think I might be interested in girls."

"What?!" The steering wheel jerks when I twist to look at Sara, causing her to slam into me. She scoots back to the passenger side of the bench seat rubbing her shoulder. "Why didn't you tell me this before?"

"It's not like I wake up in the morning with an urge to say, 'Hey, I was thinking I might be a lesbian.' I'm still figuring this out, and I'm not going to find the answer in Linden Grove. Hopefully college will give me the space to explore it."

I let the news settle and retrace the emotions that led me to believe Sara and I were two atomic love particles destined to collide. Despite her knack for helping me understand myself a little better, Sara's as uncertain about who she's supposed to be as any of us.

"I think it's cool," I say. "I mean, cool of you to explore uncomfortable questions about yourself."

She smiles and relaxes her shoulders.

"I guess this explains the Charlotte College thing."

Sara's freckles disappear in the flood of emotion that fills her cheeks.

"I mean . . . I'm an idiot, okay? Forget the Charlotte crack. I'm honored you trust me enough to tell me about this."

She looks me over for signs of sarcasm before responding. "I guess you can add my personal baggage to the rest of the shit you spent the night hauling around."

"Don't be ridiculous," I say. "I learned an important lesson today."

"You've got no chance of getting laid on prom night?"

"Okay, two lessons."

"What's the second?"

"I faced a tough decision these past few weeks over helping myself and helping a friend. I knew how much fun the selfish choice would be, but I finally figured out the right decision was about more than me."

"You chose meaning over happiness," Sara says.

"Oh, I was pretty happy tonight. Still am."

"The difference is you faced a hard decision and didn't hide from it."

"You mean like choosing to spend today doing something I'll remember forever over a fairy-tale prom that won't matter much a year from now?"

"'I went to the woods because I wished to live deliberately,'" Sara says.

"Hah! That book helped me convince Zoe to go to prom with me."

"Sorry again it didn't work out."

"It's okay. She hates Thoreau."

"You know, Bags, I've been afraid to mention the girl thing because I didn't want you to think I was weird."

I turn to see if she's serious, this time without destabilizing the car, and remember the closest Zoe came to giving me a compliment was *You're sorta weird.*

"Sara, of all the things that make you weird, I'm not sure anyone will be bothered you're a lesbian."

The laughs that fill the car confirm how perfect we are for each other.

★ ★ ★ ★

I get home well past midnight after dropping off Sara and her gear. I enter quietly, not wanting to wake Mom and Frank. As I creep into the kitchen, I kick an envelope tucked inside the screen door. The outside reads, *BAGS*. It's stuffed with cash and a note in Jed's handwriting.

Bagman—

You missed one hell of a party but did the right thing tonight. You chose substance over saccharine, and I hope you get used to the taste. No need to feel bad about coming to your senses so late in the game. It didn't take long for the crows to descend, and Zoe flew off from prom with two(!) of them.

The dough in here is the Spirit Hill Recovery Fund. When I collected money for the boat, I asked for donations to replace your bike. Nearly everyone gave something. It should be more than enough to cover a new bike, so think about getting a helmet this time around!

By the way, it's worth you knowing that as much as you fancy being an outsider, more people respect you than you realize. That includes me, dude.

Your friend,
Jed

I count the money twice on the way to my room. Six hundred twenty-three dollars. My accident destroyed me when it destroyed my bike. Recovery allowed me to see what remained when everything I thought mattered was stripped away. What I found were the people I no longer need to race away from.

"Thanks, buddy, I've been working on it," I whisper as I close my bedroom door.

"Working on what?" Frank mumbles from his bed.

57

Sunday must be the saddest day of the week in the hospital. Loneliness echoes off the empty hallways, waiting for the offices and labs to reopen in the morning. Visitors dress a little nicer, unintentionally reminding their loved ones that life on the outside waits for no one.

Marty's been in the hospital since getting locked in the school closet three days ago. Banging his head against the door left him with ten stitches on his forehead. His doctor wants him to spend another day to monitor his already weak heart and lungs. Seeing Marty surrounded by all the flashing monitors makes it harder to be a visitor than a resident in the same hospital I called home less than a year ago.

"I've got something for you." I hand him a small figurine of Greg LeMond.

"'Hanks, Sam." The oxygen tube plugged into Marty's nose distorts his speech.

"LeMond was the first American to win the Tour de France," I say. "Then he nearly died in a hunting accident. It's taken him two years to get back into shape, but I think he's got a real chance at this year's Tour."

"This guy. LeMond. Like you and me."

"That's right, Marty. A little rehab after you get out of here, and you'll be back on your bike by the Tour de France."

Marty smiles and asks, "How's 'chack?"

"Regionals are next weekend. If I finish in the top four, I go to state."

"G'luck, Sam. You're gonna make it."

Leave it to Marty to share his good luck after getting bullied and beaten. "Marty, I don't deserve your good luck. I get to run a race that's so meaningless, fourth place counts as victory, while you're in the hospital because I tried to help you and failed."

"*Wong!*" Marty responds through his blocked nose.

"What's that?"

"YOU. ARE. WRONG!" he repeats. "LeMond, Chewbacca, those guys in the Olympics"—Marty ticks through his words carefully and clearly— "Heroes. Mom says heroes are the ones no one expects to win, but they still try."

I've been searching for a reason to run beyond myself ever since Smitty shared his story of defiance and inspiration. Marty just taught me heroes are the ones who don't have to win to make the people around them stronger.

"Alright, Marty. I can't promise I'll make it to state, but I'll do my best. Is that fair?"

"Fair."

"Can I tell you one more thing?"

"What?"

"You forgot to include Marty Koppen in your list of heroes."

58

This late in the season, recovery and rest are priorities, so the five of us racing regionals on Saturday take advantage of the spring weather to venture off the track for easy road and trail runs this week. It's a return to the sort of running I fell in love with. We end Thursday's practice with reps up Spirit Hill followed by some stretching near the benches in the grassy area at the top.

"How many more years you think Coach Rip has in him before he retires?" Smitty asks.

"A couple," José says. "Maybe five."

"It would be sweet to give him his state championship this year, wouldn't it?" Smitty says.

"Sweet for him—*and* me." Leave it to Dirk to nominate himself for the team's best hope at a gold medal.

"Or me," our precocious sophomore Pops says. Pops's season is over but that hasn't stopped him from showing up to practice in a sign he knows there's more to running than having a race to train for.

"Keep dreaming," Dirk says, snuffing out the laughs that follow Pops's crack.

"Speaking of dreams . . . mine have just been answered," José says. Something over my shoulder captures his gaze.

"Isn't that your brother's car, Bags?" Smitty asks.

I turn to see the source of my teammates' awe and huff a soft laugh. While walking to Frank's car, I'm unable to shake the smile stretching across my face.

"Summer . . ."

Her hands hang in the front pockets of her pullover, as casually as if we met at this spot every Thursday. Frank throws me a hang loose sign from the driver's seat of the Guinness.

"Young Bags," she says. "You're still running, huh?"

"Heh—can you believe I made it to regionals?"

"Hmmhh. Congratulations."

I lap up every feature of her face—the jagged nose, the wispy hair which refuses to be braided, her marble cheekbones and those full, warm lips—afraid she might disappear again. "What—"

"Am I doing here?"

"Yeah."

"You didn't think I was going to miss the biggest race of your life, did you?"

"How did you—"

"I checked in with your brother. He filled me in on what I've missed over the past couple months." She raises her eyebrows, suggesting Frank told her everything. "Besides, I needed to tie up some loose ends back home. I figured why not take the opportunity to see you qualify for the state finals at the same time?"

"Thanks for the confidence. Where are you staying?"

"With my dad. He's one of the loose ends. A little space has helped me realize our relationship is more important than my feelings."

"Like the heart," I say.

"The heart?"

"The heart on your bedroom wall, with all the little pictures. I thought it meant each of the people in our lives has a place in our heart, even if none of them are perfect."

"And here I thought you were snooping through my underwear drawer."

I blush, still embarrassed about getting busted daydreaming in her bedroom.

"Can I join you for the walk home?" Summer asks. We let Frank know we'll meet him back at the house, and Summer and I make our way toward Spirit Hill.

"Are you ready for Saturday?" she asks.

"I feel like I'm hitting a second peak after injuring my foot. The problem is I'll be racing against the fifteen best runners in northern Illinois."

Summer doesn't respond. We keep walking toward the top of the hill. I look out at Linden Grove as I have countless times before. Depending on the season, weather, time of day, and randomness of everything else, the view is always different.

"I've always loved this spot," Summer says. "You can see the Sears Tower on a clear day. If you could see past the horizon, who knows what you'd find out there?"

"What are you trying to tell me?" Summer's not the sentimental type, so there must be a hidden meaning in her message.

"Do you think you've ever hit your body's limit?"

"I once died right over there." I point toward the tree that nearly killed me.

"What about on the track?"

"I've dug deep, but tell me why the right answer is no."

"I have no doubt you've pushed yourself. But you have no idea how much potential remains."

"What makes you think I have more to give?"

"You haven't died during a race yet, have you?"

"No . . . ?" I start to see where she's headed.

"Well then, your limit is somewhere beyond the horizon you know, isn't it?"

I don't have an immediate response, so I say nothing.

"Listen, there's nothing more you can do to train for Saturday's race. This isn't about your physical fitness. Do you know what your brain is for?"

"Overcomplicating my life?"

She knows me well enough to smile at my interpretation of her question. "Your brain's job is to protect your body. It forces you to pace yourself by prioritizing endurance so you make it to the finish line alive. Otherwise, your body would blow out early. There's a lot of cushion, however, between the point at which your brain starts telling your body to slow down and your full potential."

I share with Summer my various mental exercises like Smitty's mantras, Mr. O's visualization techniques, and my prerace tunes.

"This is more than mind games," Summer says. "This is about overriding your brain's emergency brake in search of your body's point of failure."

"You mean the point of death?"

"Technically, the point of collapse. Your brain's not going to let you willingly kill yourself by running."

Summer says this so nonchalantly she makes me think I've asked a silly question.

"Stop letting your competition intimidate you," she says. "You've shown more than once this season you can beat stronger runners. Your secret weapon is what's inside you. If Saturday's race comes down to a game of mental toughness, do you think anyone stands a chance against you? Somewhere beyond the horizon of pain is your body's point of failure. Go find it. Think of this as a quest for the ultimate truth—your body's full potential."

"And what if I find it and collapse before the finish line?"

"It's only eight laps, Bags." Again, with clinical indifference. "We're talking about shit that will go down in the final minute. Your brain's not going to shut you down that quickly."

Summer's made the right call at every point of my running journey, but I know the battles I've fought with my mind over the years. Negativity holds such a firm footing in my mind, I created an imaginary antagonist to help me deal with it. She has a point, though. I've already beaten death and told myself—on this same hill—I can do anything for a minute. What if I can make peace with my negative thoughts, and Bad Gorilla and I take on Summer's quest together?

59

Old timers in neon vests waving fluorescent sticks welcome our bus to the Northern Illinois High School Track and Field Regional Finals at Tony Esposito High. Athletes stand out from the spectators in their warm-up gear and the extreme physiques that got them here today. Fans give way to beefy shot putters and javelin throwers out of a sense of self-preservation, while nimble high jumpers and sprinters avoid last-minute injuries by hugging the edges of the crowd. Distance runners range from tall and skinny to short and stocky and stick close to their team buses, obsessed with conserving energy.

Mayflower Academy's bus pulls up alongside ours. It's a full-size commercial touring coach painted in the school's black and white colors with *Mayflower Marauders* stenciled on each side. The bus has been retrofitted to provide optimal comfort, preparation, and recovery conditions for its passengers. This includes tinted glass windows, a climate-controlled interior, first-class airplane-style seating, and a kitchen and bathroom.

"I wonder if Coop's going to show up today?" Smitty says.

Everyone but Dirk laughs it off. "Why wouldn't you show up when you've been given every possible advantage?" he says.

I'm not bothered. If I'm going to lose to Cooper Assel in the 3200 meters, it's not because he rode in on a fancier bus.

I tune out the sideshow and crawl into my prerace cocoon, stretch my legs onto the open seat across the aisle and put on my headphones. I've been waiting for the right moment following my conversation with Summer to rattle Bad Gorilla's cage. With forty-five minutes until the day's first race, it's now or never. I slow my breathing, close my eyes, and descend into the depths of the mess that is my mind. I travel back to my earliest days with Bad Gorilla. I created him out of fear and self-doubt, then locked him in a cage where I stored all my negative thoughts. How can I blame him for the adversary he became?

I owe it to Bad Gorilla to expose him to a full spectrum of emotions and experiences—not only the bad ones. But Bad Gorilla is one strong bastard. Releasing the embodiment of all my negative emotions from his cage to roam free in my mind sounds risky. In the end, I trust Summer and know that my ability to live life to its fullest potential—both on and off the track—requires letting go of Bad Gorilla and facing my fears and insecurities on my own. I'm ready. Ready to rediscover the rookie spirit that got me here.

Coach Rip gets out of his seat to say a few words before the sprinters depart for their warm-ups. "You can see from a look outside this is a special day. Soak it up. Breathe in the excitement. I want you to remember this day for the rest of your lives. But don't forget, every meter you run today is the same length as every meter you've run this season. And the track out there is a simple oval, like any other—"

"Except those cinders at Bethlehem High." Smitty's interruption lightens the tension, and even Coach Rip smiles. Some runners have earned enough of Coach's respect to blur his regular-season lines of authority.

"As I was saying," Coach Rip continues, "You're going to step off this bus and be overwhelmed by the noise, the crowd, the friends and family calling your name. Enjoy it and wave back. Thank everyone for coming out to support you. But make it worth their while. You are here to race, so make sure by the time your foot touches the start line you've put the circus out of your mind. And once the gun goes off, run as if it's the last time you'll ever race around a track."

"You mean run as if you won't make it to state next weekend?" Unlike Smitty, Dirk has earned little respect to justify an interruption. Fortunately, all that makes it up to the front of the bus are the various "*Shhh's*" whispered by teammates too polite to yell "Shut up!" while Coach is speaking.

"Now, you've all heard plenty from me this season, so I'm going to leave you with a few words from a guy named Bill Bowerman, the legendary coach of the University of Oregon who coached runners like Bill Dellinger, Phil Knight, and Steve Prefontaine.

"Bowerman liked to say, 'Victory is in having done your best. If you've done your best, you've won.' Wise words worth keeping in mind as you give everything you've got out there today.

"Thanks for your attention and see you at the start line."

Coach Rip departs and leaves us to process his words. Dirk wastes no time killing the mood. "My competition pulls up alongside our little yellow school bus in an Imperial Star Destroyer, and the advice for today from two old hoots is to do our best?"

With no plan in mind, I find myself standing over Dirk as he lies on his bench seat. Looking down at him with burning eyes and loud enough everyone on the bus can hear, I tell him what's been on my mind for weeks. "I don't like you. If it wasn't for your parents, you'd be off this team for violating the no-assholes policy. Try keeping your mouth shut and pretend you aren't a loser today."

No one looks at me as I walk back to my seat, although the stares tingle my skin. I interpret the silence as approval while I wait for Dirk's counterattack. Shockingly, but perhaps not surprisingly, there is none. I'm not sure where my boldness came from. Then again, Bad Gorilla can be one aggressive mother. I smile, knowing he now has my back.

The first call up for the boys' 3200-meter race scares me. I've used up all my chances to get better tomorrow. But that's the wrong way to look at things, and I now understand why Coach Rip told us to forget about our goals. I don't want this race to be the end of a story—I've come too far to allow today's outcome determine whether I look back on the past several months as a triumph or a waste of time. My unhealthy relationship with ambition, however, has always led me to judge milestones as a win or a loss. Before leaving the warm-up track, I tell myself that all ends now, and regardless of whether I make it to state I'll still be a runner tomorrow—a better runner thanks to the work I put in today.

I enter the stadium and turn to the block of Linden Grove High blue and gold. The waving hands of Mom and Frank catch my eye. Summer's sitting with her dad and mine. Jed and his prom date, Bridget the swimmer, are in the top row with Sara, who sticks out from the sea of our school colors in a white Beastie Boys tank top. Jed's booming voice shouts my name along with profanity more typical of a hockey game. I do a double take when Nurse Cooper smiles at me and almost tear up until that chicken-shit Dr. Poulet distracts me. He and our athletic director are yukking it up with a group of financial boosters.

Instead of a dual-alley start, today's race simply squeezes sixteen runners into the eight lanes across the standard start line. I get one of the outside positions. As we suffer through the final moments before the start, Rich Duffy turns to me. "Solid race last weekend."

Coop adds, "Yeah, heckuva first season, dude."

Flattery from the two favorites for today's race catches me off guard. All I come up with in response is "Thanks."

The starter begins his ceremonial walk from the officials' table. The show is about to begin.

"I'm a sucker for underdogs," Duffy says, "Best of luck today."

"Yeah, good luck," Coop says. "But not too much, right?" The friendly banter releases the last of my butterflies. I laugh without hee-hawing, and realize some winners don't need a podium to stand out from the crowd.

The starter takes his position, and we step up to the line. "On your mark!" I lean forward and draw a deep breath.

BANG!

I spend the first seven laps matching the surges of the leaders. A hundred meters ago I accepted that holding back and improvising a strong finish have never worked for me and won't place me in the top four today. This leaves me no options other than determination and endurance and their painful side effects, which pretty much sums up the last nine months of my life.

Three hundred meters to go, and I'm hanging on to the front group of six runners. Duffy and Coop lift their pace in a relentless attempt to drop each other, leaving four chasers, including me, to fight for the last two spots to state. The final trip down the back stretch is a bare-knuckle brawl with my legs and arms. I need to get to the finish line before ripping them to shreds.

Two hundred meters to go.

Inhales no longer reach my belly. My muscles begin to drown in the poisonous carbon dioxide flooding my bloodstream. I fight to hang onto Summer's polite-sounding horizon of pain, and her advice reappears in my mind. This is only discomfort. My brain is simply doing its job. I'm still upright, so I must have more to give.

I give a little more and pull alongside José and the William Murray runner when we exit the final bend.

One hundred meters, and it will all be over.

I hug the inside stripe of lane three. The stands to my right pass by in a slow-motion blur of sound, movement, and shades of gray. I can't process it but draw energy from it. The William Murray runner pushes, and José and I stay with him. We catch back up to Duffy and Coop. The Ernie Banks runner falls away. The season will be over for one of us remaining five within seconds. Coop puts down what must be his final, final kick, and Duffy somehow sticks with him. José follows. I try but am out of my mind, and my body is dead all over. Looking anywhere but directly in front of me requires energy I don't have, so I stare at the distant dot of light that is all that remains of my visual field. I can no longer see the three runners I know are in front of me and lose track of the guy on my left.

I wonder if it's possible to know the truth about something without having suffered for it. My accident destroyed me. Recovery saved me. I found the truth in friendship, love, and learning this past year after wrecking all these things through my own self-destructive flaws. I've got fifty meters to destroy myself once more and find Summer's ultimate truth—my full potential on the track.

Bad Gorilla fills the blackness in front of me. It's only an image, probably a hallucination. The finish line is still somewhere in the darkness ahead. My body has nothing left to give, like it's trapped under a fallen tree. *Help me out, Gorilla. Come on. Lift this weight off me so we can get out of here!*

Bad Gorilla looks down at me before doing something I've never seen before. He smiles. Then he thrusts his face into mine and lets out a tree-splitting roar. I inhale his energy, and it propels me forward. My knees and arms ignite in one final burn. In reality, they slow a little less quickly. I gain ground back from José, but in the end it's not enough to beat him.

It is, however, enough to pull ahead of the William Murray runner at the line. I take fourth place, and I'm headed to the state finals.

Before getting a chance to celebrate, my body crumples to the ground.

60

FOUR WEEKS LATER...

Dad makes it up the first half of Spirit Hill easily enough to convince me he's been taking care of himself. We rest at the spot I fell to the ground so many months ago, frustrated I couldn't make it to the top and weeping over all that sucked in my life.

Dad catches his breath, and we continue our walk to the soda shop. Both of us order rocky road—Frank's favorite. I add *a pain au chocolat* for Marty. He's out of the hospital and riding his bicycle again. He'll get a kick out of my gift so close to the start of the Tour de France.

Anticipation of the satisfaction ice cream never fails to deliver fills the silent wait for our cones like when I was a kid. Dad, Mom, Frank, and I would come to the soda shop on summer nights so hot I couldn't lick the ice cream fast enough to prevent it from cascading down my fingers and pooling on the sidewalk. I struggle to remember our last visit as a family and wonder when exactly ice cream lost its ability to solve life's problems.

"Tell me more about summer school," Dad says.

"It's a five-day journalism camp in Boston."

"You're lucky to have Summer looking out for you. Mom and I were happy to hear she's going to let you stay at her place while you're there."

"You're not the only one." Solace displaced infatuation as the driver of my enthusiasm to spend a week as Summer's roommate. She flew away on a plane the night after state finals. Frank stopped at a bar on his way home from the airport before driving the Guinness off the road and nearly killing himself. Frank's attorney says the good news is he harmed no one other than himself. That lawyer clearly has no substance abusers in his life.

Frank has spent the last three weeks at an inpatient recovery program downtown. His case manager says he's hit rock bottom and is on the road to a real recovery. I want to believe this, but I also know Frank avoided jail time by checking himself into the hospital.

We take our cones from the kid behind the counter and sit at a bench out front.

"Does this mean journalism is the major for you?"

"I think so."

"What changed your mind about chasing your fortune on Wall Street?"

"Yeah, I mean, I like the idea of making lots of money, but I'm not so sure I want to be surrounded by people with the same idea."

"What's different about writing?" Dad asks.

"I guess writing helps me think through questions I have about the world and accept the answers, whether I like them or not. Stuff feels more real when I write about it."

"Hmm." Dad's look as he finishes his ice cream tells me he has a good idea what I've been writing about lately. Before getting to work on his cone, he asks, "Any news on the running front?"

"I won't be eligible to race as a fifth-year senior, but Coach Rip asked me to be a student coach. With only two classes and the school newspaper next year, I'll have plenty of time to help out."

"Good for you. Have you heard any more from the college coaches?"

"A couple keep calling. They want me to think about cross-country and the longer-distance track events like the 5K and 10K . . ."

"But?"

"I'm thinking about it." I learned a lot watching the different ways Smitty and Dirk managed their conflicted relationships with running. I'm afraid of ruining what I love about the sport if I continue to compete after high school. No matter how I communicate this to Dad, he'll ruminate over Frank's failed college football career. I'd prefer to avoid that today.

"Well, you've got time. What's the latest on the scholarship?"

"I reapplied, and Mr. O'Toole has gone out of his way to rally his friends at the club to support me this second time around. I should have an answer by the end of summer."

"Hopefully your hard work at the club will pay off with some special consideration."

"Yeah, and fortunately my principal isn't involved in the decision."

Dad laughs the last bite of cone out of his mouth. Seeing him do something human gives me the courage to ask a question I've been unable to answer in my writing.

"Dad, could I ask you something?"

He swallows hard.

"When did it all get so complicated?"

He puffs the air out his mouth and appears relieved to have the opportunity to explain a piece of his life. "When I started thinking what I had wasn't good enough."

"What do you mean by that?"

"I knew *I'd* never be a big deal, but Frank had the potential to conquer the world. He gave me a chance to live a bigger life. But confusing his success for my own left me with nothing to hang onto when things fell apart for him."

"I get it. I joined the track team because I wanted to chase something that was all my own." Sara's advice to go after something that gets me excited changed my life, and by living her own advice she earned a spot on the Dodgy Knickers concert tour this summer.

"And we all enjoyed watching you," Dad says. "Which reminds me—"

He hands the picture back to me, and I stow it in my pack for the walk home. We exchange our goodbyes at the house, and he drives away.

I was always so bothered by how different the three of us are. Dad was the forgettable underachiever, Frank the golden boy, and I was the insecure headcase planning to outsmart the world. Standing on the front curb of my childhood home, I realize love doesn't give a shit about trophies, test scores, and income brackets. Love just wants to be shared so it can make us better than who we are on our own.

I take the Polaroid out of my backpack when I get to my bedroom and stare at it for perhaps the hundredth time in the past three weeks. Summer took the photo of Mom, Dad, Frank and me with Frank's camera after my race at the state finals. A flash in time and space and matter that captured the culmination of my life to that moment now exists only on the plastic square I hold in my hand. I slide it back into the frame Frank hung for me below his posters of Pre and Shorter right before he drove Summer to the airport.

A cloudy band of sunlight filters through the window blinds, giving the picture on the wall a cold, metallic sheen like the staples that once held my body together. Track is the sport of truth. Hard truths. Only one runner gets to say he won—and only three get medals that count. Some would say fourth at state makes me forgettable, but the glory was in the distance I traveled to fall a step short of the podium. If I have any regret, it's not being able to give Coach Rip his gold medal. He'll have to keep at it, and I look forward to helping him next year.

Track is also the sport of deeper truths, if you look carefully. My accident destroyed my identity when it destroyed me. My identity was a storm of fear, insecurity, and chasing the selfish wants of others. Recovery gave me a reason to run, and running led me to the change Nurse Cooper encouraged me to embrace. Running pushed me past my goals and physical limits to a place I never imagined I could attain.

I watch the band of light pass the bottom of the frame on my wall and remember slapping Frank's camera when he tried to capture the triumph I was too distracted to see during my first attempt up Spirit Hill after my accident. I think about the heart-shaped collage of memories hanging in Summer's old apartment and realize a photo captures a different version of the truth for everyone in the picture. Like me, Frank got distracted by what other people value, and I resented him for that for a long time. After trashing his stereo, however, I realized how much I need him in my life. Frank knows me better than anyone. He understands parts of me no one else ever will. I don't want to hide parts of me anymore. I wouldn't have survived the past year if I had continued to hide from myself and others.

I'm not sure if Frank stopped for a drink after the airport to hide from the superstar he used to be or the person Summer left behind. I just wish he would have called—if not to ask for help, then to explain why.

We are what we've done, and there's no going back. We're all recovering from something. The only story we get to write is the one we choose to live by our actions in the next moment.

I remember lying under that tree on Spirit Hill, my body broken, my mind clear in the hope I'd get a second chance at the unfinished business of my life. Thank God my wish was granted. A year since my return from the dead, I understand that how we deal with the hills in our lives is what defines us. In between is the opportunity to choose how we can do better on the next climb. If I'm meant to die on a hill, let it not be while coasting on the descent. Let it be while racing toward the summit, chasing another reason to run.

EPILOGUE

The sun has the sky to itself, free from its usual rivalries with the clouds, rain, and wind. Perfect conditions for a run home after my second loop of the day. School starts on Monday. The seniors will be partying their brains out this weekend. *You know, last bash of the summer and all* . . . I plan to buy a mountain bike tomorrow and ride until my legs beg for mercy and Bad Gorilla smiles.

Cycling etiquette demands you offer assistance to a rider dealing with a mechanical on the side of the road. When I see the woman messing with her wheel outside the pool clubhouse, I stop and ask if I can help.

"Not unless you're hiding a spare tube in your shorts." She shows me the slice in the sidewall of her tire that created a problem beyond the remedies of a patch kit. I take a closer look at her bike. A Gary Fisher Paragon, one of the bikes on my wish list.

"You could try this." I offer a dollar bill from my earnings today and notice her LGCC Grounds Crew T-shirt. She has the warm glow of someone who spends a lot of time outdoors. It's hard to peg her age, but I don't know many teenagers with the bike, tan, and quads of a serious rider.

"That might work," she says. The dexterity with which she reinserts the tube into the tire and reseals both onto the rim of her wheel confirms she knows what she's doing. I help her align the dollar bill between the sliced tire and tube and hold the bead in place while she pumps it with some air. The seal holds, so she fills the tire before reattaching the wheel to the fork.

"Thanks again, that was a lifesaver." She smiles, and her brown eyes soften like Hershey's Kisses.

"By the way, my name's Vera."

"Vera?" Of all the ways to respond, I insult her with surprise.

"Yeah, I know. It's an old-lady name. My family's eastern European. It means 'summer.'"

"It also means 'true' in Latin." I try not to read too much into her name. "My name's Sam. It means . . . nothing special." My accidental wit causes her eyes to melt again. "How long have you been working here?"

"Since July, when my dad decided to take a job in Chicago," she groans.

"Where'd you move from?"

"Boulder, Colorado."

"That explains the bike."

"I spent a year saving up for this. A week after I bought it, my parents told me we were moving. Now I've traded mountains for mud."

"Wait 'til you meet the mosquitos," I say. "So, are you a greenskeeper or something?"

"Hah, no. I started working as a lifeguard in the middle of the summer, and this is the only shirt they had left in my size. I'll actually be a senior at Linden Grove High as of Monday."

"No kidding? Me too." I don't get into the details of my five-year plan.

We talk about LGHS, and I ask her a bunch of questions about cycling the canyon roads of Colorado.

"So, you're a roadie?" she asks.

"I used to be, but my bike—uh—broke last summer. I've been running a lot over the past year and thought about giving mountain biking a try. You know, get away from the cars."

"A runner? I'm looking forward to the cross-country season. Hope it'll help me meet people."

"Hey, I'm headed to the Tourmalet tomorrow—that's our local bike shop. Any chance you'd be interested in helping me pick out a new bike?"

"It's the least I can do, given I owe you a dollar."

I can't believe my luck. I meet an attractive, athletic girl who'll be a classmate in three days, and she agrees to a first date at a bike shop. What else could I ask for on a beautiful August afternoon?

"Hey, before I give up on this town," Vera says, "any idea where I might find a hill worth climbing?"

"Funny you ask, Vera. Follow me . . ."

Acknowledgments

Thanks to:

Noelle for giving me the space to tinker.

Eddie and James for all the memories on Lucky's Hill in Boulder. Those days have passed, but their "spirit" lives on. I hope your mother will let you read this one day.

Mom (and Dad, RIP) for setting good examples. Sorry I didn't pay more attention. Please trust me when I say Bags's parents are fictional.

Jennifer for being the jalapeño of the family and a font of many great ideas.

Paul Lindsay. You were the first author I ever knew. Discovering that books are written by real people lit a spark in me many years ago. You proved creativity does not require a credential. Thanks for that too. RIP.

Larisa Lindsay Dodge for giving the chapters of an early draft a read. More importantly, thanks for recommending professional help with my manuscript.

Candace Coakley for teaching me about arcs while sticking to the point. Thanks also for preventing me from letting my characters off too easily.

Erik Lindsay and John Capodice for inspiring me to keep at it through your examples. Art is an arduous endeavor. I'm grateful to have grown up around lifelong masters of their craft.

John Ward, Bob Roach and your friends at LaGrange Country Club circa 1988. Thank you for your confidence in me. You gave me my first big break in life.

Western Golf Association / Evans Scholars Foundation. Thank you for trusting me with your reputation and charity. It changed my life in so many ways.

The kids I grew up with. You provided material to inspire a book and a life. You're the best people.

The various friends and family who read early drafts of this book. I appreciate your honesty and generosity. Looking back on those early drafts, I apologize for the pain I put you through.

My writing group at the Burlington Writers Workshop. You continually humble me with your mastery of the art and craft of fiction. I'm grateful to have been on the receiving end of your astute critiques.

Samantha and team at Rootstock Publishing. Thanks for taking a chance on a debut author with a quirky story and for setting the high watermark for professionalism in your industry.

About the Author

Mike Magluilo is a writer and recovering finance professional, father of three and husband of one. He enjoys clean living and dirty jokes and loves old dogs and small gestures. He grew up in the Chicago suburbs where he had the best summer job in the world as a golf caddie. Mike rediscovered an early love of writing as a way to share life lessons with his sons who, it turns out, enjoy stories more than speeches. Mike's work has appeared in *Zig Zag Lit Mag*, *Cold Lake Anthology*, and *Flash Fiction Magazine*. His story "The Golden Boy" took first prize in *Flash Fiction Magazine*'s summer 2023 writing contest. Mike currently lives in Vermont with his family. Follow him at MikeMagluilo.com

More Fiction from Rootstock Publishing:

All Men Glad and Wise: A Mystery by Laura C. Stevenson

An Intent to Commit: A Novel by Bernie Lambek

Augusta: A Novel by Celia Ryker

Blue Desert: A Novel by Celia Jeffries

Granite Kingdom: A Novel by Eric Pope

Hawai'i Calls: A Novel by Marjorie Nelson Matthews

Horodno Burning: A Novel by Michael Freed-Thall

Junkyard at No Town: A Novel by J.C. Myers

The Funny Moon: A Novel by Chris Lincoln

The Hospice Singer: A Novel by Larry Duberstein

The Inland Sea: A Mystery by Sam Clark

Uncivil Liberties: A Novel by Bernie Lambek

Venice Beach: A Novel by William Mark Habeeb